purplepenguinpublishing.com

SISTERS

Set in the attractive and mundane, seaside-town of Southport, SISTERS is a contemporary and emotional psychological thriller about conflicted siblings: Barbara Tanner and Joan Lexton.

SISTERS follows novels HIS MOTHER and HER FATHER, thus concluding this electrifying trilogy.

***

Newly formed team, Detectives Inspector Catherine Shakespeare and Sergeant Gulliver Pope must set aside their differences in order to solve the mystery behind the discovery of an alien body in a family grave, undetected for thirty-one years.

Sisters, Mrs Barbara Tanner and Mrs Joan Lexton have a problem on their hands: there is an unwelcome smell oozing from the window seat in their front lounge. Having lived the latter part of their lives relatively in peace, former nurses to a children's ward for the terminally ill, find themselves suddenly in a quandary.

It does not take long for detectives Shakespeare and Pope to discover there is more to these grizzly, sixty-plus pipe-smoking womenfolk than meets the eye. But what secrets could they have buried in their distant past that is now of vital interest to a current police investigation?

SISTERS

SALLY-ANNE TAPIA-BOWES

For Rose, Babs & Becci,

my sisters and my guardian angels.

purplepenguinpublishing.com

FIRST PUBLISHED 2019

ISBN-13: 978-0-9931919-9-2

Cambria font used with permission from Microsoft

***

'The very first requirement in a hospital
Is that it should do the sick no harm.'

FLORENCE NIGHTINGALE

'She is your partner in crime,
Your midnight companion,
Someone who knows when you are smiling,
Even in the dark.'

Barbara Alpert

SALLY-ANNE TAPIA-BOWES

1

WINTER ARRIVED PREMATURELY. His onslaught of icy gales brushed autumn crudely aside; this he did before he heartlessly blasted the historical town of Southport with a multitude of snow. Blanketed and even along the entire coast, the crisp marshes and dense farmland disappeared within hours. Once again, unable to reach a herd of sheep, a frustrated farmer grieved the loss of many ewes – the biting wind coupled with freezing temperatures, killing, not only most of her flock but their offspring too.

Thankfully, the temperature inside the township's main hospital seemed almost unaffected - the sick, recovering and dying, comforted by the artificial heat and ongoing care coming from the dedicated nursing staff. Even in the early afternoon hours, the outdoor temperature had dropped to minus four degrees Celsius – a mighty Siberian gale admonishing nature's attempt to realign the scales.

In the busier-than-usual maternity unit, the Beast from the East could be heard by everyone indoors.

Even the two women straining to manage their pain, considered him, envious of his brute strength and determination. Later, in the early hours, before either of them had gone into full labour, one was suddenly rushed from the white heat of the delivery suite, for an emergency caesarean, after her heartbeat became intermittent. The other, crouched on all fours, bellowed – her pain beyond unbearable. Eventually, on her back, eyes tightly closed, she pushed unaided, almost semi-conscious.

Scolding screams from two opposite ends of the very same short corridor filled the air: healthy girls united in their fury against the world, and the cold, and their separation from all that was fair, warm and secure. Their familiar cries brought smiles to the obstetric team; in contrast, their aggrieved mothers silently sobbed before sluggishly beginning their recuperation – both alone, having given up on the fathers' arrival.

Upon the insistent mothers' requests, the two overworked midwifes, then within sight of each other, quietly ambled towards the ward's main reception desk. Eventually, their backs to one another, both managed to reach the expectant father by telephone. Unbeknown to them, they had dialled the same number.

2

PRESENTLY, AND ALMOST an entire year earlier, the uncomplicated and sleepy town of Southport is reborn. New Year's Day re-presents herself and unusually does not disappoint. The apricity from frothy-crisp sunshine is encouraging: it promises the keen, that an altogether new beginning *is* entirely possible. Not *a* new beginning, not just *any* new beginning but *the* new beginning. This is the one that *will* be accomplished because this time enthusiasts will seize the bull by the horns and a man at his word; this time they will cross the Rubicon and run the gauntlet.

Christmas behind them, the somnolent residents of the popular coastal town stir in their comfortable beds. Stimulated by half-baked resolutions and promises, they rise somewhat determined before energetically travelling to and fro from under their bedcovers – positivity running through their veins like electricity.

Not long after midday, many are packing away their lacklustre decorations; some angrily mow their carpets with upmarket vacuums, pine needles refusing to budge. Most of these residents are childfree now. They shed selfless parenting long ago - done their duty, although their blaring consciences remind them that they could have done a much better job. Evidently, if the last few days were anything to go by, it is clearly too late to do anything about it.

Troublesome visitations over, both couples and singletons alike, take full advantage of yet another day absent from work - start as they mean to go on - possibly lose weight – eat healthier – remain faithful in more ways than one. If only their sense of right and wrong would stop troubling them, they would be able to embrace the fresh start they long for, particularly at this time of the year.

Last year was a disaster. For sure, this year will be better. But time is running out; to some, death will surely come visiting like a thief in the night. There is no escape from it. As sure as the day we were born – death is ahead of us all. It's the middle bit that counts. Our willingness to change. Be better. *A Christmas Carol* was only a fable after all. Despite its tempting and heartfelt invitation to change, *Ignorance* and *Want* still roam the streets with a vengeance.

***

In direct contrast, Mr and Mrs Evans at 131 North Lane, will leave their decorations in place until at least the tenth of January. Mr Evans' wife grew up in the capital city of Madrid. Like most catholic countries around the world, they celebrate the birth of Jesus on

Christmas Day by eating and attending mass at midnight on the twenty-fourth. On the sixth though, on the day when apparently the Magi finally arrived with gifts, after following the light provided by the Star of Bethlehem, they exchange gifts in the same way most countries do, on the twenty-fifth.

Mr and Mrs Evans are in their late forties and have a young son, aged five. Their child was what is commonly known as a *test-tube baby*. They were about to separate when Mrs Evans announced she was pregnant. They both cried.

Mr Evans calls their son Edward and speaks English and Spanglish to him. Mrs Evans calls her son Eduardo; she only speaks Spanish and has no intention of learning English. On the evening before the sixth of January, Mrs Evans barks at a nebbish Mr Evans for him to fill three buckets up with grass and three with water - for the camels, of course. She, in return, will prepare the three glasses of *Jerez* before putting their paired shoes underneath their bronze-themed Christmas tree. As Spanish tradition dictates, these will be filled to the brim with sweets by their midnight visitors.

Mrs Evans can't wait for the following day; she loves this time of year. In the afternoon, they will all sit down together and watch her favourite movie of the season: *It's a Wonderful Life* – but the Spanish version – *Que Bello es Vivir!* Her favourite part is not when Clarence, the angel, finally gets his wings but when George Bailey lassoes the moon for Mary Hatch. A long time ago, when Mr and Mrs Evans began courting, Mr Evans took a much slimmer Mrs Evans to see a re-run of the movie. His mother-in-law sat between them both. Although she is now dead, Mr Evans did eventually grow quite fond of her.

Sadly, Mr Evans no longer likes Christmas; in fact, he can't wait for it to be over. His favourite movie is *The Polar Express* but Mrs Evans won't entertain it: she claims she can't understand a word of it. For the last two years, Christmas is always coupled with some drama or another. Only it seems to be getting worse.

Only a fortnight ago, following the twenty-fifth of December, their young son cried on and off for days after he woke up to no gifts under their immaculate tree. He soon after, ate all the imported chocolates hanging flawlessly on it, before loudly throwing up, on his father's lap.

****

On the other side of the cul-de-sac, on the corner at 123 North Lane, Mr and Mrs Stone have put away their decorations. Their cat, Georgia-May, scrambled up their feather-themed Christmas tree for the umpteenth time and succeeded in bringing it down for them on the twenty-fourth. It was inevitable that the rest would follow into their organised loft.

Mrs Stone has subsequently been in a foul mood ever since. *Mrs Evans says that taking the Christmas tree down early is bad luck*, she says. Mr Stone always smiles. There is little that can ever dampen his mood. Despite all of Mrs Stone's efforts, their peach-melba painted front-lounge just doesn't seem the same – and she had spent so much money on the decorations – saved up for them all year long.

It wasn't right eating Christmas dinner without a tree to look at. Their gifts ended up on the lounge coffee table! Mrs Stone is furious; she has even banned her husband from singing carols out loud. Georgia-May is missing their tree too.

Yesterday, she turned Radio 2 on, only to find that *Steve Wright in the Afternoon* was standing in for Jeremy Vine on the day in question; like her husband, he was still in the celebratory spirit. His festive factoids informed them that the Christmas cracker had been invented by an Englishman in 1848, who having visited Paris, noticed sugared almonds were sold in twists of paper. Mr Stone winked at Georgia-May before he reminded his wife that her Roberts Revival Radio had cost him an arm and a leg.

Next door, where a child called Mara used to live, a childless young couple, bearing a heavy hangover, are arguing at the top of their voices. They have only just recently moved in. Beforehand, an investigation team waded in and out of the property for months – then no-one wanted to buy it – the neighbours didn't help.

The body belonging to the child's father was discovered upstairs on his bed; the mother had died years ago of breast cancer. At first, the police thought he had passed out, drunk. There was a large empty bottle of whisky on the floor. He had wet the bed several times.

The *Southport Visitor* reported weeks after that he had been slowly poisoned - possibly by his own daughter – who was found dead – in his bird shed. The child had been poisoned too, and beaten to death. Her fingertips were paper-thin from the grinding of poison and glass. With the exception of Mrs Tanner and Mrs Lexton, shocked residents later interviewed, remarked on the questionable fact that he had been a dutiful father – and never went out – and didn't womanise – some children were just born evil.

Mrs Tanner and Mrs Lexton from 127 North Lane didn't bother putting up any decorations. They haven't decorated anything since God-knows-when. When they were children, they lived half-way along Cider Drive – the home Mrs Lexton lived in, after she was married. Their parents put many a decoration up year upon year. Their tall and handsome father was a barrel of laughs – then suddenly, in his mid-thirties, he died of bowel cancer – and the decorations never went up again. The girls were in their early teens at the time. Afterwards, they spent many national holidays sitting outside the local pub with crisps and no tea – their mother having a jolly inside - broken.

It is almost dark now. Mrs Tanner and Mrs Lexton are almost home. They tut repeatedly as they trundle along North Lane; they spy the back of their terraced home in the distance. The frames to their windows and doors are painted a deep purple: Mrs Tanner's favourite colour. Mrs Lexton hates purple; her favourite colour is royal blue, but she cannot persuade her sister to redecorate. It's *her* house. She moved there when she married Mr Tanner. And besides, Mrs Lexton owes her.

They edge their cumbersome frames about the corner house belonging to Mr and Mrs Stone, noticing that their winter garden is filled with an interesting variety of trees and plants, before they pass *the cursed house*, as they like to refer to it.

Their purple-painted terrace is now ahead of them – it is pleasant enough to look at, but no haven. Their overgrown rose garden is thorny and wild. Every year, in the autumn, not long after the summer has ended, they go out in the evening to add manure to the rectangular beds – heaps of it – they have it delivered. The neighbours shut their windows – they daren't complain.

And although the sisters try to avoid looking at their lounge window, although they focus solely on the door before passing once it is unlocked, they cannot help but glance momentarily, before they tut and shake their heads once more in unison.

Home is not so sweet a home. They've wanted to move forever. But it's hard to pack your things up and go elsewhere when you have a body tucked away below the front-room window. In a window seat.

Home is not where the heart is either. For years they have desensitised themselves, as much as possible, from the whole horrible situation. And other things besides. But since the last summer, a growing smell is emerging from the trapezium shaped box that doubles up as a seat. It's like someone's buried a fish below the floorboards as a joke. Except no-one's laughing. With the omission of sarcasm, no-one's laughed for years.

3

CUSTOMARILY, ZITA KISSED the sentimental group photograph of her mother, father and older sister three times before she smiled absentmindedly. She did so even though it was only mid-afternoon on New Year's Day.

'Good night Mummy.'

'Good night Daddy.'

'Good night Darcy.'

At intervals, the bright sunshine warmed their cold faces – the barrier of scarves and gloves failing to fully fight the bitter cold air about them. The oval framed picture, to the centre-top of the grave's black-marbled headstone, had not long since replaced the previous, the one of Walter Folkard, taken on his wedding day.

Darcy was in the middle, her favourite place at that age. She was beaming – a tidy pigtail tucked behind each ear – green slides fixed at either side of the centre-parting – freckles speckled intermittently. Her older brother Harry had taken the photograph on her fourteenth birthday. Her front teeth stuck out slightly like some do in a cartoon. Darcy detested the photograph. It was the freckles – they were dotted about everywhere on her face – the sky at night. Her blue eyes seemed to follow her younger sister, regardless of where she stood. In life, she adored her younger sibling. Before the fire fully consumed all that ever mattered, Darcy threw her younger sister out of the third floor window. Too frightened to take flight herself, and unable to decide what to do, she headed inside to look for their mother.

Had she survived, Darcy, a middle child, she would have turned sweet sixteen by the end of the month; instead, she would be forever fixed at fourteen.

She would never be sweet anything. Never grow any older – any taller. Neither would she have the opportunity to be caught drinking before she was even eighteen. She was far too sensible for a teenager anyhow. She would have probably passed her driving test the first time – no *Well Done* to come. She'd already experienced pain before her time: she'd found the loss of her father almost unbearable, only a few months earlier, before she passed away herself - her older brother Harry by her hospital bed.

She would never graduate, fall in love - become a mother, or a wife. She was no longer a daughter. Time had cruelly arrested her promising life - all of their promising lives - forever. It wasn't personal – but cruel all the same. She was a ghost to Zita. Already Zita was beginning to forget the many memories seeded by those who loved her most in the world. It was a blessing, of course, for who could emotionally survive the horror that had befallen the perfect family in such a short time?

Harry, had not been at home at the time. Being the eldest and at university, he'd stayed over at a friend's house that same evening. Guilt pounced on him and clung to his very soul. He was sure he would have been able to raise the alarm sooner – he should have been there – his mother had needed him. Since his father had died, it had always been easier to stop over at friend's. Had remained cloistered. Sequestered from the real world. How much he missed his father. An unbearable pain shadowing him wherever he went. Doubt molesting him into the early hours even after counselling.

Catherine Shakespeare wanted to drop the bunch of yellow tulips off and return back home as soon as, but as had been the norm in the last two years or so, Zita would delay, converse and meander about the grave for so much longer than foreseen – much longer than Catherine was prepared to emotionally tolerate.

Although the cemetery on Liverpool Road was quite beautiful, it was still a place she liked to avoid. Situated on a high hill, an attractive small chapel to the very centre, it overlooked the manicured Birkdale and Hillside Golf courses nearby - beyond, an open view of the Irish sea – everything closer to heaven.

The altitude of many tombs and gravestones, on the face of it, towered well above anyone's height – solemn angels and archangels erupting from grey marble memorials supplicating with an arm raised to God.

Hermione Folkard, the mother of Harry, Darcy and Zita, had spent many days, following her husband's death, in the company of these comforting sculptures - their intricate mesmerising carvings comforting her soul. Their compassionate faces provided some understanding. It was a selective club. The dead. Little did she know then, that along with their eldest daughter, she too would become one of the crowd.

To many visitors, and in the far right corner, it was inarguably a pacifying sight, to see the angels pouring over the graves of children: protective messengers from God watching over them in their parents' absence. Catherine had wandered off earlier, in their direction, unintentionally, her impatience irritating her. Her ardent need to busy herself driving her.

One archangel stood out amongst them all, it had large triangular wings - the feathered tips almost touching the ground itself. It held its right hand as if raising a soul towards heaven. In its left it held a bunch of daisies. Catherine Shakespeare had paused over the grave to read:

SARAH

DAUGHTER TO JOHN & ESTHER BARNARD

AGED 5 YEARS

DECEASED 7 OCTOBER 1785

The little bed is empty now, the cloths laid by.

Wendy squeezed Catherine's hand at the point when she was about to call Zita over. Her patient smile communicated a much-needed understanding.

'Why don't you go and sit in the car? I'll stop here with Zita. We won't be long – another ten minutes.'

Catherine smiled briefly. Her pale blue eyes pricked as always, never on cue. She should have adjusted to the whole sorry situation by now. She'd heard time was supposed to heal, but nearly two years on, she still couldn't come to terms with the losses she had endured. She'd plenty of times castigated herself. What right had she? She hadn't been related to either Hermione, Walter or Darcy. They had been the closest of friends. That's all. They'd worked together for many years. They'd probably seen each other almost every day of their adult life. But they weren't family. Not like Harry. And Zita. The ones left behind. The orphans.

Catherine Shakespeare was no fraud. To repudiate her feelings was wrong. It was what it was. Part and parcel of the grieving process. An exclusive club. There was nothing theatrical about her. The pain she felt was vast and weighed heavy. She carried it daily: a badge pinned onto a lapel. For now, she would embrace it. To not endure was to forget. Had it been her, Hermione Folkard would have been much the same. Only stronger. And venerable to the core.

Like most little ones, Zita seemed to be doing remarkably well. She was ten now. Old enough to remember – young enough to forget. She wasn't the tallest in the class. She wasn't the shortest. Her dark hair and eyes resembled her father's. She'd recently put weight on. Her tummy bulged forward like a pincushion. The pink cheeks on her face too. She was smart, like her mother, intuitive, sensitive. Her life was full of possibility.

Alone in the driver's seat now, Catherine Shakespeare allowed her mind to wander. Like a newly-acquired sickness, she tortured herself with scenes from the fateful day that brought about the end of her most meaningful friendship. She knew that morning, that something wasn't quite right. Despite her Chief's instructions to return directly back to the station, she had taken a detour.

On her approach, to pass by Hermione Folkard's home, she was redirected – fire engines fighting a couple of houses ablaze. In the distance, there wasn't much to see – just billowing smoke. But her instinct knew otherwise.

Catherine watched herself as if in a film that couldn't be paused. First, she had pulled over and abandoned her car. She then ran along the road before turning the corner on her left, dirty smoke rising from between houses. When she reached her destination, Hermione Folkard's house and the adjoining property were on fire. The intensity of the blaze was obvious to all standing helplessly close by.

Eventually, a nearby firefighter in his full tunic, undid a long zip about his synthetic collar before he motioned for her to sit on a nearby wall. His red face had been expressionless. She remembered to replay the bit where he removed his gloves before speaking. It was important to remember it right. He then placed a rehearsed hand on Catherine's arm. Her right arm. No. Her left. It was her left. He had sat to the left of her. She was shaking all over.

'There is no-one left in the buildings as far as we know. Residents from both houses have been removed and taken to hospital.

I am sorry to say, two adults did not leave one of the properties alive – a young child is in a critical condition – smoke inhalation. That is all I know. I am very sorry.'

**

Sickened and tired by the memory of it all, Catherine took a deep breath before she began to cry. She neither saw Hermione or Darcy Folkard again: their injuries too severe. Closed casket. Closed. Boxed shut.

It was almost impossible going ahead with her wedding to Wendy, five months later, no best friend - chief bridesmaid missing - though it gave Zita something to look forward to. She recovered well from her injuries. Darcy had done well – saved her younger sibling. If only she had saved herself.

When Wendy suggested they take Zita in, she was both reluctant and elated – Hermione and Walter would have wanted that. And then there was Harry, their eldest, twenty-four now. Although settled with his wife Laura and a second child on the way, he rarely called around anymore – not even to see his youngest sister. All credit to Wendy, she visited him regularly – Zita liked the fact she was an aunt. The last time mother and son had spoken, the very last time, Hermione was struggling to live life without Walter – depression had enveloped her – cocooned her, possibly beyond help. Maybe death was not so cruel after all. They were, after all, now so cruelly re-united.

4

Trundling now into their colourful back garden, the resolute head-scarved women light up their ageing pipes before sitting on opposite ends of a wooden bench aligned to the back wall of their house. It is customary for them to spit at this point. They like to clear their throats before having a good smoke.

Mrs Tanner's pipe is a *Napoli*; it is a briar pipe and has a distinctive walnut stain with a jet-black acrylic stem. The pipe used to belong to her husband, who supposedly ran off to Africa with another woman years ago, just at the point when she'd given up on babies. Mrs Lexton's says Mrs Tanner's pipe is 'COMMON AS MUCK'. Her pipe is a *Nording Hunter* and was named once 'Pipe of the Year': it is a Bison pipe, named after the game Nording pursued. It also has a jet-black acrylic stem, but hers is longer and therefore more elegant.

Mrs Lexton doesn't know exactly what it is made of. 'IT'S NICE MRS TANNER – THAT'S ALL YOU NEED TO KNOW!' Her sister is ignorant to the fact that Mrs Lexton was told all this by the man it belonged to. He used to visit the children's ward, for the terminally ill, every day, where they both worked as sisters – as nurses. He visited until his son died of Leukaemia. He left his pipe behind on the last day – the day Bertie died. He used to let his son play with it, when his wife wasn't about. She never stayed long. Afterwards, he never came back for it. So she kept it.

Every Monday morning, like ants on a mission, they waddle purposefully towards Crossens village – it is only a few minutes away - one with a plastic bag in her hand, the other with a tatty umbrella, spokes like broken ribs. They wear their red pinafores over their long black skirts – their rigid boots go unpolished.

They head to the local tobacco shop: there they will acquire enough tobacco for an entire week. When there is more than expected, towards the end of the week, they are indifferent and uncelebratory, but when the tobacco runs out too early, they squabble more loudly than the newly-weds in *the cursed house*.

At first, accusatory sentences are flung back and forth in quick succession. Then doors begin to slam. They do the slamming with such force that the doors open right back, all by themselves, the women's strength admirable, for ladies heading towards seventy. Their neighbours don't worry too much: they suspect they are having another of their daily debates. And besides, not one of them would dare to comment.

Once and only once, an overconfident neighbour at 131, Mr Evans, acting on his wife's instructions, went around to complain about the noise and was punched full on in the face. No-one dares to intervene. Mr Evans came home with concussion and warned anyone who would listen *that they could be taking their lives into their own hands.* Only Mr Stone takes the time to speak to them when they pass his corner plot. Whilst they have grown socially awkward with age, deep down, they appreciate his kind offers to fix this and that. On occasion, he had carried the odd bag or two back to their purple house. At Christmas, Mrs Stone always brings a large packet of tobacco for them. But they know they cannot allow anyone to get too close, let alone fix anything for them. Some things at home are beyond fixing.

Only to strangers would their behaviour towards one another appear far more serious than it actually is. In reality, most of the neighbours are used to the waspish exchanges between the nondescript sisters who are not too dissimilar in age or size.

Mrs Lexton, who is sixty-seven and a year and a half younger than her older sister, refers to her sister as Mrs Tanner, and in return, Mrs Tanner refers to her younger sister as Mrs Lexton. On a rare occasion, like when they were much younger, they call each other Babs and Jo. When this changed, and not out of formality, they are not sure. Life has changed them in ways they never invited. Life has been hard on them, as it was on their parents – whom they dearly loved.

They talk like they are shouting most of the time. Each sentence is a statement or an imperative. To anyone who knows them, all the world's a stage, or in this case, a table tennis competition. Mrs Barbara Tanner, the eldest, is robust and mentally strong, despite her brutal marriage, now very much in the past. Mrs Joan Lexton, is also physically strong, but daintier in comparison – mentally troubled throughout her life – broken by the loss of Billy.

Sometimes, when their voices are raised, it is hard to tell which sister is which: like their mother, who died a few years after their father did, they are both just over five foot in height but now shaped like an apple. Once upon a time they had fine figures, and friends, and promising careers ahead of them. Once upon a time, they dreamed of marrying doctors.

Mrs Lexton has lived with Mrs Tanner for a very long time; she lived with her husband until he mysteriously vanished one day – according to Mr Stone. Mr Stone told the couple in *the cursed house*, who were not listening at the time, that Mrs Tanner had taken her sister in, out of the goodness of her heart – after her husband left her for some floozy.

In reality, Mrs Tanner and Mrs Lexton are extremely close. They were very close as children, as teenagers, as women. Circumstances have ensured they remain closer still. Bar Mr and Mrs Stone, all the neighbours are frightened of them in some small way. And neither of the sisters bother to say hello anymore: as they pass: none of the residents living in the cul-de-sac are the original ones they once used to talk to anyway – before their husbands disappeared. Most of them have moved on. Or died.

Their grunts and grumbles, as they waddle off daily to the village, are a barrier designed to warn any passer-by to keep their distance. Even the bible-bashers don't attempt calling on them anymore.

***

Mrs Lexton is now indoors; she is shouting loudly from the kitchen to Mrs Tanner, who is still sitting on the bench by the back door. But Mrs Tanner is still smoking her pipe, and refuses to budge. Like Mrs Lexton, she holds the pipe with their teeth as she talks. Regardless, they smoke both indoors and out-of-doors - they even smoke when they cook and peg out the washing.

Their cheerful garden is not far from being a haven. Like the one on Cider Drive, before their father died, and before their mother followed, it is tidy and interesting – lots of neat beds – not a weed in sight. There are different gnomes about the garden too. Only one of the gnomes ever belonged outright to Mrs Lexton. It looked a lot like her deceased husband. One windy night, a roof-tile fell, guillotining him in half. Mrs Lexton looked like she was about to cry just as Mrs Tanner started to laugh.

'COME INDOORS MRS LEXTON. WE NEED TO TALK ABOUT YOU KNOW WHAT!'

'I'LL BE IN IN A BIT MRS TANNER. I'M HAVING A WELL-EARNED BREAK!'

'THERE'S A CUP OF TEA WAITING FOR YOU INSIDE! I'VE POPPED A BIT OF GIN IN IT!'

'THEN WHY DIDN'T YOU SAY SO MRS TANNER? ALTHOUGH, I THINK I'D LIKE TO TAKE MY CUP OF TEA OUTDOORS.'

'THEN COME AND BLOODY WELL GET IT WHY DON'T YOU MRS LEXTON! THAT IS, IF IT'S NOT TOO MUCH BOTHER FOR YOU COME AND FETCH IT YOURSELF!'

EIGHT-THIRTY-TWO AND ZITA was finally in her bed. Her bedroom was the first on the left on the upstairs landing. Catherine's and Wendy's followed. Anytime between two and five am Zita would habitually enter their room and climb into bed with them. She always chose Wendy's side. Although in Year 5 now, Zita still carried her large elephant about with her – a small mouse with a long tail trapped in its soft trunk; she occasionally still sucked her thumb too.

Over time, and with Zita's expert help, Catherine and Wendy assembled a bedroom that was as good as any portrayed in the most ambitious of magazines. They did so whilst they grieved as a newly-formed family – they did so even though they weren't ready, nor felt capable. They hadn't even had time to adjust as newly-weds. No matter, they had lived together beforehand.

As sure as time passed, their once clinical environment filled quickly with furniture, toys and interesting books. Zita stopped asking the types of questions that left them both dumfounded and helpless. She cried less and laughed more.

Catherine and Wendy had always wanted to be parents - they just didn't anticipate it happening before they were both physically and mentally ready. Catherine had been one of two sisters. Her younger sister Elizabeth had married before her: they had both made their parents proud. As children, they had squabbled constantly. Even as young as six, Catherine had struggled to adjust – failed to understand her emerging feelings for the same sex. Her aunt once told her mother that she was queer, right in front of her. Her mother looked at her different from then onwards – held her more often. Her father refused to have his sister around to the house again – the cheek.

***

Wendy had headed downstairs as Catherine began reading Zita a story about a star that had lost its sparkle; it was then she heard her work mobile ring. She ignored it. When the story finished, with its predictable ending, Zita asked for another, so Catherine picked up a story called *Little Evie in the Wild Wood* – a favoured adaptation of *Little Red Riding Hood*. When Zita laughed, she reminded Catherine of her father; when she cried, she looked like her mother; when she was frustrated, she was Darcy, to a tee.

'Night Caty.'

'Goodnight noodle.'

Avoiding as always the painful photographs on the shelves, Catherine headed towards the bedroom door; from there, as always, she blew Zita a good-night kiss.

'MY NERVES ARE SHOT TO SHREDS MRS TANNER. GOD, IT SMELLS AWFUL IN THERE. AND THE USELESS CUNT DIDN'T SMELL THAT GOOD WHEN HE WAS ALIVE!'

'NOBODY'S GOING TO DISCOVER ANYTHING HERE MRS LEXTON – NOT IF I HAVE ANYTHING TO DO WITH IT!'

'IT WAS BAD ENOUGH LAST YEAR, WITH THE POLICE IN AND OUT OF NEXT DOOR FOR MONTHS ON END!'

'THAT WAS TWO YEARS AGO MRS LEXTON. MAYBE MORE! THEY MADE A RIGHT MESS OF THEIR BACK GARDEN. A RIGHT MESS.'

Washing up completed, Mrs Tanner begins to help her sister dry the remaining pots and pans on their faded draining board. The sweet aroma of tobacco smoke fills their practical and plain kitchen. Since the house was purchased nearly half a century ago, it has never been renovated; it still has a large Belfast sink. Most appliances are rarely used – even the washing machine only goes on once a week. Mrs Tanner and

Mrs Lexton no longer own an iron. Mrs Lexton once used it on her husband; they never replaced it after sticking it in the window-seat with his body.

DO YOU REMEMBER THAT DAY WHEN THE MORMON PRIEST CALLED AROUND AFTER MARA?'

'WHAT OF IT MRS LEXTON? WHAT OF IT?'

'YOU CALLED HIM A PERVERT MRS TANNER!'

'I DIDN'T MRS LEXTON! I TOLD HIM HE WAS TOO LATE, THAT WE WERE ALL GOING TO HELL, WHERE THE DEVIL'S GOT ALL THE BEST TUNES AND IT'S WARM AND FRIENDLY!'

'YOU DID MRS TANNER! AND YOU SAID SOMETHING ABOUT HIM BREATHING BEHIND THE GATE TOO.'

'THAT'S WHEN MARA LAUGHED MRS LEXTON. I HEARD HER.'

'LITTLE MARA. LOVELY MARA.'

'I HOPE HER BASTARD FATHER'S ROTTING IN HELL MRS TANNER! ROTTING SLOWLY IN HELL!'

'TWO YEARS AGO THIS SPRING MRS LEXTON. WE WERE BAKING THAT WEEKEND. FROZE FIVE LOAVES ON THE SUNDAY WHEN IT ALL HAPPENED.'

'MY MEMORY'S NOT THE SAME MRS TANNER.'

'ALL THE WHILE SHE WAS DEAD, IN HIS SHED.'

Mrs Tanner and Mrs Lexton complete their chores in silence before they head solemnly to their almost bare front lounge. The varnished wooden door is always kept firmly shut, locked with a key, all of the time. The key lies on its back like a wounded soldier above the door frame. To anyone else, it is invisible. But they know it's there. When they pass the stairs and head up, they do so in the knowledge that it is there. When they descend the stairs each day, they search with their eyes for it. Sometimes the key likes to play a trick on them; it seems that it is missing. But it is there alright – a trick of the light.

Each time one of the sisters wants to open the door, which is almost never, they have to retrieve a wooden chair from the kitchen. Today it is Mrs Tanner who unlocks the door. She drags the ladder chair with her right hand whilst heading forward; the front legs lift whilst the back ones resist, screeching. The left leg catches on the kitchen doorframe as she heads into the hallway. The chair rocks slightly before it adjusts itself, dizzy from the altercation. Rested now, before the door, it patiently awaits to fulfil its purpose before it is abandoned but not forgotten.

On the other side of the door, there is a relatively modern-looking three piece suite with purple corduroy covers that match the lined curtains; the carpet and the window-seat, with three cushions arranged like playing cards on their side. These are purple too. The window-seat once had a heavy lid that lifted. Mrs Tanner kept coal and logs inside the wooden structure for the open fire; she loved sitting in this room. The lid has since been both glued and nailed down. The fire has not been lit for approximately ten years. It has not been lit since Mr Lexton was folded neatly into the box with their only iron.

The bare walls have since been dressed with a white superfresco textured wallpaper – it has elongated grey trees on it that look like willows. In truth, it doesn't really go – it's as if the wallpaper was either chosen by someone with no taste or in a rush. There is little else in the room. There are no pictures on the walls. There are no sentimental photographs on the mantelpiece. The only ornament is a silver clock – to the centre of it. It was given to Mrs Tanner following her sudden departure from the children's ward. The time is stopped at eleven minutes past ten.

Sitting on the sofa now, facing the window-seat below the large bay, Mrs Tanner and Mrs Lexton are a picture to behold. Although they are both wearing long skirts, it is obvious from the way they sit, that underneath, their legs are parted like men.

They are both smoking their pipes. The familiar aroma helps mask the sickly-sweet smell of decay in the room. In truth, it's a terrible all-pervading miasma of sorts. A smell that is putrid and rancid – one that threatens to pervade and saturate anything it happens upon.

'GREAT START TO THE NEW YEAR THIS IS MRS TANNER.'

'I LIKED THE WALLS THE WAY THEY WERE – WHEN THEY WERE PAINTED LILAC MRS LEXTON.'

'I'VE SAID I'M SORRY TILL I'M BLUE IN THE FACE MRS TANNER.'

'NEW CARPET COST AN ARM AND A LEG!'

'I PAID HALF DIDN'T I? MRS TANNER?'

'YOU DIDN'T HAVE TO HIT HIM THAT HARD MRS LEXTON. MADE A RIGHT MESS!'

Mrs Lexton glares momentarily at her sister's contrite face before eyeing an invisible patch in the carpet ahead of her.

'I'VE BEEN DOING SOME TAPHONOMIC RESEARCH IN THE LIBRARY MRS TANNER!'

'AND WHAT THE HELL IS THAT MRS LEXTON?'

'IT'S THE STUDY OF DECOMPOSITION MRS TANNER! THAT'S WHAT IT IS!'

'SOUNDS INTERESTING MRS LEXTON – COME ON THEN – LET'S HAVE IT!'

'WELL – AS WE RARELY PUT ON THE HEATING – THAT DELAYS THE PROCESS OF DECOMPOSITION FOR A GOOD LONG WHILE.'

'ANY IDIOT KNOWS THAT MRS LEXTON!'

'WELL, WHAT WE WRAPPED MR LEXTON IN MADE A DIFFERENCE TOO.'

'GOOD JOB WE DID IT WHILST HE WAS NICE AND LIMP.'

'WELL, THE CLOTH AND PLASTIC WE SEALED HIM IN MUST HAVE PREVENTED MOISTURE FROM FORMING – AND BECAUSE HE WAS AS THIN AS A SPARROW, HE HAD NO FAT AND LITTLE LIQUID IN HIM - SO IN MANY WAYS WE SORT OF MUMMIFIED HIM.'

'YER WHAT? GOOD JOB HE CAN'T GET OUT THEN MRS LEXTON!'

'AND INSECTS CAN'T GET TO HIM – MAGGOTS AND THE LIKES MRS TANNER - BECAUSE THERE IS NO OXYGEN. IT SAID THAT THE INSECTS WERE THE MOST IMPORTANT FACTOR IN DECOMPOSITION – AND WE SEALED THE LID GOOD AND TIGHT.'

'YOU MEAN - I SEALED THE LID GOOD AND TIGHT MRS LEXTON.'

Mrs Lexton is sulking now. She deliberately averts her sister's gaze for as long as possible. She hadn't been able to help it at the time. She didn't mean to kill him right then and there, but he surprised her by turning up out of the blue. Neil, her husband, had grown restless waiting for her to return home. She'd originally said she'd be back in time for tea.

In the end, he drove around to her sister's. Mrs Tanner was in her tool shed checking her potatoes. A ten minute drive. He hesitated at first before entering the gate, then again before knocking at the door. Inside, he had a cup of tea before boldly announcing that he was leaving. That night. With the embalmer that Mrs Lexton had suspected he was seeing for the last two years. But that wasn't the reason she killed him. He did something far far worse. So she let him have it. She had no idea she could do it. But let him have it, she did.

'SO WHY THE SMELL MRS LEXTON? WHY THE SMELL AFTER ALL THESE YEARS THEN?'

'WELL – IT SEEMS THE BODY ALWAYS BLOATS AFTER DEATH AND EVEN THOUGH MR LEXTON WAS TIGHTLY WRAPPED IN TARP AND TAPE, IN TIME, SOME BONE MAY HAVE BECOME EXPOSED AND A VERY SLOW DECOMPOSITION PROCESS MAY HAVE BEGUN.'

'MAYBE MRS LEXTON, MAYBE WE'VE GOT DAMP SOMEWHERE – ON THE OUTER WALL - AND IT HAS GOT TO THE BODY SOMEHOW - STARTED THE ROTTING PROCESS.'

Mrs Lexton is looking uncomfortable now. She suddenly stands up and points to the seat before raising her voice once more.

'ARE YOU SAYING MRS TANNER THAT WE'RE GOING TO HAVE TO MOVE THAT USELESS CUNT? AFTER ALL THESE YEARS?'

'I HAVE NO IDEA MRS LEXTON. ALL I KNOW IS THAT THE SMELL IS GOING TO GET PROGRESSIVELY WORSE. AS PLAIN AS THE NOSE ON YOUR FACE. IF WE DON'T DO SOMETHING, MR LEXTON IS GOING TO SOONER OR LATER GIVE US AWAY.'

7

DETECTIVE SERGEANT POPE wasn't entirely sure whether to ring his newly-appointed line manager at all. It wasn't an emergency, but all the same, he knew that she didn't like surprises. In the little time he'd spent with her, he'd picked up that she liked to be pre-warned of any impending cases that may come their way. But it was New Year's Day. She would be most likely at home. She had never really spoken to him about her family – to be fair neither had he - but from what had been tentatively divulged by others, in-the-know, family time was a priority.

When his newly-acquainted colleagues described her as a person once full of mischief and hilarity, he unintentionally laughed out loud. Not a real laugh – it wasn't even that loud – a plangent noise in reality - but it was somewhat scornful all the same. He hadn't meant any disrespect, he really hadn't, he wasn't the sort. It had been his second day after all. Their disappointed and united expressions revealed an unanticipated response – a clearly and pleasantly loyal bunch to the core.

'Give her time. She'll be back to her old self before you know it.' Sergeant McKenna seemed sure of it although a few of the others looked doubtful. Inspector Catherine Shakespeare hadn't exactly welcomed him with open arms. His transfer to Southport station, only this past October, was now thankfully complete. His wife Carys and their two young children finally joined him soon after – their charming but in-far-too-much-need-of-repair Welsh family home now sold. The past behind him. His indiscretion unrevealed. A new start. A chance to put things right.

It wasn't long after half-seven in the evening. He very much doubted Catherine would be in bed asleep; but he'd been warned by his newly-acquainted and much friendlier colleagues, that she'd been through a lot in the last two years and that he would need to be patient.

He wanted to ask for details; he wasn't being nosey – he had never been the nosey sort - but he wanted to fit in – bond – understand what lay behind her cool demeanour – the type that categorically presents itself as a polite rejection of some sort.

Back in Wales, at Lancaster Square station, he'd always fitted in – belonged from day one – one of the family. Mind, his dad had held a senior post at the station for many years before retirement. The mood at the Southport station, since his appointment, had been somewhat volatile; it was like being adopted by a loving yet dysfunctional family.

From what he knew, which was very little, the team had lost their commander at the helm – an ugly fire he'd heard – other family members had died too. Detective Inspector Hermione Folkard had been about for many years. It was clear from the station's lingering grief and laudable commentaries that she was not just liked and respected but loved too. He did not know if Catherine Shakespeare had even wanted the promotion; she clearly had some big boots to fill – maybe she was under some immense pressure he was unaware of. Time would hopefully tell. He had plenty of it. Time. And patience.

***

In truth, Sergeant McKenna wasn't entirely convinced by his own words. He felt sorry for their new Sergeant, the new kid on the block, bright ginger hair, funny accent. Not long after their Inspector's death, two close colleagues, from their own team resigned – both had politely declined attending their own leaving party; it was eventually cancelled.

Of the two, Juliet Clark hadn't been in contact with anyone other than Luke. Over the Christmas break, they had taken a long walk along Formby beach – chewing the cud; he wasn't going to subject her to one of his caving expeditions again – she almost passed out the last time – their exciting excursion to the White Scar Cave in Ingleton ended before it had begun. They laughed together as they walked – as they remembered the good old days.

***

Gulliver Woodrow Pope hadn't always wanted to be a police officer. For a short while, he contemplated the teaching profession. His mother had been an English teacher; she had only just retired. From her he had inherited his bright red hair. His wife was a teacher too. Unlike most of his friends, in his youth, he'd excelled in every subject in school – especially in History and Science. But his father had been a *Plod* as he liked to call it and somehow, he had felt drawn to the career he felt most akin to. He had no regrets. Despite the long hours, the over-exposure to tragic circumstance and the onerous paperwork trail, he loved his job.

A Family Liaison Officer for many years, he had supported countless families in the knowledge that whilst he couldn't make things better, he could surely stop things from getting any worse. He was reputed for his compassion and sensitivity: not many FLO's went as far as to accompany victims to the mortuary. Not many were on first name terms, as he was. Family members had gone as far as dropping off gifts for him. Mostly chocolates. Once flowers.

His exemplary and caring attitude had gained many confidences and earned the respect of numerous victims. His superiors were impressed. When he was invited to join CID, as a Detective Constable, he was elated. His father had been a Detective Inspector as had been his father before him. His promotion to Detective Sergeant followed soon after. In a walled town like

Conwy, any promotion was limited. In order to grow and experience *the real world,* as his father had put it, he would have to move on – move on to a more populated area. And move on he did. But not for the reasons he had publicly declared.

Gulliver sat quietly in their newly-painted front lounge for a short while. It was a nice colour, yellow but with a strong hint of green. Green. Olives. Olive. Olivia. Olivia Bouverie-Pusey.

Pensively, he stared ahead at the roaring fire – flames licking left-overs that had been scraped onto an already burning log surrounded by coal. At times smoke spiralled forth from beyond the volcanic grate. His eyes followed one such wisp before suddenly running both hands through his thick red hair, hoisting himself up.

He was determined to never see Olivia again. They had both reluctantly agreed. It was easy to stick to such an agreement, when busy, usually during the day. But when time spared him a chance to think – his mind wandered quickly from their emotional break-up to a scene that was fuelled and energetic. Erect and frustrated by her haunting smile, he reached for the poker, he corrected the unruly pile before he placed a small log to the back of the grate.

His handsome authoritative face bore the markings of someone who was yet to make his mind up. He wanted a shower. He always felt better after a long shower – could think straight. He returned the poker to the coal bucket and headed out of the room. His wife passed him on the stairs. She held her right pointing finger to her pursed lips before she kissed him on his left cheek. She'd always suited that beige lip colour.

Pensively, Gulliver looked in on his two children. As indicated by their mother, they were both already fast asleep. Manon, the eldest, although almost ten now, still slept with her side-light on. Her main light had one of those bulbs that twirled within the fixing – an array of fluting discotheque shapes, of many colours, dancing about her rectangular bedroom. Gulliver habitually ducked before entering her bedroom. He put his right hand on the bed's metallic headboard before he leaned his six-foot-three frame forward. He planted a soft kiss on her freckled forehead before turning both lights off. Like her brother's bedroom, it was a mess.

Young Brody would be six the day before Valentine's – two days after his own birthday. This year he would be forty-five. The passing of time and age had never alarmed him. It was the thought of not making the most of it that played on his mind. In contrast, his wife, who was six years younger, was dreading turning forty in November. She'd thankfully forbidden him from arranging any party of any sort.

Brody's side-light had to remain switched on all night. Without it, he wouldn't be able to find the toilet: in the past year, since sacrificing many a training nappy to the bin, he had urinated in a number of places, having become disorientated in the dark. His hair was a shade lighter than Manon's red mop. His scalp of strawberry blonde hair was not too dissimilar to his grandmother's, but more unruly, like his father's and his grandfather before them. Another kiss planted, he attempted to remove Brody's thumb from his mouth. His mother-in-law had warned them both of the possibility of protruding teeth.

Now standing on the landing, Gulliver was about to head towards their bedroom, their en-suite beyond, when suddenly he turned before jogging resentfully back downstairs.

'Damn it. I'll call her now and get it over with. It's not as if she'll thank me in the morning for not troubling her during our last precious hours of the weekend!'

8

MRS BARBARA TANNER never cries much at all. Unbelievably, she used to cry all the time, once upon. Before that, she used to laugh too. When she was happy. When she didn't have a clue about life and men.

She used to go to the cinema with either her sister or school friends, all the time – a bag of chips on the way home. She had the world ahead of her. Like her sister, she wanted to be a nurse, and marry a doctor. Walk proud in the sterile uniform. Professional. Save lives. Cheat the reaper. An angel on the ward.

Then she fell in love. With a ride. Her favourite movies at the time, in 1969, were *Butch Cassidy and the Sundance Kid* and *Midnight Cowboy*. Both Mrs Tanner and Mrs Lexton love spaghetti westerns. When they were kids, their father insisted they all watch them together, usually on a Sunday. They were always on the cowboy's side – against the dirty Indians – the enemy who scalped the innocent – even women and kids.

Like the majority of the public, they had both changed their minds about the Indians following the movie *Dances with Wolves,* Neither of them fancied Kevin

Costner. But by 1990 a lot had changed. And not necessarily for the better.

Butch Cassidy and the Sundance Kid was a great movie. She went to see it with her sister Jo. She fancied the pants of Robert Redford, the *Sundance Kid*. Her sister felt the same way about Paul Newman who was *Butch Cassidy*. They never argued over boys. Their taste was too different. They both agreed that there was nothing like a good train robbery in a movie. The pulsing pace of the tracks juxtaposed against the rhythmic shooting of guns: Bang! BANG! Hang.

Midnight Cowboy was an X rated movie. X rhymes with sex. She went to see *that* film with Trevor Tanner. A ride. For sure. She thought about doing more than just watching the movie. But once it started, she had to watch it all. Couldn't miss a minute of it. Joe Buck was the Midnight Cowboy. Joe Buck, rhymes with fuck.

She was like the cat that got the cream – everything to live for – her whole life ahead of her. Then she got married. Most of her friends were married. Nearly twenty-one. There wouldn't be a party. There wouldn't be one the following year for her sister either. Dad gone – cancer - mum too – drink – four broken hearts.

Against the odds, she'd just become a State Registered Nurse. Her sister Jo was training too, before she had to stop. Already married. But not like her: Jo was pregnant at 18. Her sister Jo didn't wear a wedding dress. That made Babs feel better on the day. Jo looked fat too. Everyone avoided looking at her swelling stomach. Jo didn't: she was already in love with her baby. Proud of it. Proud of her husband-to-be. She was sure it was a boy. Ben. Maybe Nicholas. Billy. Yes Billy. After their father Billy Bond.

Barbara Bond's jealousy didn't last long – about six months. In the past, whenever she got the chance, she liked to warn her sister that having a baby that young was like having a noose around your neck. Her nursing career over. But her wedding ring looked lovely on her left hand, even though her finger had swollen like a loaf.

Jo didn't care. She was married. Mrs Joan Lexton. A family. The nursery almost ready. Her husband Neil walking proud. The pram ready. Filled with cellular blankets. The neighbours were on alert, in case he was out digging a fresh grave. And couldn't be reached.

But then the baby came and it was dead. It didn't move. Still like a boulder. A good size. The midwife showed her the boy before she took him away. She forgot to weigh him. Just took him away. Billy. After her father. She was sure he was still alive. She didn't let her hold him. They didn't then. *Stop. STOP! WHERE ARE YOU GOING WITH MY BABY?*

It was dating Trevor Tanner that meant, like her sister now, she was all grown up. Almost a virgin before they married. Her sister carried on with the nursing. It helped. But she was never the same. Weakened. Dependant. Changed. Different. Married. Childless. A couple, not a family. Broken.

When Barbara Bond married, and became Mrs Barbara Tanner, she went from laughing lots to crying almost overnight. The first time happened after Mr Tanner came back from the pub. And she had a go at him. He liked her being cheeky. But she went too far. Smack. Didn't see it coming. From his face, neither did he. Did that just happen?

Her left cheek was bright red for three days. She stayed indoors. Called in sick to work. He was really sorry. Said he'd never do it again. So she loved him all the more. He really was sorry. Until the next time. Sorry. And the next. Won't happen again. It was when Mr Tanner bent her index finger back-back-back until it snapped that she knew he'd never stop. Snapped. Popped. No, snapped. Twig. Seventeen years of marriage.

Before she stopped altogether crying, she stopped feeling – the drink helped. It helped a lot. She could read his mood after a few years. Began to drink before he returned home. Numbed the senses. Stopped her from saying anything stupid. Making it worse. He'd told her she was a mouthy cow.

With the exception of her sister, no-one saw what he was doing. Not the nurses whom she worked with. Nor the doctors. Nor the neighbours. No-one wanted to see. But children everywhere could see. They knew. Even on the days she wore dark glasses and thick coats in the summer - they could see. *Look mummy – the Emperor isn't wearing any clothes!*

Her boss, the ward's matron, eventually got around to having an informal chat with her. She hoped he could help. He didn't see. *The children on the ward are vulnerable. Their parents need to feel they are in good hands.* Smack. Crack. Drink.

Then another warning. The last one. Absences. Lateness. Drink. None of them wanted to see. Let go. On the record. 35. Career - ended.

The drinking abruptly stopped when Mr Tanner was gone. He went from there all the time to gone. Wiped out. Dead at 41. Her a widow at 37. Two years too late. Two years after he ended her career for good. Died on the day he was born. September 1986. He'd been out drinking of course. *Gone but not forgotten.* That's what the grave said after he was buried. *Gone but not forgotten.*

***

'God he's a catch – fitter than a butcher's dog.'

Marie Doyle fancied Trevor Tanner. But Babs fancied him too. She fancied the pants off him. Marie was a catch with the lads. She was the prettier of the two; she had long brown hair and legs like pins. She looked shyly from behind her fringe at the boys. Her eyelids had a habit of raising themselves slowly, like in a movie. They liked that. She was a senior hairdresser too. All the boys liked hairdressers then.

But Babs was picky. She wasn't tall and she wasn't shy. She was petite and feisty. Trevor liked that. He liked the way she'd turned him down flat for weeks. A challenge. She'd finally got a job on a ward after a one year pre-nursing course as a cadet. Three years after registering, she was a fully-fledged State Registered Nurse. She wasn't going to give it up just like that. Not for a man. Even though she wanted him.

When she finally said yes to a date, she thought it would all be over. The teasing. The flirting. But Trevor liked her plenty. He'd ride the milk cart like he was dancing up and down the street – and call in on the way home. Kissing. Trevor was a ride.

She came home one day nearly crying. She'd had to nurse a new-born baby with ophthalmia neonatorum – conjunctivitis contracted during birth: she had to see to the baby to avoid the risk of blindness. When she entered the lounge crying, she saw Trevor there, in a suit, like he'd been to a funeral. He looked so handsome. A ride. Her parents weren't alive to see. Her sister Joan was there though, with her husband Neil, and no baby to hold. They were all there to see. He got down on one knee. For her.

Night after night, Babs lay in bed thinking about becoming Mrs Barbara Tanner. Even after they were married and went on honeymoon to Blackpool for a week, she'd lie there daydreaming, woolgathering as her father used to say, looking at her finger bound with his grandmother's gold. She lay in bed saying the name to herself. She packed her stuff up from Cider Drive and headed to North Lane. It was a council house but it had three bedrooms. One could be a nursery. She loved the smell of him, even before he washed. She loved the bones of him. He was hers. Marie didn't come to the wedding: she had the flu.

***

But tonight Mrs Tanner isn't remembering the happier times. It is hard to remember when largely there were so few. When she first married Mr Tanner, when she said the bit before *I do* and the bit about *for better or for worse* and she did mean it then, when she said those words, and everything that went with it – she never thought she'd plant an hammer so hard on the top of his skull that it would near kill him outright.

Truthfully, Mrs Tanner hadn't meant to murder him at first. She was trying to stop him using the hammer on her. It was a game he liked to play. *Tic-Tac-Toe. Missed the toe. Tic-Tac-Toe. Got that one. What yer crying for? You need to move yer feet faster.*

Her husband was as cruel with his mouth as he was with his fists. What began as a criticism, turned into disparage. What began privately, ended publicly. Any opportunity to denigrate her, even though most accusations were unfounded, he'd make them anyway. Any excuse in the end. Although the violence was always done indoors. The walls didn't stop anyone from knowing. But then something snapped one day. And it wasn't anything physical.

Unfortunately for Mr Tanner, once she hit him, she discovered a liking for it, not for killing but for harming

Mr Tanner. Getting him back. Seventeen years. She'd always wanted babies. So she didn't stop. A fit of extreme anger that she'd stored and buried, it seemed, for far too long. Seventeen years. She'd lost three babies. After he hit her. Her nursery empty like her sister's. Hammer. Foot. Elbow. Hold her face – kiss. Hold her head – butt. Seventeen. She clubbed Trevor Tanner seventeen times.

It was Mr Lexton's idea, popping him in the grave. Once the idea promulgated, it was accepted as fact. There was nothing else to be done – no alternative – a God-send to be sure.

At least an hour after hammering him to death, Mrs Tanner picked up the phone, to ring her sister; it was her husband who answered. He'd already dug a good hole that afternoon – covered it with tarpaulin – rain on and off all night. He did it on his own – always worked on his own those days – a private gravedigger. They were all private gravediggers then.

Mrs Tanner cleaned up the mess. She was cleaning it for weeks. Kept finding something or other. Especially bits on the wall, like someone had flicked bogies onto it. Mrs Tanner never told Mrs Lexton. She meant to at first. And Mr Lexton never told Mrs Lexton. They all owed each other. Besides, Whilst finding her strength again, Mrs Tanner did something she would never forget. Something she was deeply ashamed of.

Most gravediggers worked privately before the council took over. They didn't say things like *I'm sorry, council rules.* And it earned Mr Lexton good money. Working on your own doubled the effort but it also doubled the wage. And in those days, there was always a tip. A true philistine, Mr Lexton would either head to the betting shop or the pub; he'd at least spend half – he never wasted it on his wife - on flowers, for instance – not even on special days – or days when it could have made a difference: *flowers are for the dead Mrs Lexton – for the dead.*

9

POPE'S MOBILE NUMBER lit the screen once more. Catherine Shakespeare hadn't known her newly-appointed Sergeant for long but what little she knew of him already, she liked. He appeared diligent, insightful and reliable – an encouraging addition to their recently volatile team. He was very tall though – towered above them all – and handsome too. She was sure he wouldn't have called her at home, had it not been important.

It was also fair to say that her adjustment at work, since her unexpected promotion almost eighteen months earlier, had been strenuous to say the least. Her predecessor and best friend, the late Detective Inspector Hermione Folkard, had been the barricade that had sheltered them all from the political pressures thrust upon the front-runners, leaders that could not afford to take anything personally. Here she was now, standing in her shoes.

Now that barrier, that front-runner, was herself; she had to both juggle demands and evaluate efficiently - on a daily basis - decide what was necessary - what needed to be done. In many ways, the sudden adjustment to her role was assisted by her taciturn demeanour: keeping busy on her toes, had been just what she had needed – survival through adversity.

In contrast though, altering to the sudden company of the newly appointed Sergeant was another matter. She struggled to modify – grow used to his presence about her. He was an intrusion she could not reject. Until his appointment, she'd been happy in her office alone, with her thoughts – well, not alone - she mentally ran things by Hermione almost daily.

Of course, she knew deep down that she needed him. Needed to move on. On the day when Gulliver made his closing speech to the interview panel, she instinctively recognised he was the right person to fill her own shoes – the original Sergeant's post – the right person to complement their already efficient squad.

Hermione would have liked him – she really would have. He had a good strong jawline – markedly striking - telegenic even. Although clearly not her type, she had noticed he had attracted a fair bit of attention already. He had a shy smile. More importantly, he came highly recommended.

'Gulliver.'

'Sorry to disturb you at home Catherine – I wasn't entirely sure whether to call you at home or not. All the same, I thought I'd better let you know, before you make your way in tomorrow.'

'Thank you. Ok. I'm listening.'

'I came off shift at six this evening, just before a call from the local press was put through to me – the reporter on the other end was wanting a statement. Could be something or nothing.'

'Sounds intriguing?'

'To cut a long story short – a body has been uncovered prior to a burial at a local cemetery – male – for the moment unidentified. Been there a while it seems.'

'How peculiar – how many in the plot already?'

'Two when there should have been one – the as-of-yet unidentified body appears to have been illegally buried below the coffin of a Mr Brian Brookner. His wife, Zaenab, died Boxing Day and was due to be buried with him on the day the body was discovered – her funeral on hold, I suppose. A watch apparently caught the eye of one of the gravediggers. When they looked closer, they realised it was attached to a decomposed wrist.'

'When did this happen?'

'New Year's Eve. The reporter didn't think it was a hoax call. I left his number on your desk. I said we'd give him a call tomorrow.'

'So why didn't we hear this from the gravediggers themselves? It doesn't make sense.'

'He also stated that the anonymous caller was a female – and that she believed there were more bodies buried illegally about the cemetery.'

'You're kidding right? How bizarre. Do me a favour, pay a visit to the cemetery and have a look around. Find out if there is any truth to the story. If it's true, I'd like to know why 999 wasn't their first port of call!'

'If it's true – it's a mess. Surely we wouldn't dig up grave after grave just to check such a claim?'

'At the tax-payers cost? I doubt it very much. I can't see any judge agreeing to that – certainly not on hearsay. We'd need proof. I'd better call Griffin.'

'Griffin?'

'The Superintendent. Gary Griffin. You haven't met him yet then?'

'No. Not yet.'

'Ok. Well, I'll see you in the morning then. Happy New Year Catherine!'

The pause that followed seemed to be one filled with an inexplicable air of alarm. Gulliver Pope thought he heard Catherine inhale deeply before she coughed noisily as if clearing her throat.

'Did the reporter refer to any particular cemetery?'

'I'm sorry. I thought I'd mentioned it. Sorry. I've had a glass of wine since. Liverpool Road Cemetery. The one –'

'Thank you Gulliver. I know it. I'll see you in the morning.'

Catherine did not mean to interrupt him when she did. She didn't mean to prevent him from speaking either; she just wanted to put a stop to their conversation. A stop with a clear red outline would do. The last thing she expected was to find herself launched into an investigation involving an array of illegally buried bodies, and in a cemetery that she seemed to be visiting with frequency. What a start to the New Year! Maybe for the first time she'd realised, it was time to leave the past just there. In the past. Time to move on. Time to heal.

10

LIKEWISE, MRS JOAN Lexton never cries much either. Not anymore. Time, loss and experience have seen to that emotive response. Hardened her. Dried her up. Of the two sisters, she is the one who has cried the most - since they were both blissfully married. Of the two, she is the youngest and the most sensitive.

At one point in her life, about a month after the baby was born dead, she was like Picasso's *Weeping Woman* – a suffering machine - he liked to refer to females like that. A handkerchief to her face – a security blanket. Something to cling to. Hide your face from. She'd taken a break from her career, a year. To have the baby. She wasn't even sure she would resume her nursing course. She'd have her hands full.

Empty hands. Empty arms. What to do? Grip handkerchief. Avoid nursery. Avoid mirrors. Keep busy. Her breasts leaked milk for months after. Once, a neighbour's baby cried in her pram as she passed her, trying to avoid her at all costs. Jealousy stabbing her. Her breasts leaked then. No-one saw it. But they did. She once thought about taking a baby from a pram whilst she sat in Botanic Park.

For a long while, she was a colourful and volatile nervous wreck. Her thin, calcium-depleted nails all bitten. Her cuticles, once like piping on a blazer, had been steadily groomed and torn at by her teeth - flecks of skin protruding from ridges had been pulled far too back – the pink skin exposed. Bleeding. A nervous wreck. A car crash.

Her wedding ring was loose on her finger for months. In the end she took it off, and wore it about her throat, on a short noose-like necklace that had been her mother's.

The angular lines and overlapping shapes of her face augmented the anguish. Her husband wasn't much help. He came to the hospital to see her after the purposeless birth. She never learned her sister Babs had made him. When he finally showed up, he looked embarrassed to be there. He stood by her bed wanting to point the finger. Nothing wrong with my sperm. Jo staring at the wall. No words. No holding of hands. *I do. In sickness and in health. For better and for worse. I do.* Joan staring at the open window. Jump. Just hatred for the world, and herself. Jump.

Neil Lexton was only just twenty at the time. Jo was eighteen. Two years after sweet sixteen. When she was a virgin - and her mind was filled with dreams of marrying a doctor. *I do.*

She'd aged overnight. Her skin had loosened about her eyes. Lost. Where am I? Lost. Who am I? Lost. She'd lost lots of weight. In 1968. Everything known too little and far too late. She'd only known him just over a year.

They went out less and less as a couple after that, especially after she cried in public, in his company. Embarrassed him. After she saw a Silver Cross pram down Lord Street – the one that looked like an early version of an upturned Citroen Dyane. White wheels like roulettes.

She was thrown, the first time it happened. She hadn't anticipated the pain that would follow. The shock of it. The pram was at a distance – across from them, on the other side of a black and white zebra crossing. The sun's brilliance shining. The silver metal glinted. She didn't even notice who was pushing it. She didn't even see the baby. She didn't even hear it.

It was just the sight of the pram. A large dark blue one – white *Broderie Anglaise* around the hood. The colours like a nurse's uniform. Her empty pram at home, in the cold garage – waiting to be sold. The white wheels spotless - unspun. The half-barrel of the carriage like a small coffin. Her husband Neil had stuffed it with the baby's hospital bag. Inside, the baby's clothes, nappies and the latest soft toy in the shops. A black and white Snoopy. Plush.

For almost a month, Mrs Lexton wouldn't let him near her. *Don't.* He needed her in a totally different way than she needed him. He'd even proposed trying for another baby to get into her knickers again. Lied. Said the doctor had advised it best. But she wasn't having any of it. Don't! She wasn't about to replace her child with another.

She'd loved her little Billy intensely, every day since his known existence. She'd sang to him. Felt him move, graze against her insides, push the flat of his tiny foot against the temporary barrier that existed between them. Her need to finally get her hands on him, hold him, growing more intense day by day. Billy was born. It really did happen. She was sure she hadn't made it up.

Her back was turned most nights. Don't! She lay curled like a plumeless thistle – purple discs below her eyes – her spine bent over like a beggar. Pyjamas. No more nightdresses. It didn't matter to him, for now. He wanted her from behind anyway. He was sick of looking at her face – crumpled like paper. Her green eyes sick and hard like small pebbles.

Babs, as she was called by Jo in those days, called around from time to time. She didn't fully understand her sister's depression but she could see that her husband's rejection and lack of compassion was taking its toll. She tried to help. Cover for him. Told Jo it was his job that had hardened him.

His lack of understanding was probably natural. Seeing the dead. Burying them. Sometimes day in and day out. She told her sister that he didn't meant to be so cold. And unfeeling. And selfish. She made her sister cry. She shouldn't have said the word 'dead'.

'I never got to hold my Billy. They took him away. I didn't get the chance to bury him. I'm not sure where he is. You'd think I'd know where they take them. Where they took Billy. I don't. Can you find out?'

Of course, Jo believed it was mostly her fault. She was obviously responsible. She'd done plenty wrong during her pregnancy. The wine on her birthday. The many buckets of coal that she shouldn't have carried after she'd learned she was pregnant. The hoisting of the bucket to top up the fire was straining enough. The overloaded shopping bags, some containing baby clothes. The list was endless.

'Did you find out what they did with my Billy? Did they bury him?'

Her arrogance had been proud and pregnant. She'd held her own when she found out she was expecting – although at first, she cried. Panicked. She'd lacked humility. Maybe all atheists were punished after all. Conflicting thoughts. Her confidence and sass gone. Her husband now eyeing her with suspicion and contempt. Her mother-in-law no longer interested. The neighbours. No more midwife visits. Her robust and large barren breasts weeping and seeping. No mother. No father. Her sister, Babs, was dating a milkman. Her life ahead of her. Children. Nursery. Pram.

'He was buried Jo. They bury all the still births in one plot.'

She should have said Billy. Jo's face flinched when she said the word 'still'.

'Where's Billy Babs?'

'No-one knows. They're buried in either a communal grave or in the grave of a female adult. I'm so sorry Jo. I just don't know.'

She was glad he wasn't on his own. One day she'd learn where all the babies were laid. Couldn't be far away. Somewhere to put flowers. She tried to move on. No she didn't. She didn't want to move on. Everyone else was telling her that – that she needed to move on. For her own good. For the good of them both.

Neil's mother, Eileen, said her son was a sensitive soul too. That it had broken his heart. So she went out for the afternoon. That Saturday. Almost a month after the baby was born dead. A month after they didn't let her hold him. Baby Billy Lexton. His Snoopy in her handbag.

Then she saw the blue pram. And something took hold of her by the throat – gripped her and choked her. Took her by the throat and pushed her eyes inwards. Pushed her eyes in and filled her eyes with water. Bent her double. Her chest like it was filled with trapped wind. She'd had sex before marriage. She was being punished for being the daring one. The dirty one. Plenty of eyes had thrown cursory glances bearing the same sentiment. For breaking the rules. For getting caught. For flaunting your belly. For being a whore. That's what you get. Whore.

***

But as a child, as a little girl who had a mum, and a dad, and a big sister, who loved and protected her – although she always bossed her about - she laughed on and off, lots and lots – like jelly tots.

One Christmas, a very long time ago, over a half-a-century ago, when they were five and six, and they lived at Cider Drive – the Bond family – the family that everyone secretly aspired to be - one Christmas, she distinctly remembers her sister and herself finding a flat bright-red package buried below the others. Their mother had put it there deliberately, underneath the others, so that they'd open it last.

Mouths the shape of a tall O. Inside, two nurse outfits, to dress up in. Both sisters squealed as they opened it roughly, realising what was inside. The red paper had reindeers on it. Antlers parted like wishbones. The paper was eventually burned on the coal fire alongside the rest of the wrapping. They didn't even read the label that bore their mother's handwriting. *To Babs and Jo from Father Christmas.* A hole burned through the middle of it before it was swallowed whole like the one-legged paper ballerina who fell in love with the one-legged steadfast tin-soldier.

Their mum and dad used to watch a daytime soap called *General Hospital*. With the exception of one longstanding nurse, all the other characters married doctors. They both hoped to marry doctors. Not a milkman and a gravedigger. There are no soaps about marrying them.

Nellie Oleson from *The Little House on the Prairie* nearly put them off nursing at first. Jo loved the Sunday afternoon programme more than her sister did. She was Laura Ingalls. She had two plaits just like her; their hair was the same colour.

This character of her choosing was the second daughter to her parents, just like her. She was high-spirited and inquisitive – just like her. But she hated the Oleson girl - with her blonde ringlets and her screwed up pig of a face. She was malicious and supercilious. She was always pretending to be a nurse. She bullied almost all the children into being her friend.

Jo Bond's favourite episode was one called *The Cheaters*. Finally, Nellie's mother, who was really responsible for her daughter's spoilt and vicious attitude, marched towards her in her puffed-up black dress – her hair tied tightly back – head lowered – middle parting aiming at her. She'd learned that Nellie had been cheating at cards. She was furious because she had defended her.

'Not on your Nellie!'

'Not my Nellie!'

Now she'd been made to look foolish. Her face was a picture; it always was. Lips scrunched up.

Her mother took hold of her and thankfully gave her a good spanking. Nellie cried in public. It was brilliant. Even Nellie's father had a smile on his face. No-one blamed him. Everyone liked Mr Oleson: he was kind. His face was kind. Joan clapped her hands with delight when that bit happened. Her sister and mother joined in too.

Their nursing outfits were the same size: there wasn't much difference between the two sisters at the time. Both Bond girls were petite and slim. Both had mousy brown hair and green eyes, like their mother. When they were in primary school, they had been mistaken for twins, on numerous occasions. People mistake them now in their current state. But as late teenagers, they both thankfully blossomed – easy to differentiate. Their personalities differed too. Jo was shyer than Barbara – but of the two of them, she was the most daring – the one likely to get into trouble.

Their dressing-up outfits had a long blue dress with a white apron to it – a large red cross to the middle. They also had a headpiece; to the middle was another red cross. Jo remembers now that sometime later their mother got them a plastic stethoscope and white plastic shoes. They played with their outfits until they were too small to fit into – the Velcro fastening allowing them to wear them until they were seven or even eight.

Their father didn't like their outfits at first. They were World War One uniforms. His own father had died in the war. A nurse had sent his mother a letter that had been dictated by him – just before he died. He'd always wanted to find and thank the nurse but he never did. His mother let him have the letter when he asked for it. She wanted to keep it for herself. But his eyes necessitated the envelope that carried more than just a private message. His father had managed to sign it.

Their mother felt bad – she apologised when he got up and left the room. But one day, he surprised them all by returning home with lots of bandages, nappy-pins and plasters; all of it taken from work. Before the afternoon was over, every doll and teddy-bear was sick in the house; sick with one ailment or another – a mass epidemic. Jo's collection of soft toys and dolls had been bound and dressed in time for the favoured afternoon soap. They sat fascinated with their parents who held hands - a large pot of tea and a plate of moo-cow milk biscuits on the coffee table.

On the day when their father Billy was suddenly in hospital, when they were about to become teenagers and were still in school, when they had every faith in the system that the doctors and nurses would make him better, fix him, he abruptly died – without even saying good-bye. No letter. Their mother had nipped out to the loo. 1962.

Their father was dead within six weeks of being diagnosed with bowel cancer. Thirty-eight years old. His whole life ahead of him. All of them left behind. Broken. Lost property. Lacking in purpose.

All Mrs Lexton can remember now is how he looked at the time, on the last day she saw him, the day she said to her mother that she didn't want to see him in his coffin but she did because her mother made them.

Babs said their father didn't look right: 'It doesn't look like dad!' And he didn't. He was really small and thin, like a child in a cot. The shiny pleated stuff around him didn't look right either. It made her feel sick.

Years later, Mr Lexton told his wife, in detail, what an embalmer's job involved. She wished he hadn't but it explained a lot. Her sister had ran out of the room crying so Jo followed too. Their mother eventually joined them and never went back.

At the time, Mrs Lexton had blamed the female nurse who was with him last. He'd been fine before that. Had even had something to eat. She looked Indian the nurse. Her soft eyes were as dark as her coarse hair. The Indians got him in the end. Of course, Mrs Lexton knows it was bowel cancer that killed him. A movie playing out in her head. Her father died just before the Christmas holiday. He said when he got home they'd all go to the cinema to see *A Charlie Brown Christmas*. All their friends had seen it. Everyone was talking about it. Their mother wanted to see *Doctor Zhivago*. She watched it alone the week she died.

When their mother made an effort to get the decorations out from the attic about a week or two later, Jo shouted at her not to bother – so she didn't. Jo never shouted. But she wasn't going to have Christmas without her dad. Babs agreed. Their mother did too. They all had a miserable Christmas that year. It hasn't been much better since then.

At eighteen, like her sister, Jo was training to become a State Registered Nurse: her sister a year ahead of her. She had a boyfriend she wasn't too serious about. He was nice, she liked to be seen with him. He was good looking. A head-turner. Her sister said he was a ride. After the cowboy films. She'd heard her mother say it once about John Wayne. But she wanted to marry a doctor. And someone taller, like her dad. Someone who smiled more.

Just before her nineteenth she discovered she was pregnant. And had to get married quickly. Shotgun wedding. No gun. Just the wedding. Her sister was glaring at her when she told everyone. Glaring. If looks could kill. She was going to become a Mrs before her. A mother too. Mrs Neil Lexton. She'd got there first.

On the day she got married, she was elated. It was such a rush – organised in a month. Her cream dress had been borrowed from someone Neil's mother knew; Eileen was a great help. She sorted her flowers too. A posy of cream roses. Every time she looked down at them, to smell them even, there was a ladybird somewhere in between the petals. She loved ladybirds. She was getting sick of the whole cream-theme too. A point made. White for virgins. Cream for whores. Her son – butter wouldn't melt. His mother knew he'd been about too, before her. He'd been her first. Double standards.

Her shoes were new though. Satin. Her wedding ring was new too. Thin. Dainty. Bought in a sale at H. Samuels. *I do.* Neil didn't want one: not all men wore them then. He wanted to save the money for the honeymoon. In a caravan in Wales. Two nights and three days. It didn't stop raining. It didn't matter. They hardly left the caravan. It rained outside. They steamed all the windows up. They laughed all weekend. She remembers being sore. Liking feeling sore. Needed. Married.

A few years later, when her sister got married, to a milkman, they spent a week in Blackpool in a posh hotel. Three stars. They saw all the sights. Her husband, Trevor said he'd hit the jackpot in his speech. Babs looked so happy.

Neither of them honeymooned in Paris like they planned. All those years ago. When they were supposed to marry doctors.

Neil was an only child: his mother had always wanted a daughter, she said. Jo didn't fully believe her. It was the way she stared at her that gave it away. During an argument, two days before the wedding, Neil said his mother thought her too big for her boots – up herself. She was glad when he said it. She wanted him to know she could have done better. Was punching well above his weight. Alan Smith fancied the pants off her. He was now studying to be a doctor. She could have married him. But she didn't. His two front teeth stuck out a little, and his breath smelled.

They didn't need a car to get to St John's Church: it was just down the road, a five minute walk, so she did. Walk. Proud. Shameless. Enjoyed arriving late. Her sister walked with her: moody. Jo knew why. She'd got there first. Now wasn't the time for it.

When she walked up the aisle she noticed everyone looking at her lovely bouquet. Eileen said she had to hold the flowers above her waist, with both hands. So the priest wouldn't know. She showed her how to do it. Neil was smiling nervously at the front. The priest told him to turn around. So he did. *I do.*

Joan was sure it was a boy. Ben. Maybe Nicholas. Billy. Yes Billy. After their father Billy Bond. William Lexton. Billy Lexton. Bill. Will. There was plenty of time to sort his name out. If she had a girl, she'd call her Mary, her mother's name. Mary was a lovely name.

In six months' time, she'd be a mother. They'd be parents. A family. The Lexton family living at Cider Drive. Her parents' home. Barbara's home too. There was enough room.

By the eighth month, the nursery was almost ready. The pram was parked in the entrance hall - filled with cellular blankets. And the latest must have toy. Snoopy. Plush. Only the best for Billy. Or Mary. The luckiest boy or girl in the world. Her arms empty but ready. Ready for anything. No regrets.

The neighbours were on alert, in case her husband was out digging a fresh grave. And couldn't be reached. In case Babs was out doing her training. To become a Nurse. And couldn't be reached. But the baby came at night. In the dark. It was bitter cold outside. When Joan's waters broke she awoke her husband snoring next to her. Little Billy's on his way!

She'd decided on Billy. Babs was annoyed. She wanted Billy for her first male born. Tough. My name now. Babs hoped it would be a girl. But it wasn't. She came straight around. God love her. Always there.

She knew she hadn't wet herself. Like a light had been switched on. The pain. Sharp. Bloody hell. Pant. No. Not like that. Like this. Good girl. That's better.

It was raining heavily then: everyone was ready. In the car. Pant. No. Pant like this. Like the nurse showed you. Good girl. That's better. Neil was driving his wheelbarrow of a car. He'd had Robin Reliants all of his life. The shape of an iron. The last one had an automatic transmission box. But it was yellow like a canary. He'd sold it the night he was planning to leave her. Saved them both a job. His suitcase was packed by the door. Babs took it to a charity shop.

Babs was holding her right hand when they had to stop half-way up the drive. Her two bags. Left by the front door, in the hall way, by the pram.

All the pushing. Babs holding her hand. Her eyes sorry and worried. Good job Neil wasn't there. Not allowed in back then. Had gone back home to his mother's. Didn't know what to do with himself. Too early in the morning to wet the baby's head.

Babs said Jo had wet herself twice. Tried to make her laugh between crying. The midwife liked her. Although she looked serious. Called for the doctor just before the baby came. It was a boy. She pulled herself up and saw it was a boy. Testicles like boulders. Was that normal?

Billy Lexton was here. Pain free at last. Pass him to me. Where are you going? Instinct and panic kicking in like a drug overdose. He was a good size. The midwife showed him to Jo from a distance. Fear in her eyes. Like what she saw in her father's face the week he died. She then took him out of the hot white room. Wrapped in a hospital cellular blanket. She forgot to weigh him.

Next morning Neil was in the betting shop holding a bunch of flowers when his father told him. He never bought her flowers after that. When she asked him after a row, on their third wedding anniversary, he said that that flowers were for the dead. At the time she didn't know what to say. Maybe he was right. If she had a grave for Billy, she'd have visited it, spent time with him, covered it with flowers. Sowed him a meadow. But she never saw him again. At the time she begged and begged. But they just took him away.

***

Mrs Lexton only cries now from time to time. She is far too old to cry. On Billy's birthday she lays flowers on her mother's and father's grave, five minutes up the road, where she was married, a long time ago. At

Christmas she lays flowers too. She lays flowers whenever she likes. His body is God-knows-where. That is the cruellest of all. They took him away. And she never got to say goodbye.

11

BY TWELVE the incident board was taking some shape. A stone of some weight had been thrown into a murky pond; the ripples were yet to take full effect. Day after New Year and the hangovers in the room were obvious. By far, Detective Constable Liz O'Leary's was the worse. In her right hand she held an inventory of possessions. Her left, held a half-litre bottle of water.

A close-up shot of the deceased, as of yet unnamed, was to the centre of the board. It wasn't a pretty picture. A visit to SOCO would reveal more; the corpse had obviously been down there a long time. Inspector Shakespeare paused before the board – a photograph of the gravestone in sight.

'It looks like the body may have been buried about the same time as the first official burial. The gravestone indicates that Brian Brookner, died 18th September 1986. That means the burial was likely to have taken place any time in the next fortnight.'

Gulliver joined Catherine at the board. Together they presented themselves as a formidable team. He smiled as he looked about the room.

'We're possibly talking over thirty years. Charlotte, can you get me the burial paperwork as well as the names of the gravediggers involved?'

'I'll get on to it now.'

'Liz – the list of possessions?'

'He was buried with his watch, still about his wrist, wallet and passport – unusual. Details to follow via SOCO. Mansell should have a name by now.'

'Thank you.'

'When Mansell has finished with the watch, I'd like to take it to a watchmaker and have it looked at. It looks expensive, might tell us something. A watch like that almost always has the initials of the watchmaker on the inside of the case - initialled every time it is opened for any repair. A signature amongst the trade.'

'Interesting – never heard that one before – good idea Liz.'

Luke McKenna scratched the back of his head as he began to speak.

'It's an expensive watch; I wonder what his occupation was?'

'Could have been passed down – I know what you mean though. Interesting that it was not removed and sold on.'

'We do also need to consider the likelihood that the grave was dug the previous evening and that the body was placed at the bottom and covered up before the burial the following day.'

Catherine Shakespeare, who had since withdrawn to collect something from her nearby office, now stood framed in the doorway of her adjoining glass-panelled office. Instinctively she nodded in approval of Charlotte's suggestion; Charlotte always thought outside the box – she was a valuable member of the team. Catherine had recently and finally got around to having her eyes tested. Her squinting gaze towards the incident board suggested she was yet to adjust to wearing her new spectacles full-time.

She'd complained to Wendy that wearing them gave her a headache. Like everything in Catherine's life, any modification required time. And perseverance. She advanced a few paces before she spoke.

'I am still intrigued as to why the two gravediggers did not contact the police until this morning. Someone contacted the *Visitor* before us. We have their names. Let's interview them as soon as – before they collude to such an extent that we cannot make head nor tail of the whole situation.'

'Malcolm Pearson and Michael Litt have both worked for Sefton Council for just under thirty years. They could be connected in some way. I'll pick them up and get them ready for interview.'

'Thank you Luke. Ask them about this anonymous female caller too. We are not going to start digging up any graves unless the caller comes forward and she has some proof! Let me know when you're back: Catherine and I are hoping to see Mansell this afternoon, even if it's only for a preliminary report.'

Catherine Shakespeare nodded before reclaiming her office. Since Hermione Folkard's death, she had altered very little in it. Bar a photograph of Zita in Wendy's arms, on the day of their wedding day, there was very little else belonging to herself. It was just an office after all.

In reality, to Catherine, it was a place where she had once spent a lot of time with her line manager and dear friend. When she needed to think, this is where she did it, an environment where she liked to believe that her colleague was still about, from time to time, keeping an eye on her, keeping her on her toes.

'Can I come in?'

'Of course.'

'I'm going to see if Omar can access any CCTV in the area. Unlikely but still worth a try. Samuel is out interviewing the family. We'll hear from him soon enough.'

'Let me know as soon as Mansell gets in touch. Should be interesting to say the least.'

'I used to be a Family Liaison Officer myself back in the day. Loved the job. Samuel hasn't been with us long has he?'

'No. New to the role. Doing a decent job. And Yes, I knew about your role – will be nice for you, having someone around whom you have much in common with?'

For a moment Gulliver found himself lost for words. Had she indirectly just told him to go and bond elsewhere? Was she blind to his efforts? With whom was he to develop a relationship with at work? Meet for a pint? Moan about the job? Not that he had cause to moan. He knew Catherine to have a child. As parents, maybe he could at some point strike up a conversation about their parenting roles - the highs and lows.

'Yes, maybe. I'll certainly offer my support. Fancy a pint or a drink after? Or do you need to get home?'

'I need to get home. Thanks.'

Gulliver hesitated as though he was about to say something else. His body language gave him away. It was the body language of an FLO – concerned – caring. Just what she didn't need. Catherine Shakespeare stopped him in his tracks before he had the chance to speak again.

'Another time, maybe.'

Gulliver smiled warmly as Catherine averted his gaze; instead, she looked downwardly and carried on with her paperwork. He decided, for now, not to take it personally. He just hadn't experienced this level of hostility from a senior colleague before. It crossed his mind that maybe he should have stopped in Wales.

Olivia was after all the key reason for his move. He knew that, even though he didn't want to admit it. Hadn't been truthful with his wife. How could he.

Had he stayed, he was sure his marriage would have not survived. He loved Carys. She was an exceptionable woman. A faultless mother. She was cute as a button even now. Her sapphire eyes complimented her medium-brown hair and pale skin. She was elegant and unselfish. She deserved better.

But he had fallen in love with Olivia.

Not a day went by when he did not think of her. Intoxicated. Not a day went by when he wouldn't push back the memory of that explosive afternoon together to the back of his mind. Not a day.

12

MRS LEXTON QUALIFIED as a State Registered Nurse, in 1971, when she was twenty-one. Her sister, now Barbara Tanner, had qualified two years earlier. She got her a job at the same local hospital as her – a bus ride away. She did so because she felt guilty: she had not spent enough time supporting her. Being there when it counted. Mrs Tanner had spent time coping with her own demons. She'd lost a child too - the battle never won. Her husband Trevor growing in confidence. Handy. But a ride all the same.

Work was what kept both sisters going – a reason for living. A chance to shine. Be themselves. Most people they knew worked before going home to what mattered. Then their social life started. Both Mrs Tanner and Mrs Lexton were the opposite; they lived to work.

There was nothing like the sight of children, who were truly dependant on adults, cheating death daily, to remind them both that others were indeed worse off. Both childless, the children they cared for were more than just patients – they were their children –

their responsibility. They were needed on Ward 4. They were not needed at home.

Unlike most women they knew, working in the eighties, they were able to work longer hours. Take on more responsibility. Unintentionally, they had slowly isolated themselves from everyone else. Everyone else had children – were a family. In the staff room, most women sat during their breaks knitting and sharing patterns. Their sympathetic glances helped at first. Then the resentment set in. It was easier working through lunches – getting some shopping done together.

But in reality, their lives at home where setting them both up for a fall. Their personal circumstances had pinpointed them on an unalterable timeline. Mrs Tanner – a domestic life packed with abuse - regret. *I do.* Mrs Lexton – a life of mental conflict – regret. *I do.* Two paths running side by side. Heading in one direction. The same direction. A journey filled with tragedy, doom and gloom.

For a while, Mrs Lexton worked happily on the same children's ward for the terminally ill, as her sister. But after only a couple of years, she needed to take time off. That's how it was. On and off. And no shortage of nurses then. Depression clubbing her in the morning, even before she was fully awake. Poor Jo.

Five years on. Looking better. Growing worse. Just before her thirties, she took an overdose. More than a handful of pills. Stolen from work. After little Regan had passed away peacefully in the night. A little boy she had cared for on the ward for many months. She'd left a short note for her sister Babs. She was going to join Billy. She was going to join their mother and father. *Please forgive me. I love you.*

She'd thought about jumping to her death. Ever since Billy. She'd thought about it almost daily for as long as she could remember. Sometimes she didn't even think about it. It was just there. Jump. The word popped out from her sub-conscience. Like the word God. Jesus. Jump. Jump.

She'd been to a bridge in Ainsdale, and looked over. Much higher than she'd ever realised. Timed it. Wondered if the train would just pass over her. She worked out how she needed to land. She'd stand sideways. Jump.

She knew if she drank enough she'd do it. She also knew when she was going to do it. But then one day she heard one of the girls at work talking about her husband. She was angry. He wasn't sleeping. Taking pills. A woman had jumped onto the line before his eyes. He'd ran straight over her. Made a distinctive, indescribable sound. He couldn't find the words for it. He kept waking up sweating in the night. Wouldn't take time off work. Horror in his eyes.

Jumping was no longer an option. She couldn't do that to someone. She then thought of the effect it would have on her sister. Better not to. Pills would do the job. Plenty of pills. She'd head to their parents' grave, then

Neil wouldn't find her and call an ambulance. She almost looked forward to it. To the end of torment. To peace. Everlasting peace. She thought she believed in God then.

Her stomach was pumped after it had been filled with a charcoal solution. Twice. She couldn't remember much of what happened. She'd wet herself – she could smell it. Drifting in and out of consciousness. Lolloping. Couldn't hold her head up. Head swung to the right like a cupboard opening. Vomited onto the floor. Vomit on her overalls. A cardboard-grey kidney shaped tray held by a dark hand with a wedding ring to it. She just wanted to sleep. She didn't care. She needed to be left alone. She noticed her toe-nails needed cutting.

When she awoke from a long sleep, her sister was there. She looked like she was scowling at first. Then the reality dawned. What had she done? Like a child caught stealing sweets. Shame. She looked at her toes. Her legs were open. She closed them. Folded her right toes over her left. Her legs stiff and heavy. She smelled clean now. But her hair smelled dirty. Her sister wheeled her to the shared bathroom – you couldn't talk without every word echoing along the corridor. Babs smiled as she bathed her. She'd pulled her sleeves up to do so. Knelt on the floor to wash her.

'What are we going to do with you Jo?'

'I'm sorry Babs.'

'Nothing to be sorry about Jo. It's me who should be saying sorry. We'll manage. Work it out between us.'

'Your arms – they're both bruised!'

Babs smiled. She finished bathing her before she washed her sister's hair. Jo had forgotten how much she liked having her hair washed. Their mother used to put them both in the same bath and wash their hair in the same water. She always urinated in the water on purpose. Babs would have a fit. She'd move the bubbles aside, on purpose, so that her sister would see the yellow cloud spread like smoke below the water. Babs would scream. Jo would laugh hysterically. Mum tutted to support Babs but really she thought it was funny.

During the four days she was there, most nurses caring for her spoke kindly to her – out of pity of course. She was one of their own. But damaged. Broken. Barren. Their faces said they knew. Sparks of anger awoke her early in the morning – always about 3 am. Then the image of Regan asleep. At peace. On Ward 4. Her mind skipped constantly. Who found her? Why couldn't they just leave her alone? She knew she was meant to be saving lives. How could she? She didn't even want to save her own.

But her sister Babs whispered something into her ear when she was bathing her. She thought about those three words for a long time. She said them and her eyes filled with tears. Then quick as a wink, she blinked them away and smiled.

Her husband Neil didn't visit at first, then he was there all the time. Not long after, her doctor agreed to her husband's pleas to sign the form that would magically pack her up - up and out of the house - off to Greaves Hospital for the Mentally Insane. He hoped before long, that she would return looking like her old self, sexy, sane and feisty. Maybe less feisty. After all, she wasn't the first woman to lose a baby. He'd lost the baby too.

He hadn't gone about moping. Embarrassing. That's what it was. Embarrassing. She needed to move on. She needed experts. In the field. Help. She needed help. He loved her of course.

When Mrs Lexton was sectioned, neither sister was much help to the other. One was physically broken - the other mentally. Mrs Tanner did not suspect her sister to be responsible for the abrupt death of Regan Hallworth, a little boy of seven, who had been on Ward 4 less than six months. He was always going to die. He only had a mother. She wasn't coping well. Sometimes she didn't visit: she had *other kids to see to as well*. He had CLC – Chronic Lymphoid Leukaemia. It had shrunken him. His head bulbous. His face colourless, gaunt – expressionless.

His journey into God's arms was taking forever. So one night, after his mother hadn't visited three days on the run, after the lad had cried himself to sleep, referring to himself as a burden, Mrs Lexton injected him under his right arm with a shot of Insulin. She kissed his forehead and held him whilst he peacefully breathed slowly in and out. The following day he was dead. On this awful occasion, the ward staff would breathe a sigh of relief. It was haunting supporting a child into the afterlife.

She took pills from the ward that night.

She never took pills again though, after that attempt. Just got on with it. Struggled through life. Focused on more than just herself. It wasn't just what her sister had said to her. It was how she said it. She loved her sister Babs dearly. She knew it then more than ever.

'I need you.'

***

Mr Lexton has now been dead ten years. Married thirty-nine. Not a loving or even a caring marriage but a peaceful one – in comparison to her sister's. A childless one. A marriage with little or no sex. In the last ten years, of the thirty-nine, he tolerated her; she tolerated him. Obtuse and Selfish. Didn't give a damn. They never went anywhere together. Not even to weddings. Or funerals, come to think of it. Neither ever attended christenings.

He called around to Mrs Tanner's to tell his wife, after losing his patience with her time-keeping. He'd waited for her at home for almost an hour. To tell her he was leaving. Leaving *her*. Had had enough. He was planning to leave that night. There was nothing she could say to stop him. Not that she would have.

Everyone, bar the two sisters, everyone knew he was leaving with an embalmer he had been seeing for the last eighteen months. She was twenty years younger than him. His wife was the wrong side of fifty. His involvement with a notorious gang leader had come to an end. Making bodies disappear had earned him a good crust. The house had been left to the two sisters by their parents. No mortgage. But he always held onto the cash. When you're a gravedigger, there's always a hole to bury the evidence.

He'd been stashing cash away for the last twelve months. He had nothing to feel guilty about. Besides, his wife saw more of her sister than him. His mother always said that. Before she died of cancer. In a home. But conveniently, he didn't have the time to look after her. *I have Jo to see to. She needs me.* He called around to the Hospice once a week. She left him everything like she said she would. He had nothing to feel guilty about.

Mr Lexton and Ashanti Akintola were returning to her native country, to live with her grandparents. He promised to meet her at the airport. She had the tickets in her hand. Clutching them. Kept checking the time. He had the cash.

But he never made it to that flight. Ashanti couldn't believe it. He'd come up with the idea by himself – said he was in some sort of trouble. And besides, he said he loved her. She was sure, at the time, that he did. He was married, of course. Despite his many reassurances beforehand, he had clearly changed his mind. She boarded the flight last. Doubts flashing before her. She kept looking out of the porthole window. Then to the empty seat beside her. At any point he'd surely board, full of apologies. Her heart in her mouth.

The flight was just taking off the runway at the very same time Neil Lexton was being repeatedly struck with a heavy iron by his maddened wife. In the same room Trevor Tanner had been hammered. It wasn't because he was leaving her for his mistress. There was more to it. Something unforgivable. Something far, far worse.

Ashanti Akintola was enraged too. She failed to hold back tears mid-flight - her fists shaped like balls.

13

GLAD OF GULLIVER'S company, Catherine had never much liked being present during any forensic deliberation. She was sure they made it all the more gross on purpose: Mansell had after all known her to have fainted, when she first became a Detective Constable.

There she was one minute. Gone the next. Slammed her right ear on the handle of the door. A handkerchief to stanch the flow. Hermione taking care of her from the onset Blood on both sides of the glass divider. Her ear bruised for weeks. Her leg pulled for years after. She'd been glad of Hermione Folkard's company in the past. The banter between them helped.

Above everything else, she didn't want to appear neither weak nor tense. She didn't smile much as they entered the newly-built scientific support department, their shoulders rubbing noiselessly together. Mansell nodded politely in their direction as they entered the adjoining room: the fragmented and decomposed body before them on a steel trolley. Only a glass wall, equipped with speakers, separated them now. She closed the door quietly behind them.

Mansell Beattie looked well beneath his plastic exterior – a mask about his face. He was possibly in his forties – about the same age as Gulliver. Maybe even the same height, although slighter by the shoulders. Both possessed wide defined jaws. Handsome really. Large hands too. No wedding ring though to Mansell's left hand.

Although his hands were now gloved, she'd noticed in the past how tidy his fingernails were – manicured even. At a recent get-together, he'd revealed an affection for writing poetry. He'd had two poetry collections published in the last five years. She'd meant to purchase one of them. She was surprised on her wedding day when Wendy, of all people, suddenly stood up and recited a poem she had written for the intimate occasion. She missed most of it – turned red very quickly. She liked that it did not rhyme.

'Gulliver!'

Gulliver Pope had lost consciousness. As it turned out, they had more in common than at first realised. Catherine was astounded; she was so busy thinking of herself, she had not noticed him pale into insignificance. Fortunately for everyone, it seemed he had slumped backwards onto the back wall before collapsing face down. The bridge of his nose was grazed, bleeding.

Five minutes later, he found himself seated on a plastic chair, head between his legs. He was heavy-boned too. Glass of water. Deep breath. She didn't tell him they were in it together. Two fish swimming in the same bowl. She caught Mansell smirking from the other side. She wasn't sure she'd buy his poetry book after all. Suddenly defensive, she told Mansell they'd return in ten minutes. She'd take him out for some fresh air. Wouldn't be long.

It dawned on her also, that it was the first time she had physically touched Gulliver since shaking his hand before Christmas; the time when she welcomed him to their division. She'd been present at the interview beforehand. She felt childish now. She'd avoided any physical contact with any candidate at the time. Avoided most of the application process. Mentally refused to engage. She was smiling now. Concerned. Her arm firmly on his.

'I'm so sorry. I feel such a fool. Not the first time either I have to admit.'

Gulliver thanked Catherine as she took his empty cup of water and helped him stand.

'You're not the first. You'll not be the last.'

For a moment she thought of saying more. It could wait for another time. Maybe that pint in the pub. She handed him a tissue from her pocket before pointing to the gash above his nose. Since becoming a *mother* she had learned to carry a number of things around with her – tissues was one of them: Zita had recently developed the bad habit of sneezing without covering her mouth.

Twenty minutes later and they were both before the pristine screen of glass – the wall that would reveal all - the steel trolley with the shrunken body belonging to the deceased, thoughtfully set further back than it was beforehand. Mansell's grin had now fully disappeared. His audience was ready.

'Decomposition matches the amount of time the subject was in the grave – thirty or so years – like the original burial in 1986. The subject is male and is almost fully decomposed. He was buried just below two metres of soil. His decomposure will have taken between twelve and fifteen years. We can assume that he was directly thrown and buried into the soil; he was not embalmed so there were no barriers to slow down the process, But yes. Fits the suggested time-scale.'

'The wallet? Any luck with a name?'

'Dentist records match the name displayed in the passport too: Trevor Tanner, although there is no evidence of him having travelled abroad. His wife, a Barbara Tanner, is listed as his next of kin. She is still registered at the same dental practice in Churchtown. She may still be at the same address if you're lucky.'

'Any money?'

'There was no cash in his wallet. Fragments of a pound note, a keepsake in his left trouser pocket. No photographs of any family. Traces of other paper, possibly receipts, that's all. Impossible to decipher.'

'And his watch? Sergeant McKenna thought it could be valuable.'

'A Rolex. A fake. Not in working order. A good copy at the time. As you know, hard to tell the difference these days – hands glide rather than tick from one second to the other. It is with forensics now. All valuables and possessions will be with you by morning. I'll send them to Liz with my full report.'

From somewhere behind Catherine, Gulliver stepped suddenly forward. He had some colour in his face now – mostly in the cheeks. In his left hand he held a brown notebook. He had already made several notes. Probably helped, averting his eyes from what was ahead of them – gruesome to say the least.

'No wedding ring?'

'No. No wedding ring. The flesh was too decomposed to verify if he had ever worn one. Not unusual at the time in question. My father never wore a wedding ring.'

For a moment both Catherine and Gulliver glanced at theirs before hastily returning their attention to the narrator. Mansell applied his plastic face shield before smiling candidly with his eyes. There was no doubt that he was in his element now - the glass screen separating the spectators from the action. From the tilt of his neck, a familiar range of equipment and tools, arranged on a working table to his left, seemed to be the focus now.

'Are we ready to continue?'

Both nodded. Catherine lowered the spectacles that had nested so far on the top of her head, onto the bridge of her nose. Her hands travelled decisively towards her raincoat pockets. It was obvious to Mansell that the two onlookers were standing closely, side by side. He was pleased. After Hermione died, Catherine was absent from work for a couple of months. When she returned, she looked ravished – like a farm dwelling hit by a frantic tornado – everything just about intact but forever changed. Seemed withdrawn. Angry even.

Having concentrated so far on Mansell's face, they now averted their eyes downwards towards the corpse. Looking now, it didn't seem as bad as when they had at first entered. Mostly bones. Using a more confident tone of voice, Gulliver unfolded his arms and nodded in Mansell's direction.

'Ready.'

Mr Tanner's shrunken head was now being held in Mansell's hands. Whilst he spoke, Gulliver Pope began making notes, Catherine noticed how swiftly and smoothly his hands moved as he pointed to this and that. Mansell had the hands of a conductor, graceful. His fingers glided back and forth along the body, a half-inch gap between each finger. He was a poet right there and then. He treated his subjects with the utmost respect: a true professional in his field. George Davies, his predecessor, had been much the same but not quite as elegant. More of a classical guitar player.

'I've already carried out most procedures as you can see. The subject Trevor Tanner was most likely about forty years old at the time of death. Because of the time-lapse it is impossible to estimate *the* time of death nor make reference to any distinguishing features on his body. Naturally, all the organs have decayed.

However, as you can see here, here and here, the subject received several repetitive hard blows to the cranium. His skull was most definitely fractured. This will have undoubtedly resulted in him going into neurogenic shock: severe head trauma before death.

These injuries here, and here are consistent with having been hit repeatedly with the same instrument over and over again: at least ten blows. The semi-circular pattern is consistent with being struck with a blunt instrument of the shape, size and weight of a hammer. From the angle – the person who hit him, was right-handed.'

Mansell moved around to the corpse's right side, this time facing the officers direct.

'He has two broken ribs on the left – could have happened when being moved or thrown into the grave. This may suggest that the person who moved or killed him acted alone.

'He was murdered Catherine. Rage. A hammer. Maybe not pre-meditated? We need to find his wife. I wonder what his occupation was?'

'Okay. Thank you Mansell. Anything else? What about his clothes?'

'Nothing so far. Lab report to follow. DNA on its way.'

'Thank you.'

Once outdoors, Shakespeare and Pope took a deep breath. They agreed more bone and less flesh was their preferred kind of post-mortem. They then laughed. Shakespeare passed Pope an unopened bottle of water.

'Carys and the children will laugh when I tell them. She started her new job a couple of months ago. Teacher at St Patrick's. Both kids with her too. Really handy. Manon is ten and Brody is five.'

'Zita is ten too – and at St Pat's. She mentioned a new kid starting!'

They both unexpectedly smiled before Pope spoke once more.

'Would be nice to have you around with your little one sometime. We've got a decent garden this time. Carys is delighted with the house. We're still unpacking!'

Other than when she spent time with Wendy, Catherine had not realised how little small talk she had participated in since Hermione's sudden departure. Mind, she had never been the most sociable one in the crowd back then - although, a few drinks always altered the evening's outcome. Gulliver was okay. It felt okay chatting as they had. Not at all taxing. Natural even. A welcome relief. Life went on after all. When others had asked after Zita at work, it had been accompanied by a sigh, or an apology, or some involuntary expression of both grief and pity. She hated that. But with Gulliver, it was different.

She never spoke at work about Zita, or Harry or Wendy. Maybe she should. People meant well. Grief didn't just belong to her – it belonged to everyone. It was everyone's way of saying they cared, that they hadn't forgotten. She felt bad then - at that very moment in time.'

'I'd like that. I'll speak to Wendy.'

'Wendy?'

'My wife – my partner.'

For a moment Catherine's face reddened in response to Gulliver's discomfort. Gulliver was trying desperately to look like he had moved on with the times. Of course, he had. He was taken aback, that was all. He thought he should apologise. But for what? He would only make matters worse. On top of everything else, he could think of nothing to say. The silence between them causing him to unexpectedly sweat. He began touching the graze above his nose. Anything to distract them both from the current situation.

To Catherine, the word 'wife' seemed alien, even though they had now been married for seventeen months. For whatever reason she felt awkward too. She was about to ask after Carys, when his mobile signalled an incoming text. Gulliver's face reddened further. Whatever it was, he was clearly unprepared for it. For a moment, he looked apologetic, then he looked out of his side window.

'Carys and the children okay?'

'Yes. They're fine. Thank you.' He paused as if to carefully rephrase his words before speaking again.

'Just a text from someone I haven't heard from in a while.'

14

THE DETACHED CHARACTER property on Cider Drive, a quiet road that still veers off North Lane itself, seemed unique to any other house around at the time. For Babs and Jo, as they were referred to then, it was their favourite place to be – at home – with mum and dad – and each other.

Set unusually far back from the quiet road, the long front lawn was at least one-hundred feet – a flagged uneven wide path to its very left; it ran straight from the unpainted wooden gate to the sky-blue front door. It was a great gate to swing open – you could perch on it by tucking both feet in the lower gap. It squawked before it thumped shut too. The gate would shake, made your hands sting - even in the winter, when the wood was harder than usual.

There was a square patch of asparagus to the very middle of the lawn. Their mother secretly thought herself above the rest of the neighbours – them growing their own asparagus. She'd laughed at Bill, their father, when he first suggested growing it – *my father used to – not a chance* she'd said first - *ugly sticks – no flowers – fancy sticking veg in the middle of the front garden for everyone to see – veg goes at the back.* Then she heard Dora, her neighbour to their left, speaking about their ugly asparagus patch, to the postman of all people. It wasn't pleasant what she said but her words were dripping with envy. She liked that - told Bill to expand the square by another two foot that year.

On occasion, curious children that passed by with their parents would refer to the Bond's home as the Hansel and Gretel house. Unkind boys said a witch lived there – kept children in a cage made of bones – sang a line twice from local folksong, about a hag called Edith Grimshaw, with a finger-stick-claw.

Of course there were no sweets on the Bond's slate roof; they didn't have that type of money, although they never went without. Instead, dark chocking smoke billowed from the tallest of the three chimneys – the only one they ever really lit - the only one that the chimney-sweeper cleaned twice a year.

Their chimney once caught fire – not long after Christmas. The house needed cleaning for weeks on end after. Coal soot everywhere. At first they heard the sound of a gaudy roaring fire. They were sat around it, watching the television, all four of them. They didn't think anything of it. But the roar grew louder and brasher, Their father suddenly upped and ran outdoors. For ages dark smoke poured into the wind's direction before flames eventually exited the chimney.

Before long the neighbours were all out – gawping at the top of their house like it was Bonfire Night. Two fire-engines arrived at once. There was excitement in the air. Some children cried with fear – others screamed with delight. Mrs Holding, two doors to the right, was standing in her nightgown and slippers holding a wide mug filled with tea.

Inside, the girls and their mother had managed to put the fire out by gently pouring water onto the coals. Their mother was shouting at them not to throw it on when a tall fireman entered. She'd removed all the ornaments from on top of the fireplace by now: the mantelpiece had blackened. The fireman kept feeling the chimney-breast; at one point he said if the heat didn't subside, they would have to move furniture away from it. He'd told the girls and their mother to get out already. His face looked angry. Like they'd conspired and done it on purpose.

The roof was hosed down to cool it – to prevent the fire from spreading. They ran the hose around the asparagus patch. Dora, their neighbour, looked pleased when they launched it on the grass. Then the officer in charge pointed to the patch, and they snaked around it. When the fire was eventually out, everyone went back in, subdued – the excitement over – the odd one remaining behind – waiting for a stray firework.

The black and white television was still blaring indoors. It was school the next day. The girls hadn't had their baths; Mary Bond hadn't got around to ironing their uniforms. Their father said that many clay liners had cracked inside the chimney and that plastering was needed.

From then on, religiously, their father made sure it was swept twice yearly. When *Basil Brush Services* posted a card through the letterbox, reminding their mother that the chimney was overdue its clean, she threw it in the bin: she never had it swept after her husband died of cancer – said she'd get around to it but never did.

***

From the pavement, outside the garden wall, the house wasn't facing the wavy road straight on. Slightly misplaced to the left, maybe by twenty degrees, the whole property had gained a more charming feel because of it - everywhere else had moved on with the times: modern semi-detached housing standing to attention row after row - perpendicular, current, contemporary. But not their home.

It's quaint and dated appearance wasn't appreciated much, at the time, by the energetic little sisters. To them, and at the ages of eight and nine, their cottage was old and boring, in comparison to their friends' modern homes. Yet despite their harsh judgement, they loved being at home, with their parents, baking bread with their mother, cultivating this and that with their father, playing doctors and nurses. It was a world occupied only by them – a world of lemonade and shortbread, dandelion necklaces and buttercups that said you really liked butter – bees and ladybirds – purple broccoli and new potatoes that tasted divine if you ate them straight after picking and boiling them - a world filled to the brim with warmth and affection.

Their father used to say that growing asparagus was a labour of love. In spring, each stalk could grow daily, by at least 10cm. Jo would hold mum's measuring tape whilst Babs would record the daily growth of the one right to the centre – its stalk wider than the others. They checked its progress before school, even when it rained. They'd ask their dad weekly when their lot would be ready – their mouths salivating in eager anticipation.

Its intense savoury flavour was enjoyed mostly in the late spring. Their mother said they could have made a fortune selling it. She would boil the tips under the watchful eye of their father – timing had to be precise. Any over boiling would kill the flavour. Babs wolfed her lot with best butter; like her mother, she'd mop up the yellow pool with white bread. Jo, like her father, preferred to salt hers and add lemon juice. They'd relish each and every one – suck on the hard bits like they were extracting marrowbone, the other gazing in disbelief.

Once, after they both became widows, they passed the house out of curiosity; they'd wanted to do it many times beforehand. They should have never taken the walk – they'd known it at the time. They were as shocked as they were disgusted, to see another house had been built on their front lawn – smack bang on top of their asparagus patch. In darkness, shrivelled from sight, tenebrous, the dilapidated cottage cringed at the centre of its overgrown garden – the modern edifice looming threateningly overhead.

Dad had liked to grow the vegetables - *'Vegetables! Not veg!'* - their mother would correct. He could spend hours in either the greenhouse or in his allotment - he said the back garden was big enough to be referred to as an allotment. Allotment it was. Mother attended to the flowers. She liked pots. She wanted her house to have a Mediterranean feel. She'd never been abroad. When dad built the front porch, she insisted on the orange wavy tiles – pointed them out to visitors calling in for a cuppa.

Spring sprung before summer blossomed. Their emblematic English garden was a place of true beauty, elegance and style. All four would spend many days tidying and tending the lengthy borders – a perimeter to the ever-in-need-of-mowing emerald lawn.

The girls were usually persuaded to weed between the path's flags. They hated it with a vengeance. Lunchtime took place by the front window, almost out of sight from passers-by – a retreat to sit in peace and admire. Year upon year they had managed to execute a display that was incomparable to any other garden around. Crumbs bordered the girls' busy mouths. Their mother sang a Beatles song that was popular at the time. All nails would be in need of a soapy wash. Smiles.

Crumbs. Laughter. Sitting by the hearth later in the evening. Do you remember that time when it caught fire?

Their father had an eye for design – a painter to be sure. A creator in his own right. He had mastered the values of simplicity and style. Any attainable space had its purpose; there was a separateness and a togetherness about all the borders. As the eye travelled so did the nose, from one scent to another, it needed to adjust to its height – width – demand to be caressed, experienced.

Many afternoons, especially summer weekdays, were spent together – their father at work – their mother knee-deep in washing and cleaning, baking and top-and-tailing gooseberries ready for pie and jam. There they gorged themselves on berries, bread and milk, their bellies busting and their cheeks reddening like apples outdoors in the bright sun.

Familiar visitors often brought them liquorice, a boiled sweet or even a small pastry depending on whether it was the coal man, the milkman or the postman. The odd downpour held them back indoors; then they would squabble and steal each other's toys. Babs often got her own way. You had to play her game or no game at all.

Jo was clever; she knew how to get Babs back. She copied her lines – repeated what she had said – wound her up until she went for her at the speed of an elastic band. Wet days could last forever. Eventually their mother would succumb and let them watch television. Father said no television until the weekend, *'Don't you go telling your father and getting me into trouble!'* They never did.

There was a sick boy who played with them one summer. He died later that year. His name was Fred. Dead. Neither can remember what he died of now. They were both sweet on him. His eyes were a dark brown and large like a rabbit's. His mouth was small. Like his hands. Soft and small. They played ring-a-ring-a-roses, a-pocket-full-of-posies.

'I'M SURE HIS NAME WAS FRED, MRS TANNER!'

'I'M DAMNED IF I REMEMBER, MRS LEXTON!'

It is almost midday. A succession of steady knocks catches them both suddenly unawares. Mrs Lexton is pegging out the washing, pipe between teeth, her back to Mrs Tanner. Mrs Tanner is peeling potatoes for dinner. She is also smoking her pipe; her pan is half empty – her colander is half full.

Their back garden – their adult haven, a microcosm of their childhood daydreams that was once filled with one adventure after another, is interrupted by what they always refer to as, unwelcome visitors. Thoughts of fragility and Fred, and memories of an age gone by, leave them like water disappearing down a plughole - reality dawns before they look to one another.

Although they are now sitting quietly in their sun-filled winter garden, they can still hear the successive rattle of knuckled thuds. It is a determined kind of knock. One they are not familiar with. Instinctively, they both look to their hands having chosen to ignore their caller – they often do this. Ignore callers. Then the audacity of the first, there are seemingly two of them now, becomes apparent as someone, a female, can be heard attempting to raise herself above their firmly locked back-gate whilst communicating with another.

Mrs Tanner heads quickly to the front door – she is not sure why she feels the way she does – alarmed – calm – poised – enraged – her hands by her sides – her hands held together. Something tells her that she needs to answer the door – that their callers are not going anywhere. She shuffles sideways before she is joined by her sister. Mrs Tanner is looking to the locked door. She is looking upwardly towards where the key cannot be seen. Not by them anyways.

Finally, Mrs Tanner places her crinkled right hand on the door handle. A male voice can be heard calling the female over. Their persistent dark figures appear to intermingle – like ink on blotting paper – pooling together, advancing. Their entry is unfortunately certain.

15

UNABLE TO SLEEP, Gulliver opened his eyes once again. Already awake since just before five – erect – conflicted, he attempted to soundlessly abandon the left-hand side of his bed only to be pulled back in by Carys. They smiled – his eyes avoiding hers.

WILL THIS LONGING ever pass?

Olivia's text had awoken a suppressed desire for something he had not experienced beforehand. A need he could not justify. Guilt. Carys' smile was incomparable to anyone he had ever known. It personified spring. Freshly baked bread. Warmth, and security. Every reason to go on. It had the power to change his whole demeanour. Transform him at will. His fabricated smile altered in response. How could he resist? He was a lucky man.

Olivia. Summer personified. Heat as thick and as rich as honey. Energy, and passion. Her long and dense dark hair always to the side. Wide lips. Smooth thick olive skin. He never compared. Had his wife ever learned of his indiscretion, he was certain she would have never forgiven him. She would have undoubtedly never forgotten. What woman would?

Carys loved Wales. Her accent was more distinctive than his. She had a long-standing habit of displacing her grammar from time to time. *I lives in Conwy. Where's that to?* She grew up in Cardiff. Everything was *lush* or *tidy* or even *cracking*. Moved to Conwy to be with him. Moved to Southport to support him. His career. Said she could find a job teaching anywhere. She had always been close to both her parents and younger sister. Left a chance of promotion behind. He owed her. Guilt. He loved her immensely for it.

He looked her up – medium-brown hair haloed about her head – penetrating blue eyes – wide but not needy – perfectly placed at either side of her button nose - and he looked her almost all the way down. She was lying on her side - a pale blue nightdress loosely veiled along her body – her curves undulating beneath French cotton. There was nothing undesirable about her. She was beautiful, sexy too. Why did he not want her? He wanted to want her. She still wanted him.

Unable to resist, already filled to the brim with desire, he parted her pale legs quickly and plunged far into that deep pool that negotiates and slackens - manipulated every move in response to hers – thought unintentionally of Olivia and dug deeper – pressed harder – harder until they were both overcome with the same familiar relief. His eyes filled. Guilt. He felt exposed. Dirty even.

He kissed her then. Made a point of it. Smiled. Kissed her glistening forehead before he eloped from the other side of their bed. Remorseful.

'I love you.'

He meant it. He loved her.

'I love you.'

She meant it. She loved him. She looked after him – a distance growing - her left hand outstretched towards him. For a moment she looked like she was about to speak – thought better of it. Closed her eyes.

Once in the shower, he began having the same pointless conversation with himself as the one he had had numerous times beforehand, in the last six months. He was forty-five. Was this what a midlife crisis felt like? He couldn't damn Olivia. Not yet. He wished he could regret ever laying eyes on her. Maybe one day. If he really tried. Maybe never. Had he ever really tried?

He didn't crave just any other woman. His eyes had wandered in the past – whose didn't? But until Olivia, he had never even considered what it would be like to be with another woman. To spend quality time with her. Overnight. Wake up in the same bed. Guilt. He couldn't fault Carys. He really couldn't.

Olivia. Not a single day had passed since he'd not thought of her. Some days he simply swatted the thought away. His commitments in both work and at home helped. Interrupted the thinking process. *Dad? -*

Gull? – Sarge? Hammered the desire. The throbbing. But not suppressed it. Weekends usually, especially in the early hours, he let the memory of that one afternoon play out. Reality had become distorted. Fantasy went a long way to satisfy what he ultimately desired. He'd taken her so many ways, he'd almost forgotten the original accomplishment.

Will this longing ever pass?

He wasn't sure.

He liked the longing. No-one knew. No-one could see. What was inside his head. He wasn't harming anyone.

Drop the needle. Play. Softer first. Louder. Volume cranked. Surely he was allowed that? He'd given everything else up. Like a petulant child, he felt denied. He'd given something up that was inexplicable. He'd walked away from an inextinguishable smouldering fire. Haunted. Changed. Hungry.

Gulliver habitually re-entered their bedroom to say his goodbyes. Both Manon and Brody had found a means of getting into their bed. Clad in their pyjamas, and like soft toys tucked beneath Carys' shoulders, they bathed in their mother's affection. He smiled. Their ginger mops suddenly disappeared below the lavender surface. Hands protruding from beneath the quilt. Monsters. We're coming to get you daddy.

'Shouldn't be late. Kiss! Kiss!'

'Gull? Wait! – Zita's birthday invitation to Manon's party! By the door!'

'Thank you! Got to go – running late! RAHHHHHHH!'

'Cracking.'

Screams. Back to base. Back under the lavender field. A quilt that was a gigantic cloud. Silence. Hands reappear. Freckled faces follow. Smiles. Laughter. Manon had pushed Brody out of the bed. Thud!'

On the way out, invitation now in his packed lunch bag, he noticed the *Southport Visitor* clamped in the bristled mouth of their letterbox. Gulliver yanked it free, glanced at it momentarily before he dialled Catherine's number – a look of disbelief across his face.

'Morning. *Visitor's* headline. Seen it? ALIEN CORPSE DISCOVERED IN FAMILY GRAVE. Really. Want me to put something together for the press? Okay. Will do. See you at the station.'

***

The fifteen minute drive along the coastal road, before they arrived to the village of Crossens, was over almost as fast as it had begun; it was very nearly midday. The station situated at one busy end of Lord Street they wended their way through the town, past busy department stores and numerous tea-rooms before they hit the undulating coastline. For the time of year, it was unusually bright. Most of the Irish Sea coast, that stretched from Liverpool to Preston, was visible now - not a cloud in the sky.

There were many dog walkers about the Marshide end, the declivity as the road advanced towards the coastal end notable. Unlike their subdued owners, energetic dogs sprinted to and fro. Raised wet noses indulged in the pleasure of taking in the winter sea-breeze, the air filled with interesting scents – their ears raised in response to the clamorous activity on the beach. Tails stiffened before they wagged welcome.

Hatted heads bearing taut pink faces nodded politely as they passed one another, some already losing control of their feisty hounds. A large Dalmatian suddenly defecated before everyone in sight. 'Domino! Domino!' The embarrassed owner fumbled in both pockets for a plastic bag before she reluctantly picked up the steaming mound – a bin nowhere in sight.

Not unusually, there were many joggers too. Mostly, they ran in a straight line, hips circling from time to time to avoid curious four-legged creatures. From their exhausted faces and newly acquired trainers, they had not been running long.

The freezing January tide was almost at its highest. By one, the murky waters would rise momentously, crisp and foamy edges drifting consistently in and out – the season's current strong - the beach in its full splendour. All in all, it was a great display for both the residents and the many visitors that had flocked to the town for a satisfying day out.

Surrounding the sandy shore, cushioned and embedded in the distance, was the thriving tidal wetland. Green like emerald – pooled – it was a haven for birdwatchers. From time to time lapwings tumbled in excitable displays – their planned nesting areas within sight. Parallel to the coastal road, on the driver's side, more marshland. Golden plovers wheeled about a flock of wigeons turning over the marshes. The high-pitched inoffensive shrill was mesmerising – a blue sky with a peach zip above the horizon all the way.

Earlier in the day, when the wind picked up, a flock of pink-footed geese flying backwards was photographed before they hunkered down and landed in the water amongst the long-tailed tits. The photograph was scheduled to appear in the *Southport Visitor's* Friday edition. Understandably, the front page was instead dominated with news of the alien corpse that had been found beneath the grave of Brian Brookner. His son, Paul, had already agreed to an interview.

Parked outside the familiar cul-de-sac, Catherine inhaled noisily before she spoke.

'OK. As a previous FLO – would you like to take the lead for this first part of the interview process?'

Gulliver nodded before smiling. In truth, he was delighted - wanted to get stuck in. He hadn't ever been part of an investigation such as this one. On this scale. To Gulliver, it was like a treasure hunt – he couldn't wait to discover the ugly truth. This was just the sort of crime most officers like him dreamt of. Something juicy to get stuck into. A gruesome adventure.

A few years ago, Catherine would have felt much the same. Most of their time was usually taken up with burglaries and assaults - tedious, uneventful and often unrewarding. This Christmas, break-ins were at an all-time low – home alarms had been replaced with dogs; over the last few years, petty theft had fallen too. Instead, drink-fuelled crimes, fraud and leaving without paying a restaurant bill was on the up. Managers were reluctant to put CCTV up inside premises. Customers needed their privacy when dining. Whilst unavoidable, it was frustrating the trade. Thieves of a different sort. Chancers.

Gulliver habitually brushed himself down before adopting the look of a compassionate yet professional investigating officer. In return, Catherine smiled – she was glad to have Gulliver by her side. Would be interesting watching him at work.

Together they passed a corner house with tidy beds before passing the one that Catherine once visited with Hermione during an investigation that had resulted in the death of both residents at 125 North Lane: a father and a daughter. From the diary posted to Hermione, by the child, Mara Bones, it had become apparent that not only was she deliberately poisoning her father but she was also ingesting the same poison herself: a fascinating case – and one of the saddest she had ever encountered.

Catherine looked to the tunnel; from where they now stood, the purple-clad property they were about to call upon was to the left. Almost two years ago, she'd hoisted herself above the gate to the right, to see if there was anyone home. She wasn't to know Mara had been locked in the shed – almost dead – had been assaulted – battered black and blue by her father. She could have possibly saved her. Toyed with the thought for weeks. Had she known. Her last two years had been filled with too many *if only's*.

A familiar pungent smell thankfully interrupted her thinking process. She passed through the flaking metallic gate, held aside by Gulliver and headed up the path. She didn't mind it so much now. The smell. But as a child, it made her gag. Brown clumps interlaced with straw filled every rectangular rosebush bed. Well-rotten and brittle. Crumble without the apple. Fresh from the local stables. It didn't seem to bother Gulliver. Hadn't taken the slightest notice. The Welsh in him.

'Manure. Nothing smells quite like fresh manure. My father was a keen gardener. He won a few prizes for his roses at Southport's Annual Flower Show. I remember they used to sell all the plants and flowers cheap on the last day. We used to come home with all sorts. Never seemed to rain then. I keep meaning to go, then I don't get around to it. Never regret it – seems to always rain that weekend.'

'No reply.'

'We have something similar in Cardiff, where Carys is from. The RHS Flower Show. Cardiff Castle. My grandfather used to show his leeks – entered every year, before he was made a judge. Had his photo taken, four years on the run, for The Leek Photographic Group. Has the photographs on his mantelpiece still.'

'Sorry. I don't know why I'm laughing. Knock again. Louder. I'll take a look around the back.'

'Think I can see someone coming. Oh – maybe I was wrong. I'm sure I saw someone passing. Here we go. Maybe not. Strange - looks like they're not answering.'

After trying the locked back gate, thumb hard-pressed onto the latch, Catherine threw her firm police voice over, much like the high-jump, but on this occasion failing to rouse any interest from an audience. She wasn't quite sure for a moment; she thought she'd heard the sound of a shifting motion. She could definitely smell tobacco – pipe tobacco. She was about to hoist herself upwardly on a diagonal bar, left foot raised, when Gulliver called for her return. The front door was being unlocked.

The apparition of the two women at the door seemed somewhat incredible. It was as if two characters from another time and place had appeared sullenly before them. They seemed dwarfed in stature – elbow-crinkled skin about their faces and hands – elderly - like something you'd see on a Romanian postcard - Andeans from the back-of-beyond. According to her notes, Barbara Tanner was only in her late sixties.

About their textured faces were thin scarves; their wiry grey hair had been untidily tied back – spidery wisps merging with unruly bushy eyebrows, of a similar texture and colour. Their lower arms were a similar leathery shade to their face – the colour of those who spend most of their daytime outdoors: weather-beaten.

One had a royal blue headscarf about her head, whilst the other modelled a purple one instead. A firm knot had been secured beneath their chins. They both wore long dark skirts – matching red discoloured pinafores about their waist. Stained. They were booted too. Both wore dark boots. Shoe laces - double knotted. There was something masculine. Yet their green eyes – small as they were – were as deep as wells – beautiful even.

Neither smiled nor invited them in. From the immediate smell that accompanied their whole demeanour, they did not wash very often. For a moment neither officer spoke – the women squinting in the light – maybe even scowling. Hard to tell. Their faces lined like routes on a river-map.

They stood framed in the doorway side by side – an inexplicable resilience about their posture. Both Catherine and Gulliver had an impulsive urge to laugh. Instead, they smiled and raised their identification badges. In return, the haggard women, the blue-headscarved one with a trowel in her hand and the purple-headed female with a smoking pipe in hers, began to initiate the closing of their front door.

'Detective Inspector Shakespeare. This is Detective Sergeant Pope. We'd appreciate a moment of your time. Shouldn't be long. May we come in?'

Their blank expression remained unchanged, although the one holding the trowel did slacken her wrist somewhat. A gate squealed shut. Fixated by the united front before them, neither of the officers turned to see the orderly family-unit pass behind them - Mr Evans straining to listen to their one-sided conversation.

'We believe a Mrs Barbara Tanner lives here?'

For a moment, it looked as if neither were prepared to respond. Then the top lip belonging to the purple-scarved woman lifted slightly before her eyes blinked several times in succession. She lifted her right hand upwardly and placed a dark pipe into her mouth. Her fingertips yellowed like the few teeth that remained in her mouth, nails unwashed but neat. It seemed obvious now that they had both been attending to their sizeable back garden.

'May we come in?

Standing aside now, the purple-scarved woman signalled for them to enter whilst the blue-headed one stared at them in disbelief. She adjusted her headscarf momentarily – soiled fingernails trimmed by teeth – before she too, moved out of the way.

Catherine and Gulliver entered the plain hall before allowing the purple-scarved woman to pass by them. Sluggishly, she led them through the hall, to the back of the house where a square-shaped old-fashioned kitchen led outdoors into the garden. Immediately behind Catherine and Gulliver, followed her sister, a trowel in her left hand.

Awestruck by their tidy outdoor haven, Catherine accepted a seat on a sage-green metallic bench whilst Gulliver chose to stand. Certainly their outdoor plot of land was a stark contrast to their indoors. Their hall most definitely smelt like someone had buried a fish beneath the floorboards.

'Mrs Tanner?'

'THAT WOULD BE ME!'

'We'd like you to take a seat, if you don't mind. And you are?'

Both pulled forward plastic seats within six feet of the officers. Right now, it seemed Mrs Tanner was the more confident of the two – her body language defensive – to be expected: they didn't seem the sort of women who ever entertained – even ventured out much.

'THIS IS MY SISTER, JOAN LEXTON.'

'Is it just yourselves, or does anyone else live here?'

'JUST OURSELVES.'

'It's a lovely garden.'

It was obvious from their expressionless faces that they were unwilling to entertain any further polite conversation. Their penetrating glare willed them to get on with it - pupils like hard pebbles surrounded by a deep green sea.

'A body was recently discovered at the Crematorium on Liverpool Road. We have since been able to identify the remains of this body. It is the body of your husband, Trevor Tanner. We are, of course, very sorry for your loss.'

An incredulous look spread across the face of Mrs Lexton; she looked to her sister who seemed equally as shocked. Mrs Tanner appeared to stand before she sat back down. Her left hand moved from her leg to the side of the bench. Her pipe dropped suddenly from her grasp and cracked onto the concrete flag. At first, she did nothing to retrieve it, then, as she began to lean forwards, Gulliver secured it before handing it back.

'I appreciate this question must be difficult, given the lapse in time, but when did you last see your husband Mrs Tanner?'

'A LONG TIME AGO, THAT'S WHEN! HE WENT TO WORK ONE DAY, AND THEN NEVER CAME HOME! HE JUST UPPED AND LEFT ONE DAY – NOT THE FIRST TIME - MIND. NEVER HEARD FROM HIM SINCE! MUST BE NEAR THIRTY YEARS AGO!'

'Thirty-one to be precise. Did you report him missing? Our records indicate that he was never reported missing.'

'I MADE A FEW PHONECALLS, TO THE POLICE – HOSPITAL TOO – DIDN'T BOTHER AFTER THAT! THOUGHT HE'D BE BACK IN HIS OWN GOOD TIME. IT WAS ALL SUCH A LONG TIME AGO. I CAN'T REALLY REMEMBER!

Mrs Tanner paused visually distressed. 'I WAS UPSET AT THE TIME - HIM NOT COMING BACK HOME. ARE YOU SURE IT'S HIM?'

'We are certain Mrs Tanner.'

'WHAT WAS HIS BODY DOING IN THE CEMETERY?'

'It was discovered by a couple of gravediggers preparing a former grave for an additional burial. His body seems to have been deliberately placed below another coffin, in 1986, like I said, thirty-one years ago.

We are sorry to inform you that he died following a storm of blows to his skull. As of yesterday, we began conducting an official murder investigation: we believe your husband was killed not long before he was buried. Anything you can tell us to help with our inquiry, would be greatly appreciated.'

Mrs Tanner did not respond. Instead she looked to her sister. Until now, Mrs Lexton had remained silent – a curious look about her face – a sage green trowel firmly held in her left hand. For a moment she locked eyes with her sister. Habitually, and to the astonishment of both Catherine and Gulliver, Mrs Lexton gathered phlegm in her throat, and was about to spit, it appeared, when she thought better of it.

Suddenly, Mrs Lexton stood up. As if perturbed, shocked somewhat herself, she headed for the kitchen, spat into what was probably the sink and could be heard switching the kettle on.

'Your husband, what was his occupation?'

'HE WAS A MILKMAN. CAN'T THINK OF ANYONE WHO'D WANT TO HARM HIM THOUGH. HE'D PLAYED ABOUT. I KNEW HE HAD. MANY TIMES. CAME HOME REEKING OF ALCOHOL – AND CHEAP PERFUME! JUST THOUGHT HE'D LEFT WITH SOME FLOOSY – HIS PASSPORT WAS GONE – JUST THOUGHT HE'D LEFT WITH HIS LATEST TART!'

'And yourself? At the time, 1986, did you work? Stay at home with children?'

'WE HAD NO CHILDREN. NO. I DIDN'T WORK.'

For a moment Mrs Tanner seemed to be about to say something else. She looked upwards, to the kitchen window – her sister still indoors.

'IS THAT IT? ONLY I NEED TO GET ON IN THE GARDEN – GOES DARK BY FOUR!'

Catherine looked in the direction of the glass-panelled kitchen door; Mrs Lexton hadn't moved from the kitchen. The kettle had now boiled; there was no sound of a brew being prepared. She returned her attention in the direction of Mrs Tanner. Surely the woman had a hearing problem: she spoke so loud.

There was so much that could be misread from their body language. Mrs Lexton was yet to speak. Had the cat got her tongue? She certainly seemed agitated. Maybe upset. Certainly she seemed stunned. More stunned even than her own sister. Their response was difficult to read – like a jigsaw, it was proving difficult just locating the corners.

'Does your sister live with you?'

'SHE DOES.'

'Would you mind calling into the station tomorrow to identify a few items we believe belonged to your husband? Maybe we could get a written statement, if you feel up to it, at the same time? We can always arrange for you to be picked up, if that helps?'

Mrs Tanner's eyes lifted in search of her sister. The officers expectation clearly unaware of the sisters' inner discomfort – an unusual lack of synchronicity on their behalf. The kitchen was still silent.

'CAN'T WE DO IT NOW? GET IT OVER WITH?'

An hour passed before Mrs Tanner's statement was complete. Fifteen minutes before completion, her sister re-emerged looking drawn. It seemed strange that at no point did either sister comfort the other. Maybe that was just how things where between them. They hadn't appeared to be the touchy-feely sort in the first place.

Regardless, something about their physical distance seemed odd. Like something was amiss. At the door they had stood side by side, united, a barrier to encounter at your peril. Right now, they seemed out of tune – ill-at-ease - a cat amongst the pigeons. Unsupportive even.

Mrs Tanner closed the door quietly behind them. She stood at the side window watching them go before she opened the front door and headed for the gate – looked after them until they drove off – made sure the gate was shut. A curtain twitched next door to the right – Mara's old bedroom. She hoped they had not been overheard by anyone as they spoke frankly in the garden.

Shakespeare and Pope entered their navy unmarked car to confer, unaware that the two sisters were now engaged in an almighty row – a row that took place upstairs, indoors, once the back door was closed and locked. A row that lasted on and off for hours. The bitterness between them would last for days.

***

It was late when Gulliver finally made it home. Exhausted and exalted from the day's events, he took a deep breath before he turned the engine off. It had been dark for hours. Bitter too.

As planned earlier on in the day, he re-read Olivia's message a number of times. He'd avoided responding until now, had done well. Avoided entering into what could spark up a never-ending conversation. Begin something that would never rest. A test of some sort. A test he'd fail. They couldn't move again.

He needed to be honest with himself, at least. Deep down, he knew that he was always going to respond. He was incapable of letting it go. Had almost texted a few weeks ago. The longing irrepressible.

He sent it. He reminded himself that you only lived life once. That life was too short to ignore the obvious.

Carpe Diem. Seize the day. For a moment he hesitated – then remembered – placed his mobile on silent, like he had done in the past. He couldn't help it. He didn't want to help it. Flashback. That afternoon. They didn't even make it upstairs. The curtains drawn back. The summer heat drawing them both together. What harm could it do?

16

MRS TANNER AND Mrs Lexton have been arguing on and off for hours. After the detectives left, they sat separately - in silence - for a lengthy while before the questions began – an unfamiliar tension building between them - like gravy and cheese sauce touching on the same plate.

At first the table tennis exchanges were measured – the ebb and flow predictable - the build-up certain; then the rowing commenced, before the tsunami hit. Unsuccessfully, Mrs Tanner pointlessly exasperated the defensive approach, her self-justification wasted. Then the tears came. Both of them at once. Anger interlaced with doubt. Fear interlocked with regret.

When rage took over, the pan containing two over-boiled eggs was flung against the wall by Mrs Lexton. Mrs Tanner stood up ready, although she wasn't entirely sure what she was ready for. When she sat back down, and her sister took herself upstairs, thump, thump, thump up the threadbare staircase, she thought long and hard about what had happened in the last few hours. She thought long and hard about the decision she'd made decades ago.

In many ways, it was a welcomed relief – everything now in the open. She'd never kept any secrets from her sister before. She regretted that more than she regretted killing her own husband. And now, she'd probably go to jail for it. And her sister would be on her own. Alone. At least she could not be accused of being an accomplice. Silver lining.

The worst times of their lives had been spent separate from one another. They'd both agreed on this on many an occasion. Their marital homes a gehenna of dashed ambitions, futile dreams and unfulfilled potential. Trevor controlling her every move, her every word. Slap. Punch. Kick. What time do you call this? Look at the state of yer? Bastard.

Neil - the opposite, ducking and diving, playing the field – selfish – devious – lazy. Useless cunt. If they'd hung on, they'd have married doctors. Had their parents lived, they wouldn't have been in such a rush. They were sure of that now. When their parents died, they had both pined for that familiar cosiness – a nest of some sort – a family unit - tried to recreate the life they once had – a childhood filled with hopes, dreams and sunshine. At least they had each other.

They'd laughed the hardest when they lived there - at Cider Drive – all of them together. They had laughed again once they were reunited, after they both became widows - just them. Nobody else but them. Had been widowed for what seemed such a long time.

The thought of leaving her younger sister behind troubled Mrs Tanner greatly. If she were jailed, if they put two and two together, she'd never see Jo again. She'd probably do life. Not a lot of life in her anyway. And they'd die alone. Like their parents had. No-one to hold Jo's hand. She wasn't going to let that happen.

***

'I'VE SAID I'M SORRY UNTIL I'M BLUE IN THE FACE MRS LEXTON!'

Mrs Tanner and Mrs Lexton are both back in the kitchen. The back door and window are now closed. Mrs Tanner is sitting at the table smoking her pipe, listening, stopping herself from opening her mouth. In contrast, Mrs Lexton is pacing back and forth, waving her pipe with her right hand as she speaks. The room is filling with the pungent smell of Virginian tobacco, grey smoke escaping into the front hallway.

'ALL THESE YEARS, YOU MADE ME FEEL LIKE YOU'D DONE ME THE WORLD'S GREATEST FAVOUR - HIDING NEIL'S STINKING CORPSE IN YOUR HOUSE – AND – AND – YOU'D BOTH COLLUDED TO BURY YOUR OWN HUSBAND - AND NOT TELL ME! YOUR OWN SISTER!'

'I TOLD YOU – I – I.'

'BOTH OF YOU – THICK AS THIEVES!'

'I RANG HOME. I ASKED TO SPEAK TO YOU. YOU WEREN'T THERE. HE DIDN'T KNOW WHERE YOU WERE. I WAS IN A STATE. BLOOD ON MY HANDS. BLOOD ON THE WALLS. NEIL TOLD ME TO SIT DOWN.

I COULDN'T STOP SHAKING. I HADN'T PLANNED IT. HE TOLD ME HE'D BE AROUND SOON – THAT HE'D TAKE CARE OF IT – THAT HE KNEW WHAT TO DO. AND HE DID. TAKE CARE OF IT. I ASSUMED WHEN HE'D COME AROUND, YOU'D BE WITH HIM. BUT HE SAID HE HADN'T BEEN ABLE TO FIND YOU. AND HE ARRIVED ALONE.'

'AND IN THE SAME BLOODY ROOM NEIL'S IN! I CAN'T BELIEVE IT! NO WONDER YOU'D DECORATED. YOU HATE DECORATING! YOU NEVER GOT THAT USELESS CUNT TO DECORATE IT DID YOU?'

Mrs Tanner pauses before she speaks once more. She shifts her body uncomfortably from left to right as if trying to adjust herself on a toilet seat. Her hands adjust her red pinafore before she speaks.

'I DID. WELL I COULDN'T JUST ASK ANYONE ELSE TO DO IT, COULD I?'

'THAT LAZY, USELESS CUNT NEVER LIFTED A SINGLE FINGER TO DECORATE OUR HOME! I ASKED HIM FOR YEARS ON END TO JUST PUT ME UP A FEW SHELVES IN THE KITCHEN – IN THE END I PUT THEM UP MYSELF! HE LAUGHED AT ME BECAUSE THEY WEREN'T STRAIGHT. I PUT HIM STRAIGHT IN THE END MYSELF THOUGH – DIDN'T I MRS TANNER?'

'I DIDN'T SEE YOU FOR DAYS AFTER – ONE OF YOUR EPISODES. YOU WEREN'T WELL. NEIL SAID IT WOULD BE BEST IF I SAID NOTHING, IN CASE IT MADE YOU WORSE, OR YOU TALKED TO SOMEONE WITHOUT MEANING TO – SAY A COUNSELLOR.'

'DON'T YOU GO USING MY EPISODES, AS YOU BOTH CALLED IT, AS AN EXCUSE FOR KEEPING ME IN THE DARK! YOU AND I KNOW YOU COULD HAVE TOLD ME AFTERWARDS! WE'VE BEEN LIVING IN THE SAME HOUSE FOR YEARS!'

'WHEN I EVENTUALLY SAW YOU, IT SEEMED EASIER TO SAY THAT HE'D DIED OF A HEART ATTACK. YOU DIDN'T LOOK WELL. I ALWAYS PLANNED ON DROPPING HIS ASHES IN THE NEAREST BIN ANYWAY. HE WAS A SELFISH BASTARD. AND A THUG. YOU KNEW HE WAS A THUG. WHAT I WENT THROUGH.'

'AND - AND YOU WOULDN'T EVEN LISTEN TO ME ABOUT REPAINTING THE HOUSE BLUE – HELD IT OVER ME ALL THE SAME. ALWAYS GETTING YOUR OWN WAY. I HATE FUCKING PURPLE!'

'I'M VERY SORRY MRS LEXTON! I REALLY AM. IT WAS AWFUL OF ME. I LOVE PURPLE – YOU KNOW I DO. NO EXCUSE – TO BE SO SELFISH. WE'LL REDECORATE THIS SUMMER – YOU CAN PAINT THE HOUSE ANY COLOUR YOU WANT!'

For a short while, both sisters call an unverified truce. Mrs Tanner is visibly shaken; her weathered paper-thin hands grip the edge of the table as she slowly stands. Moments later, steadier, she is up and about; she shuffles towards the kettle before she switches it on. Carefully, she lowers two mugs from a make-shift shelf. The brown checkered mug has a chip the shape of a smile on the exposed rim - the other, white china, says *Lancashire Tea* in red. Mrs Lexton does not refuse the gesture. Their throats are dry from shouting at one another – their minds awash from the day's events. Mrs Tanner is about to get the gin from under the sink when Mrs Lexton half-laughs.

'DID YOU BURY THE HAMMER WITH HIM? IN THE GRAVE? IT WILL HAVE YOUR DNA ALL OVER IT MRS TANNER!'

'I WASHED IT. I WASHED IT MANY TIMES AFTER. WASHED IT LIKE I WASH MY HANDS. USED IT PLENTY OF TIMES SINCE TOO. THE ONE HUNG BETWEEN THE TWO NAILS IN THE SHED. THE ONE I ALWAYS USE. THE ONLY ONE WE HAVE!'

'BLOODY HELL. THAT'S GRUESOME MRS TANNER!'

'I'VE GOT NO REGRETS. OTHER THAN NOT TELLING YOU MRS LEXTON. NO REGRETS. SELFISH BASTARD HAD IT COMING!'

For a moment, standing side by side, they look on through the kitchen window ahead, at the shed, planted in clear sight at the bottom of the garden - to the far left of the back garden. Mentally and clearly, they can both picture the hammer. Light and handy. Brown wooden handle – black head – solid iron. Hung by the neck between two nails. Hung like a cross on the back wall about three quarters of the way up. To the left.

'WHICH END OF THE HAMMER DID YOU USE MRS TANNER? JUST CURIOUS!'

'TO BE HONEST, I COULDN'T SAY. I JUST PLANTED IT SO HARD ON HIS SKULL. MAYBE THE BLUNT END. MIND YOU, IT DID STICK IN HIM TOWARDS THE END. MAYBE I USED BOTH.'

'JESUS-MARY-JOSEPH MRS TANNER!'

'I REMEMBER COUNTING OUT LOUD – UNTIL I GOT TO SEVENTEEN. I STOPPED AT SEVENTEEN. I COULD HAVE KEPT GOING. I HAMMERED HIM FOR EVERY YEAR OF MY LIFE THAT I'D WASTED ON THE SELFISH, USELESS BASTARD.'

'AT LEAST WERE NOT STUCK WITH HIS STENCH MRS TANNER!'

'THE FRONT LOUNGE – WE NEED TO DO SOMETHING ABOUT THAT. THOSE OFFICERS MIGHT BE BACK. WE CAN'T KEEP MR LEXTON IN THERE INDEFINITELY.'

'I THOUGHT IT WAS A JOKE – SHAKESPEARE AND POPE. ANY OTHER TIME, I'D HAVE LAUGHED IN THEIR FACES!'

'BEST GET OUR THINKING CAPS ON THEN!.'

'I USE THAT HAMMER ALL THE TIME! BLOODY HELL MRS TANNER! I EVEN LENT IT A FEW YEARS AGO TO MR STONE! YOU KNOW – THAT TIME MRS STONE WAS AWAY AT HER MOTHERS AND TOOK THE KEYS WITH HER. MR STONE COULDN'T FIND THE KEY TO THEIR SHED – AND CAME ROUND TO BORROW OURS! BLOODY HELL MRS TANNER!'

'HE HELD ONTO IT FOR DAYS MRS LEXTON. I WAS HALF HOPING HE'D NOT RETURN IT – BE RID OF IT. BUT IT'S A FINE HAMMER MRS LEXTON. I'M QUITE FOND OF IT YOU KNOW.'

For a moment Mrs Lexton looks at Mrs Tanner with an incredulous look on her face. She unscrews the lid on the gin before she adds a splash to her bottomless mug. Having taken a gulp, she stumbles forth towards her sister to fill her mug.

'I'M SORRY – I'M SORRY I WASN'T THERE FOR YOU MRS TANNER. I WAS TOO WRAPPED UP IN MYSELF. I KNOW NOW I COULD HAVE DONE MORE.'

'NO MATTER.'

'MR LEXTON WAS A USELESS CUNT – AND A SELFISH SHIT, BUT HE NEVER LAID A FINGER ON ME. NEVER.'

'LOST THREE BABIES BECAUSE OF HIM.'

'BASTARD DESERVED IT!'

'BASTARD'S TOO NICE A WORD FOR HIM!'

'WE'LL NEED TO GET RID OF THAT HAMMER TOO, MRS TANNER!'

'BEST GET OUR THINKING CAPS ON MRS LEXTON THEN!'

'MORE TEA MRS TANNER?'

'MORE GIN I THINK MRS LEXTON!'

'DROP OF GIN IN OUR TEA IT IS MRS TANNER.'

'MOTHER LIKED A DROP OF GIN IN HER TEA FIRST THING – AFTER FATHER DIED.'

***

It's dark and silent outdoors but the air is cool and crisp for the time of year. It is almost midnight now. There are no lights to the upstairs windows, at either side of the house; no windows left carelessly open. The smell of coal fires still lingers in the winter breeze. Mrs Tanner coughs before she spits ahead of her. In return, Mrs Lexton spits too – much calmer now.

The shed is invisible from where they sit, in their garden – the dark is no barrier to them. If necessary, they could find their way blindfolded. The hammer has been retrieved from its place – the nails pulled; it is now on the paved floor between the two women – their feet parted like cowboys ready to draw – their pipes firmly held between teeth.

'HADN'T WE BEST GET RID OF IT FIRST, BEFORE WE MOVE THE USELESS CUNT?'

'YES. I SUPPOSE SO. MIND, THEY MIGHT BE WATCHING US – WAITING FOR US TO DO SOMETHING STUPID – LIKE GET RID OF A HAMMER!'

For a moment they intentionally laugh before they lower their voices once more – their whispered exchanges pregnant with anticipation.

'WE HAVE NO CAR! HOW ON EARTH ARE WE TO MOVE HIM?'

'WE NEED TO BURY HIM SOMEWHERE ELSE. WE CANT HAVE HIM TURNING UP LIKE MR TANNER DID!'

For several seconds the women are silenced by their troubled thoughts; the only sound to be heard is of the burning tobacco, sparking and crackling as they partake in their usual habit, deep in thought – a wispy white smoke furling in the breeze, after they have methodically pumped the smoke several times around their oral and nasal cavities. Twice, Mrs Tanner finds herself in need of relighting.

'LET'S DISPOSE OF THE HAMMER FOR NOW – THE USELESS CUNT CAN WAIT.'

'BUT WHERE?'

'HOW ABOUT POPPING IT IN SOMEONE ELSE'S BIN? THEY'RE DUE THE DAY AFTER TOMORROW. MR STONE'S GOT HIS BIN OUT ALREADY - LIKES TO BE FIRST. WE COULD STICK IT IN HIS MRS LEXTON!'

For a moment a familiar silence grows between them: they are picturing their plan – weighing it up. It's a risk – but a risk worth taking. The fact is, the sooner they dispose of the hammer, the sooner they can start thinking of what to do with Mr Lexton's corpse. Neither is relishing the thought of cracking open the window box. The smell. What will Mr Lexton look like after all these years? Where on earth will they hide him?

'I'LL COME OUT WITH YOU THEN. WE'LL GO LATER – WHEN EVERYONE'S ASLEEP. WE'LL WRAP IT IN A

TOWEL AND BAG IT. SEE IF WE CAN GET IT IN MID-WAY.'

'WHAT ARE WE GOING TO DO UNTIL THEN MRS TANNER?'

'I'VE THOUGHT ABOUT IT MRS LEXTON. WE COULD WATCH DR ZHIVAGO. WE'VE NEVER WATCHED IT – WE'VE SAID FOR YEARS WE'D WATCH IT – AFTER WE PICKED UP A COPY AT THE MARKET – BUT WE NEVER HAVE. HOW ABOUT IT? SEE WHAT ALL THE FUSS WAS ABOUT.'

'WE COULD MRS TANNER. THAT WE COULD.'

'IT'S ABOUT THREE HOURS LONG, FROM WHAT I REMEMBER. THAT WILL TAKE US UP TO HALF-THREE. TOO LATE FOR ANYONE TO BE UP. TOO EARLY FOR ANYONE TO RISE. WHAT DO YOU THINK MRS LEXTON.'

A half-painful look passes from one sister's tired face to the other. The night before her death, their mother – Mary - their mother who was everything to them, like their father Billy - the night before they found her, as teenagers, she'd watched the entire film alone. Told them she was going to. Sent them to bed for nine. Early. Said she had a headache. They knew she was sending them to bed to drink. She didn't like to drink in front of them. She'd stopped going to the pub, with them. Someone spoke to her from social services.

In hospital, their father promised, in front of them, that he would take their mother to see Dr Zhivago at the cinema – said it when he was still alive, in 1965 – and they were the witnesses; but he was dead first week in December. Years later, their desolate mother swallowed lots of green and white tablets with a whole bottle of Russian vodka. They both wondered if she did it whilst watching the film, or afterwards. They knew she'd cried. Mascara all over her face. Vomit and urine on the couch and carpet.

She was buried at the graveyard down the road, at St John's with their dad. The priest arranged it all. They'd never seen Father Hickey smile until then. He seemed filled to the brim with pity – and kindness. Genteel. No homiletic sermon to the service either. Just kind. They had no idea what to do. Had paid no attention as to what their mother had done, when their father died. Anger. Anguish. Fear. Why them?

***

The hammer in its plastic bag takes pride of place on the coffee table – at either side two mugs of coffee to keep them awake. Although they eventually managed to stay awake for most of the film – they both nodded on and off at intervals, for short periods of time. Impatient and clockwatching every twenty minutes or so, they agreed that one of them needed to stay awake – take turns cat-napping. Mrs Tanner nudged Mrs Lexton awake. Then Mrs Lexton nudged Mrs Tanner. In the end, they both slept a good thirty minutes. It was beyond them why their mother had wanted to see the film so ardently. Maybe they just didn't get it. It was boring as much as it was complicated.

As soon as the film was done – both agreed Omar Sharif was no dish. There was nothing quite like a western. Good old Clint Eastwood. He wasn't useless and he wasn't lazy. Years later, when *Play Misty for Me* was released at the cinema, they saw him in a very different light. He was a disc jockey then, not a horse in sight. They felt sorry for the crazed fan who stalked him; the character, Evelyn, attempting suicide when he severs ties with her, having used her for sex. It all gets out of hand, of course. Mrs Lexton already knew of Edgar Allan Poe's poem *Annabel Lee*; Evelyn made reference to it during a phonecall before she attempts to stab Clint Eastwood's character, Dave Garver, to death.

Quietly now, Mrs Tanner carrying the hammer in disguise, and Mrs Lexton on the look-out, they headed outdoors – the bin belonging to Mr and Mrs Stone in sight.

17

AFTER REPEATEDLY NAPPING on and off, and not much after three in the morning, Gulliver found himself wide awake – when asleep, his mind had wandered like a lost child in an unfamiliar lamp-lighted city – a smog-ridden labyrinth of sorts frozen in time. No matter what turn he had taken, house after house had been the colour of liver, street after street seemed uninhabited. He was lost. Misplaced. And he knew exactly why.

Olivia was yet to text back. She would, of course she would – he was sure of that – but the anticipation – the cat and mouse game, it was tormenting him both physically and mentally. This was a game for teenagers, not a grown man, married, a father. His mind pirouetted absentmindedly. Maybe he was paying the price for not having responded instantaneously.

For some forsaken reason, when he first took to his bed, Carys already asleep by his side, he could not reject from his disquiet mind a childhood memory from a time gone by. He wasn't even sure if he had remembered it right – a flashback of a moment when he was caught up in a trance-like state at a local fair – an innocent game of thimblerig before him – at eye level with the table. His father had unbeknown moved on and left him behind. Bewitched.

The rigger – an elderly man with a long nose and face – his white hair tied like a Viking, braided ponytail and beard alike – had placed a large hard pea below one of three cups. They were plastic. The white cups. The noise of the pea made them sound like they were made of plastic – and the scrape of them on the wooden table, as they whooshed in circular shapes dancing before his eyes in the figure of a number eight, confirmed this.

When he finished scooting them, Gulliver had been sure which cup held the quiet pea that held its breath. He lifted his right hand to point to the cup in the middle when doubt ceased him. Child after child had failed in their attempt beforehand. He'd thought of going for the one that seemed less obvious – the one the rigger had handled the least.

The rigger had trickery in his eye. Was the pea elsewhere? Where all three cups vacant? Had he moved or manipulated the pea unfairly? He somehow knew, despite his age, a singular number, that he was one in a long line of guileless players who had never stood a chance of winning. But he held his nerve – even though he knew the pea wouldn't be there. And he chose the middle cup after all.

It was dark. Shadow had now married shadow. The sound of Carys' breathing only served to underline the silence in their bedroom. He thought about rising once again before he decided against it. He was too tired. His loud and troubled mind was willing whilst the flesh was too weak, for now. He needed his sleep - needed to concentrate on their present investigation. He was yet to prove himself.

So far, he'd successfully managed to alienate fellow officers by cracking a joke about their previous Inspector – a dead one at that - and had embarrassed himself before his new boss by collapsing at the sight of a bloodless dead body. He had more than one bridge to build, although pleasantly, he did sense, for the first time since he had met Catherine, that she was somehow warming to him. He needed a friend. He'd made none so far.

The appearance of the two sisters had already haunted him earlier that evening; he'd been eating at the table when Manon entered holding a life-like doll under her arm. Their frozen scowls and narrowing glances were like reflections from mirrors at a fairground. Dolls on a shelf abandoned shelf at a museum. They had made their unmistakeable displeasure obvious. He'd studied *The Strange Case of Dr Jekyll and Mr Hyde* as a student – hated it. But he had never forgotten the descriptions of the dwarfish deformed character of Hyde who lurked in dirty corners, trampled on children and murdered the guiltless for the thrill of it. He remembered a few quotations still – he had been compared to a *troglodyte*. It was the two sisters he had pictured earlier in his dreams that bore such a likeness.

But now fully awake, he thought of Olivia and Olivia only. Gulliver was all too aware that Carys was naturally close by. Parallel, and with her back to him – her breathing sounded peaceful – her body rose and fell between intervals, at times ever so slightly. He was secretly glad of it – thinking about Olivia was easier if he could physically separate himself from everyone else – even the children - the guilt was less cumbrous. The duplicity easier to uphold.

There was, of course, only one way to rid himself of the guilt, but he was clearly not prepared to put a stop to what had once more ignited between them – their brief separation one of the hardest things he had ever experienced. Maybe now, with the distance between them, they could manage their feelings for each other better. Control the uncontrollable. They both had their careers to think of. Although childless, Olivia too was married.

Mobile on silent, he glanced at the screen in the certain knowledge that Olivia would not have yet responded. He re-read his last message. *I need to see you.* He re-read it again.

At the time he thought it was a good message, simple and direct. He'd thought long and hard about it. Had re-written it in different ways. Doubt and uncertainty had now grown to such an extent, that he had convinced himself that his message could have been misinterpreted – had had some adverse effect – hadn't sounded like he had missed her to the same extent she had. She had, after all, taken the risk to contact him first. Why didn't he just say what he had wanted to say all along. He sent another message: *I need you too.*

***

He'd first seen her in a library. They had really met by chance. He wasn't meant to be there – he'd had to stand in for a sick officer – the theft of two of Gladstone's own annotated books taken from a small reading room – a room that housed a distinctive collection of rare 18th century items. Within an hour of the theft, it had already made the regional news.

He'd lived in Wales all of his life but had never heard of the world's only residential library. And in Wales, of all places. The two books had been given to Gladstone himself as a boy by his father, had originally been kept by his bedside at Hawarden Castle, until he died. They were both botanical books, he was informed. One was a large book on the nature of porous mimeographed paper entitled *Seeing the Light* by Dr David S. P. Manzi. Brick-Red covers. The other was on Japanese Botany: *The Period of Wood Block Printing* by Dr Harley T. S. Harris. Green-Morocco. *I'm sorry?* Confused, Gulliver was also too embarrassed to ask for help with the spelling of a couple of words. *The covers Detective. Brick-Red. Green-Morocco.*

When he was assigned the job, he naturally frowned. A library. He'd never been too fond of books. What he had pictured in his mind, as he set off towards North Wales, could have easily been summed up as a generalisation of a clinical contemporary setting – technology ridden, with the ambience and pulse of a doctor's surgery. Possibly the odd plant thrown in too – oh – pencil pots – little natural light – sparseness – bleakness – oblivion. Must. A musty smell. A building filled with must and dust – like a cemetery, idle and dated. He'd also pictured the residents he'd have to interview. A line-up of shop dummies, a uniformity in their faces, the staff moving anxiously making small birdlike gestures. Apologies. Silence. A warning sign of some sort, blue-tacked to each stack of shelves.

Years ago, he'd attended a weekend training session, for his Sergeant's exam at the University of St Andrews. It was there he read two of the most outrageous signs he'd ever come across so far in his lifetime. Carys hadn't believed him. He'd sent two photographs to prove it after a long phone call. Manon must have only been three.

The first was one about keeping the doors closed during the evening so that bats did not come into the building. Surprisingly, he didn't see a single bat at the time. But in the toilet was a sign that was headlined <u>MASTURBATION NOTICE</u>. It warned that the act of *masturbation in the toilet was a violation of the University of St Andrews University Library Regulations.* The mind boggled as it has since.

He'd promised Carys he'd be home early. The first week of the summer holidays promised much sunshine according to the BBC; in the past, they frequently took to the beach for a walk and possibly a picnic – he'd promised to take time off before the end of July. He would, of course he would. Carys, being a primary teacher, would grow tired of childish company, understandably, pester him to take time off, spend some time with her.

It was on a blistering hot day, the day he arrived to the Library's grounds that he met Olivia. He was not in any way prepared for the awesome building in site. It wasn't colossal, although it seemed much bigger than it was. The emerald grounds too had had the same effect – wider rather than longer – expansive. Panoramic. The three historic statues outdoors elevated its overall appearance and position. They stood tall, and green, the ageing process making them even more attractive and rustic.

Shaped like a punctuation bracket from the front, the reception and entrance was to be found in the middle, on the ground floor. The wooden and iron two-storey library rooms were to the very left. How elegant the tiered windows were. Indoors, the light landed diagonally across the parquet flooring whilst the sound of summer and the smell of roses fluctuated in strength as visitors wandered amusedly, as he did then, along the side path entrance.

To the right of the edifice was a smaller structure, a pretty and timeworn church made of the same dark-red sandstone. Surrounding it were many flowerless gravestones, some tilted sideways like sinking boats or upturned teeth. Directly in front of where he stood, to the left of the church, was a vast looming tree; it cast a welcome shadow over the oldest of gravestones. Each branch rose upturned, tier by tier, like a dog's nose – shorter – shorter - each layer reaching upwards – dark green leaves – thick like carpet - the widest of trunks was to the middle. Gulliver was sure he'd never seen such a wide tree.

And from behind the hulking trunk appeared a young woman. He hadn't anticipated that. A woman possibly in her thirties. It was her dark hair that he noticed. He had not yet set eyes on her face. It was lowered, immersed in a book. Her long hair was to the side – disorderly – thick – wavy – tied three-quarters of the way down twice. Gulliver had stepped through a porthole. He stepped back. Looked away. A strange and unrecognisable surge causing him a pleasant discomfort.

She was engrossed in what she was reading. She paused, leaned on the dense trunk – she'd done this before – leant on it like she depended on its actuality. Folded into it. Some part of her disappeared. Dissolved. Suddenly, she raised her head to laugh bemused – smiled as she turned a page. He didn't hear her – her facial expression and tilting of the neck had told him. That's when Gulliver saw Olivia's face for the first time

- when she raised her head ever so slightly to turn the page – her smile – it's slightness. Her long neck arched gracefully like a willow tree. In an orange and white tea-dress – buttoned from top to bottom – a white belt about her waist.

Then a permanent photograph of a moment when he unintentionally locked eyes on her – was too embarrassed to look away. He apologised, retraced a few steps – his face had surprisingly reddened. He turned away and continued on his path to the front entrance. She hadn't smiled either. Just held his gaze. Why had he struggled to find something to do with his hands? His absurdity did not amuse him in the least.

Quite intentionally he spent the rest of the day busying himself – like a spot needing to be scratched, the fleeting visualisation threatened to turn into an almighty rash. He pressed on. An hour later he'd acquired names and addresses of all recent visitors and residents to the library. Fortunately, there were not many. But as certain that the sun would rise, he knew at some point, they would meet again. He flicked through the list of names several times at first; it was difficult matching a name to such a face. It seemed ludicrous to crave after someone in such a manner, on the basis of a fleeting moment.

Gulliver was sure he would be disappointed. He told himself that as he glanced deliberately at his wedding ring. That fleeting instant was just that. The past. Gone. The magic had been in the silence – enveloped in the snapshot – the appearance of it all. Reality always disappointed. Curiosity after all, killed the cat.

It made more sense to interview the residential visitors first; after all, most would be leaving by midday. By half-past twelve, none the wiser, following a short lunch, he began to interview the ones who would remain overnight. It was difficult to ascertain who was telling the truth. Most people visiting the library seemed to be cut from the same cloth – they seemed as honest as the day was long. However, they all had one thing in common – the love of books.

Many admitted having an impressive collection of their own at home. Two admitted to not having returned books from a university library. Absolved on the spot, he left them nursing troubled thoughts. What would a book thief look like? Surely it would be more likely that an expert book-lifter looking more like an art thief had deliberately wandered into the library, the desk often unattended, the building having no CCTV, and effortlessly managed to acquire the two volumes with ease?

Some visitors had written themselves, many needed the library's resources to support their studies, few were in residence to simply read and relax. Miss Marple would have done a better job. Any one of them could have stashed both books into their holdall. Short of searching them one by one, he had no idea where they were, although he did assure the director that his investigation was going well and that he was confident both volumes would soon be returned, unharmed.

Before he left the grounds, later in the afternoon, Gulliver took a stroll along the left wing corridor and headed to the library, the wooden parchment floor betraying his arrival to the place where the books had originally been taken – the very scene of the bodiless and bloodless crime.

The ancient library was divided into two reading rooms – both had an upstairs and a downstairs. Wooden shelves stocked with rare books decked out every shelf from floor to ceiling. Accessed only by the less weighty, the circular and narrow concrete steps in each corner spiralled upwards. At a slit of a window, Gulliver paused to take in the beauty of the place both indoors and out. He was unsure at first, then he knew that it was so. He had located the wide berthed tree by the churchyard. He watched for a moment before he moved on.

There was a singular desk between every two shelves – both on the ground floor and on the first. Many of these desks were occupied – familiar faces nodded politely as he wandered about the library. One of the self-confessed thieves smiled nervously before she lowered her gaze. Had he imagined her leaning on the tree? Possibly bewitched, he continued the tour.

It would be on the following day that he would conduct his final two interviews – early in the morning, before checking out time. In the knowledge he would most likely get nowhere, he would then travel to visit the three remaining names on his list, at their home – those whom he'd missed prior to his arrival. Two of them, male, lived poles apart - a fifty-two mile round trip ahead of him. The single remainder, was listed as a Mrs Marjorie Higginson. It was hard to match the name Marjorie with the face of the woman he had seen that afternoon. She lived only an hour away; he would call in on her on the way home. In any case, she was married, like him – probably a parent likewise.

Gulliver then made his way across to the second reading room. The grained door was surprisingly light to handle; he was unsurprised by the groaning that ensued following every footfall, heavier as each landed, lighter as it lifted.

An impressive window was ahead of him – it was almost as wide as the wall itself. It was tiered like the others but none of the windows could be set ajar, open. Its beams highlighted the north end of the library floor, widespread diagonal rays slicing volume after volume, the faded gold lettering reawakened – a particular and familiar shade to the mummified hard covers – pomegranate reds, slate greys, hunting greens, navy blues – classic cloth bound leather covers, in penitential colours. At a nearby desk, a young man, most likely a student, held a latticed volume in deep gold.

There was an air of respectability to the room. Whilst gross shadows lurked anywhere else, undisturbed, the cinnamon light spread far and white – almost everywhere, bar the beamed ceiling. It was a warm library yet unstiffling. A public building for the private. A haven of many sorts. A place to showcase the beauty of books. To touch was to intimately partake in a sacred ritual. Gulliver admired from afar.

As he passed by, stepping on the arched pools of warmth, he suddenly noticed, immediately across from where he stood, a familiar face. Lifting her head ever so slightly above her laptop screen, a young woman, looking momentarily like a trapped animal, looked unintentionally both ways. Seeing no easy way of avoiding him, she sat back upright, casual-like – her folded bare arms had already given her away.

Gulliver turned aside before he afforded himself a smile. He was pleased in a way that he did not understand; it thrilled him to have witnessed her discomfort – she had behaved as though she had been caught out. He wondered for how long she had been watching him.

He deliberately moved slowly from one section to another, looking at this and that – one book had spelt the name Shakespeare as *Shakesphere*. How odd? He was making his way towards her at the pace of his own choosing – her desk cornered between two darker sections – the only way out behind him. At that moment in time, he did not know whether he would simply pass by or stop to make some enquiry. He stopped and fingered a thick and heavy teal volume gilded in bright gold: *The Government of the Kingdom of Christ* by J. Moir Porteous, D.D. 1888 – opened it. He was enjoying himself.

The chase was as attractive as the hurt coming from a loose tooth. He only managed to remain composed because he had told himself he was there on business. But as he neared the section of the library she was caged within, he felt the need to take a deep breath, acclimatise. He was sure at this point she would rise and leave.

It was warmer now; hands clammy, book returned, he moved towards her chosen area of work. He had no idea whether they would communicate – he only knew that he would pass behind her to access the opposite corner available before he would spontaneously descend the turret-like staircase, before heading for the exit.

She stopped word-processing as he neared – he heard the tapping of her fingers stop. Without looking directly he had already seen the sight of her fingers hover over the white keyboard – her unpainted nails short, the whiteness contrasting against her olive hands – a wedding ring on her left. An inexplicable energy, like electricity, a ghost of a space in time passed. He afforded himself a side-long glance. Did either of them breathe as he quietly passed? No scent. Her bare white neck exposed – the same dress, a little higher now, clinging uncomfortably above her knees. Her face visibly red. The sound of birds. And unusually cars. And then he stopped and turned around. She hadn't moved – not an inch. And when he spoke he not only surprised himself but clearly herself too.

'I believe we are to meet tomorrow morning - before you check out?'

'We are?'

Like an obedient child, she turned right and faced him as best she could. Of course, she had since learned whom he was, as well as his purpose at Gladstone's. She had anticipated she would be one of the last to be interviewed – having stayed the entire weekend in order to complete an assignment. He was bound to interview the first to leave. She could see now, that in many ways, the wait had been worth it. After their earlier encounter, she had in earnest hoped to catch a glimpse of him again.

'Ah, the mystery of the missing books! Will you be conducting a search of my quarters?'

Initially Gulliver was taken aback. She was smirking. He hadn't realised until right then, just how beautiful she was. Her jaw seemed masculine in comparison to most – suddenly she was strong, aligned, yet dignified, poised – the redness to her face having fully disappeared. Her large eyes seemed intense, mischievous even. In the dimming natural light penetrating the arched windows, her pupils looked as black as the oncoming night.

'Well? Do you have them?'

'Of course not!'

'Then that is the end of my investigation. I'll thank you and bid you good day!'

Then he smiled. And she laughed. And she spoke.

'Do you have time for a cup of tea before you leave? The premises have a café and I am ready for a break.'

18

MRS LEXTON AND Mrs Tanner were like cats on a hot tin roof until the maroon bin was finally collected. On many an occasion, either singularly or in unison, they looked out of the front room bay, or even Mrs Lexton's bedroom window, in order to catch sight of the lonesome bin, on the very corner of the cul-de-sac, patiently waiting to be collected.

On many an occasion they allowed their overactive minds to wander. Their intake of breath coincided with either a passer-by or even worse by the sound of a police siren. Relief and dread had been the only two sides to the invisible coin that had constantly tossed in their troubled minds – which side it would land on was very much dependant on lady luck.

It was such a relief when the steel lorry reversed into their expectant cul-de-sac. Of the eight to be collected, it was the first to be emptied, then one bin followed the other – solid waste pouring from their mouths. Churning. The engine still running. Bins once positioned neatly outside each household now littered carelessly on the pavement like children released from a primary school awaiting collection. The truck turned the corner. The hammer was gone.

***

Mrs Lexton places her mug in the sink; her head aches and the gin has made her sleepy. In turn, Mrs Tanner removes herself from the kitchen and heads outdoors. She remembers with distaste what followed after he had painted her lounge lilac and fitted her a purple carpet. It is a memory she tries to avoid like the plague. She excuses herself as best she can. The conversation is ongoing inside her mind. It is a secret that can never be shared. It had been nice having Neil at the house, being there, popping in and out during that fortnight. There were times she did not see him as her sister's useless husband.

Neil had thought of everything. He told her what to say and what to do. She rang Trevor's employer; he'd been driving milk carts since he left school. She told them he'd left her a letter. That he was gone. It was all unbelievably easy. He wasn't liked. Like her, both his parents were dead. She didn't touch his money – she kept his belongings in the attic. He'd left her – would most likely return at some point for his clobber.

When he put his arm around her, after she had begun to cry, worrying about money, she rejected his advance. She wasn't stupid. If she had been honest with herself, she should have seen it coming a mile off. He was a decent man compared to Trevor. But a useless cunt all the same. And just the once, she relented –

frustrated and lonely – weak and tired of the past. He wanted her and at the time, truth be told, she'd wanted him too – a pent-up frustration building over a few days when he just didn't seem to be anyone's husband and she wasn't anyone's wife. The shame of it was, it was all over before it had begun. Dirty. Selfish.

As if standing in a courtroom, she would argue her case quite unconvincingly to herself. Reprehensible. She was grieving, vulnerable – she had refused him several times. She knew she should have told him to stop coming around. She only had herself to blame. *Mia culpa.* Like a baby with colic, nothing would ever placate or mollify her. She hoped-to-God he wouldn't tell Jo.

In the end, when she thought of her sister, and their parents – wrong was wrong. There was no excusing what she had done. She knew he'd move onto someone else eventually – so she told him – warned him – and he laughed. Accepted it was over. All the same laughed at her. She deserved it. Dirty.

Her sister Jo had been in and out of Greaves Hospital on many an occasion – depression flooding her existence – drowning - drowning. Mrs Tanner knew her time had been poorly spent. She needed to make amends. Right the wrongs. Support her sister. Spend time with her. Neil wasn't going to. He was a useless cunt after all. Their parents would have expected it. Especially after they found Jo hanging from one of the asylum trees.

19

THE INVESTIGATION AT Gladstone's Library was over not long after they had sat in the café drinking tea. The management triumvirate, looking both relieved and embarrassed at one another, relayed that the two books had been found when their evening staff clocked on for the evening. The books in question had been set aside in a drawer for a customer wishing to use them that Sunday. The assistant had not noted this in the ledger. He did reiterate that the books were invaluable and that he hoped he had not wasted too much of his time.

Gladstone's was an hour's drive from Southport; from Conwy it was almost exactly the same amount of time. Olivia lived with her husband, a History lecturer at Bangor University almost as far as he did, but in the opposite direction. Olivia studied there too; she often used Gladstone's to study or complete assignments. When she met Gulliver, it had been her fourth visit to the place. She loved it there. She was about to complete a Masters of Studies in Theology – her specialism on Christian Doctrine and Patristic Theology. Her father had read Theology at Cambridge.

When Olivia left the reception the following day, he watched her grow smaller and smaller. For an insignificant moment he followed her, but he couldn't think of anything to say. His mind a blank. His body restless. Then, after placing her belongings into the boot of her sanguine-red sports car, she paused, returned, growing larger and larger, until she was there, not too far from where he stood, breathless from having walked a lot faster, her desire uncommunicative. He promised to stay in touch.

Their courtship was like a slow Rumba. More texts than anything else. Within a fortnight, he thought he knew all that he needed. Their texts had changed dramatically. No more inquisitive questions. Desire and hunger kicking vehemently in. The summer heat making them restless and moody. Their imaginations failing to satisfy them. An emotional and uncontrollable avalanche of some sort.

Then one morning he received a text asking him to come to her house. *I need you.* He couldn't get away until midday. Was he really going to brazenly enter her marital home? When he arrived, he did not wait long until he arrived to her door. Olivia was waiting for him. She looked peasant-like – and restless. She was wearing a long casual dress – thin – white - her left shoulder almost obscured by her dark hair, untied – a tincture of the light warming her. It looked longer – stronger. He had never seen her hair fully down. He moved towards her. Neither spoke. She was breathing noisily.

They didn't even make it upstairs. The curtains drawn back - the August heat drawing them both gently together, at first. Apart. Together. There was no breeze. Only the noise of them coming together again. Their mouths clashed at one point and they laughed nervously. There was plenty of time before Olivia's husband would be home.

Agitated, neither felt fully satisfied by the time they parted - despite their attention to detail and their ardent hunger. Restless, both Gulliver and Olivia knew this was only the beginning of something bigger - something that would willingly and undeniably consume them, despite their best intentions.

***

Gulliver knocked on Catherine's half-open door as he entered her untidy office. She moved a little away from her computer screen before she lifted her spectacles upwardly to rest them on her head. She looked both irritated and tired.

'It's not easy adjusting to wearing spectacles! At the moment I'm getting at least one headache a day. Wendy's wondering if they've given me the right prescription. I'm unfortunately at the point in my adjustment where I need to wear them now, but I also desperate for a break from the damned things. I've started driving home without them on. I can do that with my eyes closed.'

'Possibly? An invitation, for Zita. It's Manon's eleventh birthday on the 15th – a Sunday – if you can all make it. We've hired a bouncy castle – for the kids – although I often end up in the middle of them myself. Mind, I'll have to behave. Other than our families, they'll be folk neither of us know too well.'

'I know the feeling. Thank you. I don't think we've got much on that weekend – I'll pass it onto Wendy – she'll give – I'm sorry – what's your wife's – partner's name again?'

'Carys. My wife.'

'Sorry. Wendy will give Carys a call. I'll pass the invitation to her as soon as I get in. Thank you. She manages the diary. She's always moaning at me for not putting things in it. Changes you. Having a child. Responsibility.'

For a moment they both fell into an awkward silence. Then Catherine pulled her seat away from her desk and stood up as if to leave the room. It seemed when she smiled that it had taken some effort.

'Toilet break.'

Gulliver had news. The information on the watch belonging to the deceased would at least break their ridiculous discomfort with one another.

'Liz has since had the watch of the deceased examined – nothing to go on – a fake – too much erosion to tell if it was ever worth much.'

'What about the gravedigger's name? Any luck with that?'

'No gravedigger's name was ever assigned to the job at hand. There's no real paperwork. However, we do have the names of two men who worked for the cemetery at the time. Neither were employed by the council. Both were self-employed gravediggers – most were in those days – could earn them a pretty packet apparently!'

'Fingers crossed they're still above ground themselves.'

When Catherine returned she found Gulliver still patiently waiting. A headache looming, she located a sheet of paracetamol in her desk drawer before swallowing three tablets with water.

'I'm sorry. It's not you Gulliver; I genuinely don't feel so good today. Can you try to find these gravediggers? Get a statement from them?'

'Charlotte is trying to locate them – a Mr Lesley Litt and a Mr Neil Lexton. I also spoke to Mr Brookner's son, in case he remembers anything significant about the gravedigger. He may have been too young, could remember nothing. But we'll give it a try.

If you want I can cover here. I can ring you at home with any developments?'

'I might take you up on that. Thank you. Really.

Litt is an unusual surname – American I think. Any chance this Lesley Litt fellow is related to our current gravedigger Michael Litt? Father and son possibly?'

'Charlotte is onto that already. We wondered ourselves. When we looked back over the interviews, Mr Litt did not mention his father may have been the gravedigger at the time. And the surname – it's unusual – someone said American.'

'Maybe he knows something. If Lesley turns out to be any relative of his, bring him in again – there is no reason why he should forget to mention such an important fact.'

'Agreed.'

'And Gulliver, thank you for the invitation. It's all new to us – Zita's last birthday, her first birthday with us, went almost uncelebrated. We are only now getting to grips with the demands and expectations of children at such an age. Birthdays mean a lot to the little people. Wendy mentioned Manon and her were getting on great in school. To be honest, I'm not so great at these social events – will be nice to mingle with someone I know for a change.'

Gulliver was arrested by Catherine's frankness. He wasn't expecting her to open up in such a manner. He was pleased she had. Selfishly it made him feel in some strange way privileged – like she had confessed something – shared a secret. He knew Carys would be pleased too. If they were to settle in Southport, they needed to make new friends – move on – leave the past behind. Easier said than done. He recalled just then something his mother used to often say. She believed that the past was part and parcel of one's own landscape. For a moment he thought about this. Then he smiled sympathetically at Catherine who was now miserably clutching her head like a football in both hands.

'I'll make you a hot drink.'

He was heading to the kitchen, having just seen Charlotte enter it when his mobile rang. It was Olivia. He allowed the phone to ring. Guilt. He was no good at this stuff. What was this stuff? Charlotte pretended not to notice his odd behaviour, the way he just stood there, staring at the screen.

He had no idea why he did not know what to do right then and there. He'd waited long enough for her response. He looked at the screen once more before he turned his mobile on silent. He couldn't think. He then realised Charlotte was staring at him. Managing a half-smile, he excused himself and left the kitchen. Despite the sudden urge to ignore the call, Gulliver found himself answering it.

'Hello you!'

'Hello you. You ok? Is it a good time to talk?'

'Of course. Now's good.'

Her voice alone penetrated his exterior shell and softened him to the touch. He edged towards the back of the corridor. It was great hearing her voice again. Like an insect that had volunteered to trespass the spider's web, there he hung – onto her every word – entrapped and pensive. He needed her more than ever now. Her every word a magnet. The energy that surged within him unstoppable. When she suggested they meet, he did not hesitate. He hoped for somewhere private – more private than her own home – he had little desire to meet and talk. They could talk later.

When Olivia suggested the following weekend, he agreed, of course. Saturday evening. He hesitated. Then agreed. The day before Manon's birthday. She would be staying at Gladstone's Library, overnight. She would be waiting for him. How early after work could he get there?

'I cannot wait to see you.'

'Neither can I.'

20

MARRYING A BASTARD is far worse than marrying a useless cunt. Mrs Tanner has had another sleepless night. Guilt, interlaced with a deep regret prevented her from getting a good night's sleep. Mrs Lexton was still in bed when Mrs Tanner left for the shops. Last night, they agreed that when this whole sorry business was over, they were going to repaint the whole exterior of the house - a royal blue: Mrs Lexton's favourite colour.

At the corner shop, Mrs Tanner bought a plug-in air freshener, tea-bags, tobacco and a large bottle of gin. It was whilst they were drinking the tea-laced gin that she agreed to let her sister repaint the house blue. She also promised that there would be no more secrets.

As Mrs Tanner arrives to her single gate, she notices Mr Evans in his bay window; he is finally taking down the Christmas tree. Mr Evans' wife originates from Spain. The Spanish celebrate Christmas Day on the sixth of January. Mrs Tanner already knows this – Mr Evans has explained over the years that the Spanish receive their presents on the sixth, on the Epiphany – when the three Kings gifted gold, frankincense and myrrh to the baby Jesus.

In Spain, no-one takes their tree down until after the sixth. From the tone of his voice, the explanation sounds more like an apology. Indoors, Mrs Evans is by her husband's side now - Eduardo is nowhere to be seen. She scowls at her through the window. Mrs Tanner would like to tell her how handy she can be with a hammer, just to wipe that disdainful look from her face. She'd be doing poor Mr Evans a favour – she's sure of it.

As Mrs Tanner closes the gate, Mrs Evans is standing to the side; both of her hands are on her hips. It seems from the look on both their faces, and the way she is waving her arms that she is shouting at her husband. In turn he is just standing there – taking it. How odd life is? Mr Evans is the sort of man who constantly looks as though he is about to apologise. On the odd occasion, when she has heard him speak, as she passes by, she has noted that he seems to be a kind and patient man. Not like her bastard of a husband.

Mrs Tanner is now indoors making a cup of tea. Memories flood her mind two-fold. She once spoke her mind when she was newly pregnant, not long after they had married. Her husband didn't react like Mr Evans does. She hadn't been feeling well – morning sickness. She was tired of feeling nauseous, tired of vomiting, even though she'd eaten nothing that day.

Her husband was clearly tired of her moaning. He'd been working since the early hours – being a milkman – she'd caught him unawares.

At the time, she wasn't entirely sure she was that pleased to be pregnant. Trevor certainly wasn't. When she told him she'd missed her period by two months, he walked out and went to the pub. But when he came back, he had a bunch of daffodils in his hand. She wasn't sure how her sister Jo would react either, when she told her the news. She needn't have worried: she never had to – never got that far.

It was when she started bleeding that the panic set in. It was when she lost the baby that she realised how much she really wanted it. Began to relate to how Jo had felt losing her own. Incomparable but all the same, the pain real. When she started to bleed, Trevor's face filled with panic too. His clenched hands relaxed. He was her old Trevor again. Her ride. He hadn't meant to push her that hard. Hadn't slept all night. Milkround. Tired. She'd caught him unawares. Overtired. No excuse. He had no excuse he said. Wouldn't ever forgive himself he said. Could she ever forgive him? He was a ride.

At the time, her figure was still something she was proud of – skinny with legs like pins. Trevor loved for her to stand naked in front of him – her long brown hair draped on each side – her eyes peeping sheepishly from behind her fringe. It wasn't just her though, her feisty nature attracted him to her. She didn't realise he must have picked her because she was a challenge. The one he would break, come what may. She'd played hard to get.

Little by little he whittled her down though – if she put weight on – if she had sugar in her tea – if she was seeking attention by wearing the wrong top. It was all her fault. He never said it at first. He was clever. He ignored her too. Nobody had ever ignored her before.

When exactly the shoving became a throw of a punch, she cannot recall – and her feistiness regressed until she almost disappeared. A caged fox. Once a ward nurse. Now a killer. A killer living with another killer. It wasn't fair. Life hadn't been fair.

She must have been about ten weeks pregnant when he hit her for the second time – too early to have a scan – when she spoke out of line. Went too far. There was nothing much in the fridge for their tea. Trevor was hungry. *Famished. Starving.*

He was always hungry. He'd come in after his shift and sit there all afternoon in front of the television whilst she was feeling sick upstairs. When he called her down, in the voice that warned her it was coming, she thought she'd better drag herself out of bed. Before he came after her. The baby.

Mrs Tanner suggested a walk – a breath of fresh air for them both. To the corner shop. Get something for their tea. *A chippy tea.* He was tired. She wasn't feeling too good. She was tired too.

Tired? You've been sat on your fat backside all day!
And she whispered it. Loud enough so that he'd hear it.
Quiet enough so that he wouldn't be sure she'd said it.
Like a schoolgirl. Only teachers don't lose their temper
like that.

*What did you say? Nothing. What did you say? I said
nothing.* Push. *Get off. Or what?* Shove. *Get off. So I'm a
selfish bastard am I? Get off!* He was angry. They'd kiss
and make up like they always did. Shove. Fall. *Selfish
bastard am I?* She stood up quick. Her face red – unsure
– angry. *You selfish fucking bastard I said! You can't
even hear straight yer that pissed.* His face. She hadn't
seen that face before. Apoplectic. She noticed he
couldn't get his words together. Shit.

She was all grown up now. Had the house, and the
husband and the job she'd always wanted. He hadn't
meant to lose his temper. He wasn't like men who
really battered their wives – they lived on the other
end of a fist every day. It was a one off. Well a two off
but the second didn't count because it was a shove to
be honest and she'd started it herself. She was a
mouthy cow. He wasn't looking for a fight. He was sat
resting after a hard day's work when she started
calling him names. He bought her cheap flowers then.
He was sorry. He was still her ride.

A few years later, when she'd let her figure go a little,
and she had no fringe, he started to drink both after
work and at home. And his face changed. And his
kindness disappeared. He liked it when she flinched.

He was in control. She was no longer a challenge. Tamed like a wild horse. He was no longer her ride.

He'd developed a liking for something she never understood. Not the shoving. Nor the punching. It was a liking for cruelty. Belittling. Slapping. Especially her face. He liked the sound of it. In full swing. You could start small and build it up. The crying and begging bated him. Shut her up. She was winding him up. He'd told her to shut up.

And when he was sober – he sometimes said he was sorry but his eyes said he was not. He was changing. He stopped saying it wouldn't happen again. And he knew everyone at her work knew – everyone she worked with - at the hospital - but he didn't care. And they didn't want to see. Or care. She was up herself he said. *I'll bring you down a notch. You think you're too good for me. I don't Trev. I love you.* I love you worked for a while. Like slowing a steam train down. She looked to the sky many a night – cried for her parents – couldn't bother Jo. The infinitesimal glow of stars unreachable. When she spoke to the priest, in confidence, he urged Christian tolerance.

He knew the neighbours knew – that seemed to bother him least – he skulked back from work now and then. The women glared at him and some of their husbands stopped letting on to him. God please don't ignore him. He'd say she'd said something. It wouldn't matter if she told him she hadn't seen a soul. He'd say she was lying. She'd been talking. Seeking attention as always. A disloyal wife. Smack. Bitch. Fucking bitch. Slap. *What yer crying for. Whore. Fucking keep yer crying down. Mouthy cow.*

The police called because the neighbours did. Mrs Tanner looked at them so they could see but their eyes said they didn't want to know. They'd called because they were obliged to. Told her husband that. Saw her face. Didn't bother looking into her eyes. Mrs Tanner pleaded with them in her head. He closed the door and laughed.

Once he pissed on her. Honestly. He closed the door after they went. One of them was a woman. She thought the female officer would at least see. Before they'd even shut the front gate, he pissed on her. He pissed on her because she fainted. Mrs Tanner was pregnant for the second time. And he pissed on her. A month later, she'd miscarried.

She stayed pretty much indoors from then on. Called in sick to work. He was no longer a ride. He was a bastard. She'd put more weight on. Her legs weren't lanky. He beat her for cutting her hair. She hadn't asked if she could get her hair cut. Dragged her by the new bob and sat her on a kitchen chair. Took the scissors – chopped at it this angle, then at that angle. She didn't care. She thought he was going to cut her ear off. Stab her. He was furious. Bastard. *Who're you trying to look cute for?*

It was when he bent her index finger back-back-back until it snapped that she knew he'd never stop. Why she hadn't realised it sooner, she'll never know. Snapped. Popped. No, snapped. The drink helped. It helped a lot. She could read his mood. Drank before he returned home. Numbed the senses. Stopped her from saying anything stupid. Making it worse. He'd told her over and over again that she was a mouthy cow.

He beat her for answering back. He beat her for cutting her hair. He beat her for looking at him. He beat her for being in bed. He beat her for being a lazy cow. He beat her for being a mouthy cow. He beat her for being drunk. And because she stunk.

He beat her black and blue. She'd lost babies. She'd had multiple broken ribs. More than three times. Once, when she couldn't breathe, he had to drive her to the hospital. *She fell down the stairs*. His breath stunk of alcohol. But nobody wanted to see.

With the exception of her sister Jo, no one *saw* what he was doing. Not the good nurses whom she worked with. Nor the qualified doctors. Nor the neighbourly neighbours. No-one wanted to see. No –one wanted to look her way. God didn't want to look her way. Jo pleaded with her to leave him. But she couldn't – she really couldn't – was afraid to think of it. He'd know. He'd look at her, and he'd know.

But the children could see. They knew. Even on the days she wore dark glasses and a thick coat in the summer they could see. *Look mummy – the Emperor isn't wearing any clothes!*

Her superior, the ward's matron, eventually got around to having an informal chat with her. She hoped he could help. He didn't see. *The children on the ward are vulnerable. Their parents need to feel they are in good hands.* Smack. Crack. Drink. The children could see. It wasn't fair on them. Then another warning. The last one. Absences. Lateness. Drink. None of them wanted to see. Let go. On the record. 35. Career - ended.

She was last pregnant when she was 36. Had almost stopped drinking. After she stopped being a nurse. When she became nothing. When she was just a wife. She couldn't believe it. He hardly touched her in the last year. In bed. He'd been hitting her less. She hadn't realised herself but she'd grown from within. He only really hit her when he was drunk. Even then, he sometimes went straight to bed. Bed rhymes with dead. She wished the bastard dead.

She didn't think she'd lost the baby because he'd hit her this time. She didn't tell him on purpose – Jo's idea. A good idea. She was almost four months pregnant. Kept the black and white scan picture at Jo's. There is nothing that compares to that feeling – that answer to a longing – that magic – an unborn's heartbeat. It hadn't been real until then. Jo went with her. Their secret. Jo was great. Much stronger now. She'd looked on the pregnancy as great news. She'd be the best aunt.

Babs had made her mind up. If the bastard came at her, she'd be ready. There's nothing more dangerous in the animal kingdom than a mother who feels threatened.

Then she began bleeding.

The drinking stopped all together when Mr Tanner was gone the following year. He went from there all the time to dead at 41. Her a widow at 37. Two years too late. Two years after he ended her career for good. Died on the day he was born. 27th of September 1986. He'd been out drinking, of course. Hammered. Seventeen years married. Started on her. She'd even bought him a card. To stay on the right side of him. *Tic-Tac-Toe. Missed the toe. Tic-Tac-Toe. Got that one. What yer crying for? You need to move yer feet faster.*

So she took the hammer from him and didn't stop. Served him right, the selfish bastard. She'd lost three babies. Her nursery empty like her sister's. Hammer. Bastard. *Have yer cake and eat it bastard.* Blow after blow after blow after blow after blow after blow after blow after blow after blow after blow after blow after blow after blow after blow after blow after blow.

For a moment he looked reproachful. The cheek of it. Then he lay there smashed to pieces – blank and stopped as a dead baby.

21

THE WEEKEND HAD thankfully passed. It did so rapidly – there had been plenty to do. He'd needed to mow the lawn; he couldn't have put it off any longer. Gulliver felt guilty. That morning Carys had risen early in order to surprise him – the smell of bacon filtering under the door. She was making him breakfast whilst he was lying in bed - thinking about Olivia – thinking about an amazing time when he'd taken her from behind – after they'd had breakfast themselves - at Gladstone's.

Like animals. Thought about it then and there, played it again. Her on all fours on the floor. Rewind. Played it again. The point when she surprised him. He'd not expected that. She'd begged for it. He needed her - then and there. It wasn't right. Manon and Brody still asleep in their beds. Carys thinking of them all.

Their relationship had lasted months – not years. But the intensity of every liaison – the quality time they had spent together, had changed him. Maybe one day he'd look back and feel embarrassed – he'd risked so much already. The possibility of being arrested for lewd behaviour a reality. How many times had they met in her car? He couldn't say. Like feral animals.

Most of the time they hadn't even participated in penetrative sex. Sex in the car meant something all-together different to Olivia. He'd never resented it. Olivia rarely spoke beforehand – she communicated with her eyes, not her hands. She communicated with her mouth – and her voice – the deliberate pace outwitting him almost always. She needed it first. He grew used to that. What he received in return was indescribable. It really was. Belted into place. Erotic. And challenging. How could any man give that up?

There were at least fifteen people coming to the house he had never heard of. Most of them colleagues of Carys, from work, with their own children. There were parents too – parents of children who played with Manon, in the same year. Fortunately he'd know someone other than their parents. He hoped Catherine hadn't changed her mind.

No sooner had they purchased something for Manon's party, did Carys remember something else they had forgotten. He had been assured at first that it would not be a big affair. It was Manon who informed him otherwise. Manon was one of six girls in her class – all of them had been invited – all of them had accepted. Wendy had called Saturday to thank them for their invitation.

On the bright side, Carys had said that everything was on track. Even the roller-skates Manon had pleaded for were in stock. She wasn't expecting the bicycle though. Gulliver had picked it out himself – checked all the safety features. He knew she'd burst into flames when she received the bike.

Monday was five days short from Saturday. Saturday preceded Sunday's much anticipated event. He truly hoped he would not be needed that afternoon – the day when he would meet up with Olivia. Their first meeting since they had separated last year. He hoped dearly that no disaster would befall.

He was yet to come up with an excuse for his absence from home. Catherine would be there at the party; he couldn't exactly claim he was on duty the previous day. Regardless, he would be there Saturday – come hell or high water. Wild horses wouldn't keep him away. His mind was filled with everything that was Olivia. Had he ever felt that way about Carys?

'I have Mr Litt in the interview room Sergeant.'

'Gulliver please.'

It was almost a quarter to ten. Gulliver arose from his chair where he had spent the last ten minutes in deep thought; he signalled with a wave of his right arm towards Catherine. Composed, they headed coolly downstairs; they very much hoped Mr Litt would provide them with some useful information. Catherine was about to enter the interview room when she paused momentarily. From the look on her face, whatever she needed to say or ask, had some urgency about it.

'Wendy forgot to ask Carys what Manon would like for her tenth birthday. We're not entirely sure what to buy her – we don't want to buy her something she has already got. If I forget, I'll be in trouble when I get home. I hope you don't mind me asking.'

For a moment Catherine's skin turned faintly pink. It was obvious from their recent conversations that, whilst she cherished her family unit and would defend it come what may, she was yet to arrive to that point in time when you stop worrying so much and learn to chill – go with the flow. He'd been much the same with Manon, his first. By the time Brody came along, he'd relaxed a fair bit – took fatherhood in his stride.

He wanted to say that by the time they had another child, she'd be more relaxed about it all. But he couldn't exactly say that. Was it normal to say such things to a same sex couple? And in such circumstances? They weren't exactly the child's biological parents. Mind, neither were couples who adopted. He wanted to say more but lacked the right words. Or even the confidence. Instead he smiled kindly before he spoke.

'Thank you. Unbelievably, I have only just realised that I have not bought Manon a bicycle helmet. How stupid of me! And she can't ride her new bike without one? A helmet would be great! Is that okay?'

'A helmet it is!'

Michael Litt possessed the stereotypical look of a guilty man. He was a bulky man with curled dark hair. His eyes were large and pooled with a culpability of some sort or another. On the top of the table, he held his left hand in his right. As Catherine and Gulliver entered the room, he shifted nervously in his plastic chair before he moved it nowhere forward – his large stomach pressing against the table's edge.

'Good morning Mr Litt. I am Detective Inspector Shakespeare and this is Detective Sergeant Pope.'

Michael Litt attempted to shift his chair forward again. Being the only observer, Gulliver seized the opportunity to glance in more detail at the interviewee's ears. It just couldn't be helped. They had both noticed them as soon as they had entered the room; being enormous and shaped like a butterfly's wing, they had both corrected their involuntary attention by refocusing on the speaker's eyes, just in case he had noticed either of them staring.

It took Gulliver at least a couple of minutes to figure out what was so unusual about the detainee's ears – it was most odd – it was as if they had been placed lower down on his face than everyone else's. Almost half-way down, he anticipated. And to add to that strange irregularity – the top of them curled naturally forward like a pig's ear. Obviously the cartilage was thicker; despite this, the ears themselves gave Mr Litt an overall caveman appearance.

'My father is dead. He passed away four years this summer. Heart attack. My mother died soon after – 67 - that's no age to die. He was a good man.'

'We are sorry to hear that Mr Litt.'

Silence. Mr Litt shifted uneasily in his chair. For a tall man, and a man of his size, it seemed tragic-like, the way he was physically positioned, sitting like a schoolboy at his desk – uncomfortable and with a look of sorrow unfit for a man of his age.

'I did not mention that my father had been a gravedigger at the time because I did not want his reputation tarnished – my father was a good man.'

'I am sure he was Mr Litt.'

'If he was ever mixed up in something – which I am sure he was not – I do not want his name all over the *Visitor* – blaming him – he's not here to defend himself. I said nothing, not because I know something, but because I do not. And I don't want my father getting the blame for something he did not do.'

'I'm sure you can –'

'I know nothing. I worked alongside him since I left school. He was a decent man – hard-working. He went to church every Sunday. I do not believe he is in any way mixed up in this body business.'

'Understandably Mr Litt, I am sure you can appreciate our need to follow any line of enquiry.'

There was a long pause. Michael Litt released the hand he held before he moved his chair back a little. Sitting straighter now, he placed both hands on his wide legs, palms down. His nails were unusually clean, although from the look of his hands, it was obvious to anyone that he was a manual labourer.

He unfolded his legs and stretched them ahead of him. More relaxed now, he appeared to have grown in stature within seconds. He yawned before his left hand lifted and scratched behind his left ear. Gulliver smiled. His story seemed genuine.

'Do you recall the name or names of any other men who worked with your father at any point in time?'

'Only Mr Lexton. Neil Lexton. They worked together for years.'

'Do you happen to know the whereabouts of Mr Lexton, Mr Litt?'

'Africa. I think it was Africa. About ten years or so since he moved abroad. We all went to the pub the night before he left. I wasn't in the know as to where he was going but my father told my mother that he was going there with a woman – hadn't even told his wife – was moving there for good.'

'I don't suppose, when going through your father's private papers, following his death, that you ever came across an address for or a postcard from Mr Lexton? We'd appreciate anything you can give us to clear this all up.'

'Never heard from him again – I'm sure. I can't speak for my father. He spoke of Mr Lexton as though he'd shifted abroad for good. After my father died, my mother couldn't face the paperwork. I've binned everything - didn't come across anything from Mr Lexton. I am sure of that.'

'Thank you Mr Litt – do not hesitate to contact us if you think of anything else – any detail whatsoever – it could be important. And as you said, if your father is in no way connected to this business, then it would be in your best interest to help us, then your father can be eliminated from our enquiries.'

Michael Litt remained seated until he was shown the door. When he elevated himself, he seemed shorter than at first thought. His wide torso gave him an impression of massiveness but in reality he could have only been about six foot two. He put out a large right hand to both officers before he thanked them and left. On the plastic seat, a damp patch remained behind where he had once sat.

'I'll speak to Charlotte and Liz – see if they can locate this Neil Lexton. His wife or children at least. Feels like we're chasing our own tails.'

Habitually, Gulliver removed his mobile to check for a text from Olivia. He smiled to himself when he saw she had sent him a message. Waiting for any communication was like waiting for the sun to rise. She could not wait until Saturday evening. Neither could he. He had rehearsed so many times how they'd spend their precious time together. He'd rehearsed and corrected. Began again. Slowed the whole sequence down.

For many, waiting was as much part of the fun but for Gulliver, it was torment.

22

MR LEXTON WAS a useless cunt. To the year, he has been dead ten. In the thirty-nine years they were married, she only received an anniversary card once. Like her sister's, it wasn't a loving marriage. But in comparison, it was a passive union. He did buy her a couple of birthday and Christmas cards. But he didn't believe in buying flowers, not anymore. *Flowers are for the dead*, he'd say.

Like her sister's too; their marriage was a childless one. In time, she healed – healed as best she could. Managed not healed. It took a lot of time. In and out of Greaves Hall. The asylum for outcasts. The asylum set aside from society. The corridors like long streets. The more hopeless you were, the further they hid you.

When they let you out, if they let you out, after you'd been a good girl, and promised to behave yourself, you accepted the stares and glares whilst society suspiciously watched your slow reintegration. The urge to howl was great. Irresistible. Those who howled were returned. Mrs Lexton was not the first leper to be released with a warning bell. The cured living on the fringe of society. Watched by everyone. Nobody let you forget. Greaves Hospital. Anyone could have driven past, confused it for a stately home. Surrounded by anthropomorphic asylum trees. The wind always rattling. The windows nailed down.

Her sister's troubles helped. She refocused – tried to comfort as best she could. When she was around. Babs had always been stubborn. Nothing she could say would convince her to leave her home. But it was more than stubbornness. *He'd find out,* she'd say. He'd make her pay. Fear. That was something she didn't truly know. Her sister knew fear. Despair is what the two had most in common.

Mrs Lexton qualified as a State Registered Nurse, in 1971, when she was twenty-one. Babs, who was a year older, had got her a job at the same local hospital. Ward 4: Christiana Hartley - named after the first female Mayor of Southport, her father the famous jam and marmalade maker. Their mother said John Lennon was born there in 1940. Eight years before she met their dad. She knew this because Christiana herself died that year, that Christmas in 1948.

She wasn't needed at home. Her husband was always out – supposedly digging a grave – *can't put a time on death. I'm like a doctor, on call all hours.* If only. If only she'd married a doctor. If only she'd waited. But turning the clock back meant no Billy. And despite all the pain, she would never wish him away.

Unlike most women they knew working in the eighties, they were able to work longer hours. Maybe intentionally they increasingly isolated themselves from everyone else who worked with them. They all had children – were part of a family. In the staff room, most women sat knitting - sharing patterns – in the days when nurses smoked whilst knitting, and eating their lunch. At least one of them was always pregnant.

They all knew each other – *your Eddie – our Martha*. If it was the birthday of one, they'd all attend, husbands and all. Christenings. *Think I'm having a girl this time.* Mrs Lexton and Mrs Tanner, as they were known then, were unintentionally rejected - left out in the cold. Childless. Barren. But in it together at least.

For a while, Mrs Lexton worked happily on the same children's ward for the terminally ill as her sister. Death didn't frighten her. Nor her sister. They'd contended with a lot worse. But after only a couple of years, she needed time off again. That's how it was. On and off. Off and on. And no shortage of nurses then. Depression clubbing her in the morning, even before she was fully awake.

Just before her thirties, she took an overdose. More than a handful of pills. Stolen from work. On the ward, little Regan passed away peacefully in the night. She put him out of his misery. Left a short note for her sister. She was going to join Billy – and their mother and father. *Please forgive me Babs. I love you.*

Pills would do the job. Plenty of pills. She'd head to their parents' grave. She almost looked forward to it. To the end of torment. To peace. Everlasting peace. The wreckage of her life coming to an end. She wasn't sure if she believed in God then. It was cold. A patch of sunlight warmed her before lights flashed and her breathing quickened. She thought she was going to be sick. No matter.

During the four days she spent in hospital, most nurses caring for her spoke kindly to her – out of pity of course. They whispered rather than talked. She was one of their own. Her mind was blank for hours at first. Surreal. A white light. A blue light. Everything went black again. Then the image of Regan asleep returned. At peace. Had anyone noticed?

She kept hearing at intervals someone moaning. Then her sister's voice. *Jo – it's okay – I'm here.* Someone was lifting her head. Maybe rearranging her pillow. She wasn't sure. Her eyes weighed heavily on her face, had sunk beneath her eyelids. Her throat was dry. No matter. The moaning returned. More voices. A disagreement but not a quarrel. She was being moved. Something told her she was being moved. Rattle. Rattle. A long white corridor. She tried to roll away from the light. Metal. Keys swinging against a metal frame. Clanking. Rattling. More flashing light. The sensation of levitating. Then the darkness returned.

Her husband convinced her doctor to sign the form that would magically pack her up ready for Greaves

Hospital: an asylum for the Mentally Insane. She heard him say that she wasn't the first woman to lose a baby. *I lost him too.* She needed help. He loved her of course. But he didn't know how to help her. Useless cunt.

Her sister told her on a visit, after she'd asked, that little Regan Hallworth, who was always going to die, passed away the same night she'd taken pills. A Post-mortem had found a needle prick under his arm – there was an on-going investigation. Nothing would come of it. Her sister Babs also told her, whilst sobbing, that she needed her. Jo promised. She'd try harder to live with the need of dying.

As the years passed, Mrs Lexton's crying slowed down. The smoking helped. The pipe smoking. And the drinking too. Her heart that was once as soft as sand, was now turning to stone. On Billy's birthday she continued to lay flowers on her parents' grave. She'd join them in good time – she was only five minutes up the road now. Living with Babs.

Her sister accompanied her from time to time. She still does now. At Christmas she lays flowers too. They lay flowers whenever they like. It still bothers Mrs Lexton that his body is God-knows-where. They took the dead babies away in those days. She never got to say goodbye. It was wrong that.

Neil Lexton was a useless cunt for many, many years. He was part of her landscape. She'd lost count how many times he'd played away. Never anything serious, or so it seemed. Despite everything, he never left. She'd come home and his stuff would still be there. If he wasn't with a woman, he was mixed up in something she didn't want to know about. Some faces that had called to the door over the years hadn't been friendly.

They didn't communicate. She preferred it that way. They rarely ate together – even on Sundays. He was usually at the pub. Pub or digging a grave. Or on a job. *You can't put a timing on death.* He never lifted a finger at home. His nails were always dirty - no matter how many times he scrubbed them. In those days, nobody asked for a divorce. She should have divorced him. Moved in with her sister sooner.

Then one day, out of the blue, he called around to the Tanners, after waiting for his wife in their own home for almost an hour, and told her that he was leaving. Leaving her. Had had enough. He was planning to leave that night. There was nothing she could say to stop him. Her sister, a widow now, was in the kitchen keeping out of the way. She'd put the kettle on before she checked on her sister.

Jo's anger rose. Like a bucket filling. Filling and reaching the point when the water spills away and over its side. What chance did she have of ever finding happiness now? She'd stayed with him despite the neglect, despite the lack of love, despite the deceit and lies. Why was she that surprised? She'd be better off without him.

She was fifty-nine. Married almost forty years. And he was leaving her. Not the other way around. It would of course be for another woman. Or he was on the run. No. It would be a woman. She knew him like the back of her hand, or so it seemed. *You've got some girl pregnant haven't you?*

Then he said it. She couldn't believe it. The shock of it hitting her like the back of a hand. *I've had the chop stupid. Had it many years ago.* Disbelief. *What did you say?* It made no sense. What had he said? *A vasectomy stupid. Whilst you were in the hospital.* Silence. She heard her sister retreat back into the kitchen. His mother had said it was for the best. His mother was dead now. Died of cancer in a home. He hardly visited her. She died before he got there. Of course.

Silence. Disbelief. Grief.

And then the useless cunt turned his back on her. She'd just finished ironing a pair of dark purple curtains for her sister. All those years wanting a baby – sleeping with him in the hope – no hope – there was never any hope. Mrs Lexton was speechless. The iron in her hand. Weightless now. He had nothing to feel guilty about. He'd stuck it out as long as he could. Stood by her through thick and thin. That was good of him.

Silence. Disbelief. Grief.

She'd blamed herself for years. If there was a God, he'd done it to punish her for killing Regan. Or there was something wrong with her – barren – one baby dead. Her clock no longer ticking. Stayed with the useless cunt out of guilt. In comparison to Trevor, he hadn't seemed that bad.

It was when he turned around again she let him have it. The look on his face. The smirk needed wiping. What a pathetic feeble wasted life she'd led? And here she was, childless, rejected, old – and he was leaving her – moving on. Grief. Anger. Let him have it. Wiped that smirk off his face. Put the iron flat on it and held it – pressed down hard on his face whilst he screamed and groaned. Her sister came running in as she smashed the corner of the electric iron into his skull. The cord came away from the round pin plug with ease. The useless cunt wasn't going anywhere.

23

'MR NEIL LEXTON, son of Eileen Hodge and Sydney Lexton. Both parents deceased. Born, schooled and lived his entire life in Southport. Supposedly left for Africa, in 2007, with a young embalmer by the name of Ashanti Akintola – unmarried – worked at Manchester Road's funeral directors: Massey & Sons.

She gave her notice a month beforehand, Planned. She'd said she was visiting family. According to Mr Massey, the owner, everyone knew they had been carrying on for at least a couple of years.'

'Great Charlotte, do we have a forwarding address for Mr Lexton?'

'I'm afraid not.'

'We need confirmation from the flight records that they both ascended that flight. They may even have an address on record. Charlotte, try to locate her address as well.'

'Miss Akintola's – already onto it – but I've had no luck with the flight record. Sorry Sarge. Too far back.'

'Gulliver please.'

'I do have some good news though.'

'You've got that look Charlotte – I know that look when I see it!' interrupted Catherine.

'His previous address in the UK - 79 Cider Drive. Previous address to Mr and Mrs Lexton. After Mr Lexton left, Mrs Lexton moved out, sold the property and moved into an address already known to ourselves.'

'The suspense is killing us – should we know that name?'

'No. But you recently met her sister.'

The suspense brought about by Charlotte's dramatic delivery placed them all on tenterhooks. Charlotte pushed back her spectacles before she spoke.

'Mrs Lexton moved into 127 North Lane – with her sister – Mrs Barbara Tanner.'

For a moment both Catherine and Gulliver looked at each other open-mouthed.

'Never!'

'No way!'

'Yes way.'

Charlotte's face was beaming. Having completed her mission, she removed her spectacles before heading back to her desk. She walked like a woman satisfied. If there was a needle in the haystack to be found,

Charlotte Cunliffe was the woman to find it. And found it, she had.

'Would you like me to arrange a time for a revisit?'

'No thank you Charlotte. I think Gulliver and I will call on the two sisters unannounced.'

'I think that's a very good idea – first thing tomorrow?'

'First thing.'

***

Gulliver was alerted to a text just as he pulled up, with some difficulty, onto his drive – Carys had parked at an odd angle. He had to reverse and park ever so close to the outer brick wall – the non-existent passenger trapped overnight.

'Aching to be alone with you x.'

That was it. That was all Olivia had said – in many ways he wished he had received the text earlier – had a chance to pull over – think aloud. He reread the text several times. Pictured her aching. Guiltily he looked towards the front lounge window before he returned to his mobile.

He wanted to say many things – he wanted to show her then and there that he too was aching for her too. He typed something before he erased it. Instead, he'd show her when he next saw her. Saturday was within their grasp. He paused then as if lost in time. He deliberately pictured her half-undressed – her blouse unbuttoned - black lace on olive skin – he pictured her topless then – he'd never seen nipples that dark before – erect and dark. He was hard now.

'Dad!'

Manon stood at the open door. It took a moment to fully register who had spoken. Her voice muffled. His mind returned to what mattered most. Where was Carys? For a moment he hesitated – he'd text later. He'd never seen Manon open the front door before – not alone. She looked small and vulnerable in all the dark space that surrounded her – the bright yellow light of the kitchen in the distance. He looked behind her as he exited the car. No Carys.

'Where's Brody? Where's your mother?'

'I was waving at you from the window. I was waving at you for ages dad! You didn't see me waving! Dad! I was waving my sword – Brody was too but he got tired of waiting. Dad, mum's ordered a bouncy castle for Sunday!'

'She has! That's great! Where's your mum?'

'She's ordered one that looks like a pirate ship! She showed me on her computer!'

'Wow Manon – so not a bright pink one this year!'

Manon shrugged before she pulled away from her father's embrace.

'Look!'

From her back pocket she produced a black eye-patch. She was demonstrating how it should be worn whilst Gulliver headed towards the front-lounge. Brody ran towards him brandishing a toy sword. Gulliver habitually kissed him, enforced a smile – put him down. He ignored any further questions. He called after Carys. No response.

When he entered their bedroom Carys blushed. Semi-naked, she was taking off a dress before their wardrobe mirror. She took off her party stilettos – not her usual stilettos – these were black. Gulliver smiled before he kissed her. She looked radiant in pale blue.

'The door was closed. You didn't hear me call.'

Carys folded her dress before she dismounted from her newly purchased shoes. Alongside with the blue dress, she put them away in two separate boxes before placing both items at the bottom of the wardrobe.

'Manon opened the door.'

'She didn't!

She wouldn't have opened it if she hadn't known it was you.'

'Yes, of course. Overcautious, I know.'

'Not a bad thing.'

'Something for Sunday?'

'Possibly. I'm not sure it's the right outfit for then. Maybe for another day. We'll see. Sorry, I didn't mean to worry you. How was your day?'

'Thrilling as always – death – sordid affairs – the usual.'

He'd said it and felt guilty as soon as the words had escaped. So judgemental. Matter of fact. Even Carys looked surprised by his outburst. For a moment she stared after him. Then she was gone.

24

DECEPTION HAD BEEN at the very root of most of Mrs Lexton's and Mrs Tanner's insurmountable problems. For better or for worse was one example. In sickness and in health was another. A third example was Greaves Hospital – the place where Mrs Lexton was sectioned after her husband insisted she be detained until she be cured. You only needed the one doctor's signature in those days.

Greaves Hospital was a beautiful country house; it had been expediently chosen by the powers that be, the powers that knew best. It was set conveniently aside from Southport's caring community – on the outskirts - an excellent example of a Tudorbethan mansion. Why to look at it, anyone in their right mind would be sold on the spot: the vision and mission presented on a plaque to the left of the door - IGNIS REGENERAMUR. *From the fire, we are re-born.*

Mr Lexton himself took his wife to the asylum as soon as she was discharged. Mrs Tanner was with them too. She'd heard stories about Greaves Hospital. Dark stories. Incredulous stories; she hoped none of them were true. She was glad she was sitting in the back – it was hard holding back the tears. She almost envied her sister to some extent. At the time, nursing a broken rib, anywhere seemed better than home sweet home.

The seaside drive did much to alleviate both Mrs Tanner's and Mrs Lexton's reservations; Mrs Lexton wound her window down, the fresh air fighting the car's progress. Waves drew back like hands. One after another. Go back. Go back. Stones and broken shell clanked like money. They smiled. Maybe it was for the best.

Mrs Lexton hadn't spoken since entering the car. She'd nodded from time to time. It was the medication. Her sister had suggested that the stay in hospital would give her some much-needed rest – provide the help she needed. The expertise. They'd passed the road to home a while back. At The Plough roundabout. Mr Lexton had said it was best they didn't call in. He'd packed everything she needed. He hadn't. Her sister added a few essential items. Billy's Snoopy too. She'd want that.

As they entered the high gates, they were acquainted with a series of sculptured lawns with many ornamental trees and flowering shrubs. The impressive and charming building was then suddenly ahead of them – looming. The entrance was dated 1900. It was bright outside – cloudless. No sooner had they parked, than a nurse appeared in the doorway. She was smiling like nuns do.

'Just Mrs Lexton please.'

It was odd how Mr Lexton passed the bag to Mrs Tanner rather than to his wife; he was probably distancing himself from the whole predicament – an *I didn't put her in here* moment. For a singular moment, he looked as if he were about to kiss her on the cheek before he thought better of it. Her sister hugged her. Mrs Lexton's eyes were like black tunnels. No smile. She looked dead before she'd even entered. Her mind as frangible as an egg.

Some memories are hard to remember – it's the passing of time – and the ageing process. Some memories are never forgotten. Greaves Hospital was one of those memories. A memory as sharp as a glass splinter in your finger. Something that leaves a bad taste in your mouth for a long time. It seemed to rain every day hereafter. It didn't even sound like rain from the inside – from where they lolled day in and day out – it was more like the sound of a tap running.

Dr Pancreas had showed her around. It wasn't his real name. Sour Tits called him that to the patients. Because of his skin. All scaly and bumpy and yellow. He told her where she could go. And where she could not. He wasn't that bad. At least he smiled. He told her without smiling that in time she'd meet Dr Lowe. A martinet: he'd insist on an absolute adherence to the rules.

There was an odd smell about the whole place as well. From the moment you entered everything changed. Everything was a shade darker. Colder.

Deader. She looked back – saw nothing over her shoulders. Her sister gone. Her husband gone. Free of her. Heading home alone. Her sister heading home to her bastard of a husband. She was tired. Her head ached like she had a hangover.

The sun was on the outside now – especially summoned to fool her. Deceive her. It couldn't penetrate the thick brick walls. She was on the inside. Mrs Lexton was instantly struck by everything she saw. Something didn't add up. Maybe it was the staff. They didn't look like nurses – more like caretakers. At first it looked like a hospital – but something told her it just wasn't. Nobody smiled.

It wasn't the faint odour of urine that lingered everywhere – inescapable – it was something else. Something familiar. Couldn't put her finger on it at the time. None of the windows opened. Many of the doors didn't either. Under lock and key. *For your own safety*, said Dr Pancreas – *God forbid if there was to be a fire*. Everything wooden. Solid. On the inside.

There were so many rooms – fifty-five in total she'd been told - *some never to be forgotten*. There was a basement and a cellar too. There was something rubbery about everyone there – not the staff though – they were like walls. The walls said nothing. Nothing penetrated them. Nobody knew what happened on the other side of a wall. Everyone had legs like jelly. No rubber. Tiny fish nibbling at the inside of your stomach. Mrs Lexton held her breath. So many closed windows. Panic attack. Hard to breathe. Windows that didn't open. Asylum trees on the outside.

Patients whispered to one another when Sour Tits wasn't looking. Sour Puss was far worse. She told on you, like they did in school. She was the one who wheeled the trolleys that ended up in the shock-treatment room. The lucky ones, the really difficult ones, had been transferred to Ashworth Hospital. That's what Philomena told Mrs Lexton. Don't get on the wrong side of anyone. Tiny fish nibbling at the inside of your stomach. Legs like jelly. No fresh air.

There was a nurse called Arthur that everyone liked. Even Mrs Mop, who never spoke, would wave at him when he finished his shift. Smiles. He'd eventually leave them. Everyone that could remotely help them eventually left.. Sour Tits and Sour Puss weren't going anywhere. Tiny fish nibbling at the inside of her stomach. There were so many patients – men and women – mostly women – some of them didn't look like women. You weren't allowed into the men's rooms. The basement had a cellar.

At the time, in the eighties, there were as many there with learning disabilities as there were patients with mental health. Everyone looked much the same. Tractable. Flexible. Flowers that hadn't been watered. Rubbery people with legs like jelly. Nobody's hips moved from side to side. No-one danced. There was one way of telling the difference though. The mental shifted quickly when told. The disabled were dragged

– or pushed – or both. The disabled were washed less often too. No-one fed them if they didn't do it themselves. Nurse Arthur said we were lucky. They kept kiddies too before the war.

The best staff were the trainees: they were polite, smiled. None of them stayed. When they had done their stint, they almost always said they'd visit but they never did. Their smile said they wouldn't visit. Their hands wrung guilt-ridden. Washed their hands. Who could blame them?

A young woman with Down's was once tied to a chair in front of them. Lucy. She'd bitten Sour Tits when she medicated her. You couldn't say no to the medicine. It was for your own good. Everyone sedated – lolloping – wilting flowers - everyone trapped in a labyrinth with the minotaur running the show. Doctor Lowe. Everyone obeyed Dr Lowe. He had a peremptory call that no-one could afford to ignore. From the staff's response, it was obvious that he was a man that expected to be obeyed on the spot – and without asking questions. His office was in the basement – in the opposite direction from the cellar. Tiny fish nibbling at the inside of your stomach.

Mad. If you were mad, you went to Greaves. Bad. If you were bad, you were sent to Ashworth. If you were both, you went to the basement. When you returned from the basement – you were usually just mad. If you were still bad – after three visits – and a new insulin trial that had failed – you went to Ashworth.

The clinically depressed were all mad. The lonely and dysfunctional were mad too – insane. The Down's were insane. The epileptic – the old – the weak – the disabled – the broken – the one's in need of love – and help – all mad – insane. It was just the right place to drive you mad. When someone said they'd been abused in the cellar – they were mad too. Mad bitch. The staff never changed. The patients didn't improve. The mental could end up disabled. The disabled could be mental too. Open your mouth. There's a good girl.

'When can I go home?'

Mrs Tanner visited her sister every week for three months. She'd been one of the lucky ones. She'd been a nurse. Even Sour Puss felt sorry for her. No more nursing. Couldn't nurse a baby either. Nursing over. No room for lunatics in hospitals for the sane. It was important to be a good girl. The medication was great; it stopped you asking too many questions.

Only the once was she given shock treatment. Electro Convulsive Treatment. Or ECT. She still didn't know if any of her chemistry had been altered after it. The basement. No windows. Wide corridors that led to a wide room painted grey. In the cellar. She walked there. She was taken there. Intimidated into it. She didn't like the way Dr Lowe smiled at her - before he gave her an anaesthetic. After she lay on the bed.

Dr Lowe said something. He'd strapped her in. She'd feel much better. Then he rolled a trolley on wheels towards him and sat on a chair that was taller than the bed. There was grease on her temples. She could smell Dr Lowe's breath. Chewing gum. She tried to smile. His face stiff like papyrus. His dilated pupils black. She bit on a wire whilst a metal plate pressed down on her forehead. Cold plates on the side of her head. Eyes shut. Blue light.

Her hair and flesh felt like it was tingling – like it was on fire. Her body seizing forever. One big jolt followed by another. Her bones shattering under a bright blue light. The smell of grease and mint. When she woke up, Dr Lowe told her she'd been a good girl. She didn't know who she was. She couldn't remember her name for two days. But she remembered whom he was. He never treated her again.

Mr Lexton never visited. He was busy recuperating himself. Dr Ford who signed the papers to section Mrs Lexton, also consented to him having a vasectomy. When he told Mrs Rogers at number 117 what he'd been through – his wife in an asylum – she almost broke down in tears. Mrs Rogers drafted in any willing neighbours in one fell swoop. *He's recently been in hospital himself. Won't say what for. Seems he is in some pain. Poor man. He's utterly broken. His wife in an asylum. Greaves Hospital.*

Mrs Dalby brought him fish pie on Mondays but Mr Lexton doesn't like fish; he scooped mouthfuls of the delicious cheddary-mash into his mouth before binning the rest. Mrs Eccleston brought shepherd's pie on Tuesdays; Mr Lexton loves lamb, as does Mr

Eccleston. Mrs Dhaker brought a chicken curry on a Wednesday; Mr Lexton never lets Mrs Dhaker in. Mr Doyle and Mr Smith dropped off a vegetable bolognaise; they dropped out after one week – fuming that their dish had been returned chipped – and no apology.

Mrs Stone brought lasagne on Fridays; Mr Lexton doesn't let her in either: she is always accompanied by Mr Stone. Mrs Murray brought steak pie on Saturdays; her husband died last year so Mr Lexton has invited her in to join him on the odd occasion. Mrs Rogers usually brings a roast on Sundays. Mr Rogers says he is going to the pub after he has eaten but Mrs Rogers knows he is going to see his mistress. He has been doing this for three years. Mrs Rogers brought desert too one Sunday evening. She didn't leave until eleven Mrs Murray said.

***

Once discharged, Mrs Tanner took Mrs Lexton fortnightly to a scheduled appointment that couldn't be missed. If she said anything – asked after Lucy, or Philomena, or Mrs Mop – whose real name she does not know – got their backs up in any way – she knew, they'd have her back in. Their eyes warned her. Dr Lowe held the pen that made the notes. She'd seen him twice since she first met him – small icy-cold hands. Black eyes. She remembered to smile. She nodded – agreed. Her sister smelt of alcohol once. They saw it.

Every time she left she felt guilty – had left them behind to it. She tried not to look at the windows – their rubbery faces on the other side. Most didn't have anyone like she did. To fight her corner. Perhaps she'd go back. There was something there too that she liked. Being amongst others like her. The living dead.

Her next appointment was thankfully cancelled. The snow had blocked many roads. Her sister Babs couldn't walk properly, a broken toe; she smelt of alcohol again – the bastard on her back. The local newspaper informed them that a great fire had started in a basement of Greaves Hospital – there was to be an investigation.

The asylum had looked beautiful on that day. Frozen like a wedding cake, the sky bellied with the promise of more snow. The asylum trees appeared frozen on the spot; they glistened in the moonlight. The many layers of snow looked deceptively clean. How quickly footprints could disappear – snowfall erasing traces of the past that the mind never could. A level state of topography fit for a Christmas card. *Season's Greetings.* An arrangement of natural features at their best. An ardent fire licking its way through all the corridors. Some of the patients danced on the spot.

A third of the patients died in the fire. Where were the keys? Dr Lowe's body was found in the cellar. In the cul-de-sac of a shadow. In the furthest room. Afterwards, a fire officer reported to the *Visitor* that he looked like Frankenstein's monster, on the bed, still strapped in. Someone had given him Electroconvulsive Treatment. Repeatedly.

Among the dead where five more staff. Sour Tits. Sour Puss. Dr Pancreas. Shirley Wesley and John Manton – two trainee nurses. Arthur, the kindly nurse, had been unable to reach the hospital. His vehicle had failed to start.

The beautiful mansion was too far out for anyone in the community to help. Especially because of the snow. And the road blocked. Took the two fire-engines forever to arrive. It was difficult manoeuvring a twelve tonne vehicle at the best of times. No-one saw anything. No-one heard. Too far out. Too many residents didn't even know of its existence – until the *Southport Visitor* printed story after story.

When the fire engines eventually made it, from the other side of town, the roads treacherous with ice, the building was ablaze. Bonfire night at its best. The wind picked up in time and the startling fire showcased the attractive grounds for few to ever see nor remember. Fire fighters climbed the back walls were most patients sedately slept on. They smashed many windows. Couldn't lift the sashes. They'd been nailed down. Dr Lowe's orders. The fire burned from the basement up.

There was screaming. There was praying. There was singing.

25

THURSDAY MORNING BEGAN badly. Brody had urinated in the middle of the night, as usual in several places on the landing. No-one had heard him. Carys looked shattered. She seemed more tired these days; the new job, she said – understandable. Gulliver blamed himself: he'd forgotten to turn Brody's side-light on, after he'd kissed him good-night.

There Brody lay, in a comfortable heap outside his bedroom door, thumb in mouth, fast asleep, warm like toast. Butter wouldn't melt. His unruly scalp of strawberry blonde hair needed cutting for the party. Gulliver managed to bathe him and clean the carpet before he set off to work. Carys was fast asleep, that was until the bath was poured – air trapped in the pipes resonating – the sound like the arrival of a battleship. He needed to bleed the pipes.

***

Neither Mrs Tanner nor Mrs Lexton appeared to be in that morning; they'd called early enough. Maybe they were still in bed – curtains open though. Both Catherine and Gulliver had looked forward to hearing what they both had to say – watch their response. The likelihood that Mr Lexton had buried Mr Tanner seemed incredulous now – comical even. Could Mr Lexton have even killed him himself? How did the two men get on? Did either of the women know anything? It was unlikely that there would be any DNA to tie either of the women to the scene. Regardless, a sample needed to be taken – just in case – to rule them out - if they were innocent.

Card posted through the letterbox, they headed back to the station. If neither of the women called within twenty-four hours, they would revisit. Catherine had had a strong inclination that they were indoors – no evidence – almost too quiet – just a hunch – and if in, what or whom where they hiding from? Next time, they would wait until they showed – possibly climb the back gate too. She always had a good reason to climb a gate uninvited – a cat stuck up a tree was one – the sound of a scream was another. They couldn't stay in there forever.

***

When Gulliver was eleven he locked himself in his bedroom for almost twenty-four hours. He was both stubborn and curious, like his mother. Had become a vegetarian. His father was furious. *HE'LL EAT WHAT HE'S GIVEN OR NOT EAT AT ALL!*

There'd been a visitor that year – an assembly that haunted him for weeks. The film showed how caged hens were kept – a few children cried. It exposed the shocking, cramped and filthy conditions chickens lived in on farms, in cages, that then provided every supermarket in the UK with eggs. When a hen was shown dead on the soiled floor of a cage, there were gasps of horror.

Worse was the snippet filmed on a pig farm in Italy – they were all in the dark – to keep them calm – the conditions deplorable - hemmed in so they couldn't turn around, bite anyone. Like the chickens, pigs had taken to fighting with one another.

He thought at first he might become a Muslim or a Jew – he was sure they didn't eat pork – but then he decided he didn't want to eat meat at all. Nor eat eggs. He was going to become a vegetarian. He'd forgotten how much he loved fish and chips.

He was still a vegetarian come the following Saturday but by Sunday morning, when his mother cooked best streaky bacon for breakfast, he salivated and gave in. By twelve-thirty, when roast lamb was served for dinner, he'd decided to settle on not eating meat unless he really wanted to. His mother said she'd only buy free-range eggs from then on. He smiled and tucked into his dinner. Best gravy too. *NEXT YOU'LL BE TURNING QUEER LIKE THE CHAP UP THE ROAD!*

They don't turn queer dad. They've always been queer.

LESS OF THE CHEEK!

Women can be queer too.

His father looked incredulously at him. He folded his newspaper and left the room, but not before he looked long and hard at his wife – where was he picking up all this garbage from?

***

'And Luke has finally traced the whereabouts of Mr Lexton's mistress: Ashanti Akintola. Not so hard to trace. Returned to England only eleven months ago.'

'And Mr Lexton?'

'Nothing as of yet. Should I contact her and arrange for you to call around?'

'Not yet. If I call – I may do so without warning. We don't want anyone getting away do we? Thank you Charlotte. Great job – thank Luke for me. What would we do without you both?'

Charlotte returned Catherine's warm smile. At last it seemed they were getting somewhere – the pieces of the puzzle coming nicely together. From what Charlotte had discovered so far, neither Miss Akintola nor Mr Lexton were on the voting register. Neither were registered as either working or claiming benefits. What where they doing back in England? Why return now? Was it all one hell of a coincidence?

'Do you think Mr Lexton has made contact with his wife since his return? We assume he's returned as well? How did Charlotte find his mistress?'

'Facebook I think – I'll ask her. I'd like to listen to the call made by our anonymous caller. It was brief I know but maybe this caller has a distinctive dialect or accent?'

'You think it was her? His mistress? – Doesn't make sense – why would she implicate him? Why now?'

'I don't know. Let's listen to the call before we call in on her. I'll get the address from Charlotte whilst you trace that call.'

As Catherine walked away from his desk, Gulliver felt a pang of guilt – mistress sounded like a dirty word – society judged and rarely understood the reasons why men and women, since the beginning of time, became involved with another whilst already committed. There was more to it than sex. It was possible to love two children as a parent – why was it so hard to believe that a person could love more than just a partner. He loved Olivia. He was sure of it. He hadn't known her long though. He couldn't wait to be with her. He didn't set out to upset Carys. He loved her too.

He longed for Olivia.

Saturday was just two nights away.

26

MRS TANNER AND Mrs Lexton sit rigidly in their kitchen chairs. Since their last call, the call that said it all, when the officers came to tell Mrs Tanner about having found her dead husband's body, they've decided to keep the door between the kitchen and the hallway closed, so no-one knows whether they are in or not. The hammer is long gone; it is a huge relief to them both. If only they could rid themselves of the body. Mr Lexton is as much use dead as he was alive.

Knocking. There is knocking at the door before they hear their names hollered though the letterbox. There seems to be two of them. From the sound of their voices, it is the same two detectives that called last week. Mrs Lexton leans over before she whispers in her sister's ear.

'IT'S THEM AGAIN MRS TANNER! CAGNEY AND BLOODY LACEY!'

'CAG AND WHAT MRS LEXTON?'

'CAGNEY AND LACEY MRS TANNER!'

Mrs Tanner nods in her sister's direction before she affords herself a smile. They sit quietly drinking their tea laced with gin. The alcohol helps calm the nerves. Like naughty schoolgirls, they exchange a wink and a nod of the head before the uncross their legs below their dark skirts only to end up crossing them again. Mrs Tanner lifts her red pinafore to wipe some unexpected excess saliva just as Mrs Lexton considers copying her in turn.

'CHARLIE'S BLOODY ANGELS MRS LEXTON!'

'COLUMBO MRS TANNER. I'M PARTIAL TO A BIT OF COLUMBO MYSELF!'

Like children they afford themselves a half-smile before some unforeseen terror sets in. More knocking. More calling. Mrs Lexton holds back nervous laughter whilst Mrs Tanner looks about like an alert cat checking its surroundings. Their back kitchen door is ajar. They hope they will not call around the back.

'WHAT DO THEY WANT I WONDER MRS TANNER?'

'NO IDEA MRS LEXTON! WE KNOW NOTHING MRS LEXTON - NOTHING!'

'WE KNOW NOTHING MRS TANNER - NOTHING!'

The tension in their untidy plain kitchen is electric. No light. They have been moving like the walking dead for hours. Just shadows. Shadows loom from almost every corner, envelop them and keep them safe. How strange they behave, the shadows. Sometimes they walk like obedient children, behind them. Other times they surprise them, to the side, like a car waiting to take over. On occasion they dare to walk ahead of them. It's the passing of time that does this. Light and dark conspiring against them.

It is now raining outdoors. The officers may give up and leave. Nobody likes the rain. The winter draught coming through the kitchen door chills them to the bone. Only their feet are truly warm – boots – nothing as cosy as boots. Mrs Tanner looks to Mrs Lexton before she shows her an empty mug. Mrs Lexton in turn shows her that she has almost finished. Mrs Tanner winks before she stands and takes both mugs to fill with gin. Mrs Tanner has noticed her sister is suffering with her nerves again. Little wonder.

Unbeknown to them, Inspector Shakespeare and Sergeant Pope left five minutes ago. The rain sending them on their way. Off to the car – the warm metallic shelter more appealing. A rectangular card was fed through their letterbox. *If they could telephone them directly, it would be much appreciated.* There is also a phone number. And the lead Inspector's name, printed in a serious font.

Twenty minutes pass and the sisters feel tired with anxiety and gin. What began as spitters of wind-driven rain is now falling more heavily. Having closed the back door now, they both agree they are in need of a decent nap. Mrs Tanner grabs her briar pipe and tobacco before she releases herself out of her chair. Mrs Lexton needs some help in order to stand; she is already half asleep. They never used to drink so heavily during the day – but a change is as good as a rest. Mrs

Tanner picks up Mrs Lexton's Nording Hunter and looks at it for a moment. It really is of superior craftsmanship; maybe she will ask her sister for a go – they could swap and see.

Yawning now, the two of them creep upstairs not having noticed the blue business card trapped in the letterbox mouth. Up – up - to bed.

'I CAN'T BELIEVE HOW TIRED I AM, MRS TANNER!'

'NOR I MRS LEXTON – NOR I! I'M EXHAUSTED!'

'SWEET DREAMS MRS TANNER!'

'SWEET DREAMS MRS LEXTON – DON'T YOU GO SMOKING THAT PIPE IN YOUR BED NOW!

'I LIKED HART TO HART BEST MRS TANNER!'

Mrs Tanner has paused on the stairs to think. 'REALLY? I NEVER KNEW THAT! I LIKED THE ONE – UH – THE ONE I LIKED WAS THE ONE WITH THE MOUSTACHE – YOU KNOW – THE ONE WITH A LOLLY IN HIS MOUTH!'

'REALLY? KOJAK? THE BALD ONE! REALLY MRS TANNER?'

'NO MRS LEXTON! NOT HIM!'

'WHO THEN?'

'MAGNUM P.I. MRS LEXTON!'

'P.I.?'

'PERSONAL INVESTIGATOR MRS LEXTON! STOP SHOUTING DOWN MY EAR! KEEP YOUR VOICE DOWN PLEASE MRS LEXTON!'

'MRS TANNER, I NEED THE TOILET – I HAVEN'T HAD A WEE IN HOURS!'

Mrs Tanner is trying very hard not to laugh: she too needs the toilet now that her sister has pointed it out. They begin an impromptu dance before they do a jiggle, still holding onto each other, and their pipes, and a bag of tobacco that is threatening to spill all over their dark upstairs landing.

Within five minutes of having laid on their beds, both Mrs Tanner and Mrs Lexton are fast asleep. Mrs Tanner sleeps in the back bedroom – the largest of the three. She has taken her boots off and laid flat on her back in the middle of her wooden double bed. She is still fully dressed. The pipe remains unlit on the bedcover.

This was the bed she shared with Mr Tanner – she always meant to get rid of it but it was her parents' bed, and over the years, it has become their bed once again. The bed that both her sister and herself climbed into when they were small enough to still sleep with them – the bed where everything felt safe and loved – a haven by all accounts. It's one of those beds you see in antique shops – the head and foot are almost as tall as each other – the frame is solid and made of iron, like the springs. Mrs Tanner is so exhausted that she dreams of nothing.

Mrs Lexton is also lying fully dressed on her bed, but as usual, she lies on her stomach – in the recovery position. She is still suited and booted. Her pipe lies unlit, loose like a dummy in her mouth. When she moved in with Mrs Tanner she brought her three-quarter bed with her. It was her childhood bed.

Mrs Tanner and Mrs Lexton went from sleeping with their parents to sleeping with one another – in this very same bed – two peas in a pod. Then they went from sleeping together, to sleeping with a wife-battering milkman and a two-timing gravedigger. How ignorant they were then. How ridiculously naive and impressionable. Considering they weren't soft either. If only they could turn back time. If only they could make a small change here and a small change there. How different life could have been? If only.

27

CATHERINE SHAKESPEARE HAD stood thoughtfully before the incident board for almost ten minutes - the photographs and profiles of the two sisters ahead of her; she then rotated herself left before aiming her pointing finger directly at Mr Lexton's long-term mistress: Miss Ashanti Akintola.

'Are you certain she is our anonymous caller?'

'The sooner we visit, the sooner we'll know for sure.'

'Then maybe we should leave the sisters until last. Get a fuller picture. After all, we could be waiting all day for them to open the door – this way – hopefully - we'll have made some headway today. I don't want this dragging out over the weekend. We need that DNA sample. We'll review the facts and possibilities then - move forward Monday.'

'Agreed. Anyway, I need to be at home this weekend. Carys has got more than a few jobs lined up for me. It's only a kids' party, I know, but it feels like it's getting a little out of hand. We've bought an equal amount of food for the parents! Alcohol too!'

'Good! I don't like parties much. The alcohol will help me socialise with a smile on my face. Zita hasn't stopped talking about Manon's party. I had to take her for new shoes yesterday – apparently her current party shoes are not sparkly enough!'

'I take it you don't do sparkle.'

'Gulliver, do I look like I do sparkle?'

Catherine smiled before she headed for her office to grab her coat. Dutifully, Gulliver followed. Ready for the off, their bodies moved in unison towards the exit. Outside, it was beginning to rain. Drops of water that were more like slashes – a bleak winter's morning after all.

Gulliver, in the driving seat now, punched the postcode into the *Sat Nav*. Broome Road. Eleven minutes away. No diversions. Off Cemetery Road, into Birkdale village. He'd not long lived in Southport. It wasn't a large town - he already knew many of the main roads. But Broome Road, and the area surrounding it, was still unfamiliar to him.

Number 117 was situated on the far left of the road's lengthy cul-de-sac; recently, they seemed to be going from one dead-end road to another. The field ahead belonged to the secondary school of Christ the King. Catherine had been here before – a case she would never forget – she was a constable at the time. Afterwards, she thought about it for years. As did everyone else in Southport.

A young mother had disappeared overnight – not unusual, the police supposed. Not the first time either. She'd finished her shift as a croupier, headed straight home in a taxi and wasn't seen since. Then one night turned into more nights. Her family frantic – the parents of the missing mother overly concerned. Her husband said she'd left him. They'd rowed earlier in the day. They'd rowed again that night. It was true they were always rowing. She'd abandoned them all just before Christmas. *She'd never do that.*

Her parents said nothing when the *BBC* and *Granada Reports* aired the appeal; her shaken husband begging his dead wife to return home. He loved her. *Please come home.* There was something to be said about the way her parents looked at him – especially the father. He looked like he was going to launch himself at him. His red face contrasting against the husband's pale complexion. It was so pale, he looked almost green.

The young mother's husband and his brother, local butchers to the Birkdale community, had chopped her up in the bath and buried her all over Southport. In bin bags. First sign was when they found an arm in a black bin bag, by the railway line. Everyone about the village thought there'd been a suicide – a jumper on the track. But it wasn't.

They never found all of her. A family broken in so many ways. A dead girl smashed to pieces. On Stamford Road – parallel to Broome. They'd dug the school field opposite. Nothing to be found. The father had stood there watching with both kiddies at either side of him, in the knowledge they'd never find her. Horrible business. Before her time as a proper detective. Thank God. To this day, her head and hands have never been located.

'Do you have the recording with you?'

Gulliver nodded as his personal mobile rang. For a moment his face looked agitated.

'Sorry. I need to take this. I won't be long.'

Catherine thought it a little odd how Gulliver exited the car and stepped a safe distance away. On the odd occasion he seemed to turn around as if he were checking she had not wound the window down or exited the car without him having heard. Strange. When he returned to the car he seemed flushed although smiling.

For a short period of time both Catherine and Gulliver said nothing. Gulliver turned the ignition – they were on their way. Moments later Catherine had abandoned the thought of asking him if he was alright. She wasn't sure why she had dismissed that there had been a row between Carys and himself.

She texted Wendy to check if Harry had been reminded about the party; she did so whilst Gulliver thought long and hard about Olivia. She'd called to check he could still meet her the following evening. She just wanted to hear his voice. Wendy had texted straight back. Harry was yet to reply. In the last two years, since the death of most of his family, he rarely attended social events – pity intermixed with an uncontrollable dread to lose his temper at the root of most problems. His wife Laura was his rock. Catherine texted her instead.

Try and hold me back. I'll be there. I'll be there as soon as I can. I can't wait to see you. I, I have to go. Olivia had said nothing in return – she didn't need to. Tension between them had reached a point where there would be no return. Time had cheated them both; it deliberately dragged its heels – thick like condensed milk. A familiar nightmare. But if time could only be stalled, it could most definitely not be stopped. The delay was temporary. In just over twenty-four hours he would have her in his arms. He would have her, come what may.

***

The slim terraced house seemed somewhat different to any of the others on either side of the short road. The cement gateposts had been painted a deep green before a series of hand-painted roses, of different colours, ascended from half-way. The gate itself was a crimson colour; there was nothing garish about it – just different – if anything, it seemed to welcome them – suggest this was a home worth visiting.

Equally, a large variety of ceramic and metallic pots and containers, below the bay window, caught their attention. A few were decorated with fancy butterfly patterns – pottery bells immersed in the dark soil. The grass was certainly greener on this side of the fence: in comparison, next door's flagged front seemed bleak and clinical, despite its minimalist and tidy demeanour. A quaint sign hanging above the doorbell advised that one should LIVE THE LIFE YOU LOVE. For a moment Gulliver thought about its meaning; a feeling of resentment caught him unawares. Guilt-ridden he busied himself by looking about. There were many parked cars riding the pavements. The people who lived in this neighbourhood were neither wealthy nor poor – probably just getting by.

It was also obvious from the outside, that the inside of the house was as colourful as the garden itself – the walls a radiant orange – green and crimson curtains, at either side of the wide bay window, throttled mid-way up by curtain tassels, the colour of gold. Before they'd even taken the knocker into their hand, two young girls, twins it seemed, appeared from nowhere – they peered on their knees from the convenient seat that took up the bay – smiles as wide as watermelons – their decorated braids jiggled as they giggled.

The first child made a face. Laughter. Then she encouraged her sister to press her dark button-nose against the window, like hers, *like this*. Catherine and Gulliver waved and smiled before a large woman with a kind face abruptly opened the door. The giggling continued until the dark-haired woman hushed them with her wide eyes.

For a moment she seemed elsewhere; she did not smile at first – her large frame moved forward as they stepped politely back: she had a watering can in her arms – some of the water had already escaped – spilled like milk onto the concrete flags ahead of her.

Catherine and Gulliver offered their identification.

'This is Detective Sergeant Pope. I am Detective Inspector Shakespeare. May we come in?'

Probably unintentionally, she glanced over her left shoulder before inviting them in. The can was left outdoors; the noise from indoors quietening as the girls were encouraged to leave the room.

'You may take a seat. How can I help you detectives?'

'Thank you. We are trying to trace the whereabouts of a Miss Ashanti Akintola. This address is listed as belonging to her mother, and her last known address in the UK before she travelled to Nigeria in 2007.'

Gulliver was about to ask with whom he was speaking, when the large woman called into the back of the house. 'Ashanti. Ashanti! It is for you.'

The room fell silent. Like synchronised swimmers, everyone looked to the back of the room, the sound of hefty feet approaching – flip flops – a slow approach – heavy, steady, certain. As Ashanti moved a thick corridor curtain to the side as she entered, the older woman exited the room. For some reason both Catherine and Gulliver stood to attention. As they shook hands and introduced themselves, Catherine could not push a certain irritable thought to the back of her mind: Hermione would have remained seated, unnerved – in control - imperturbable. For whatever reason, they were already on edge.

Seated now, Ashanti commanding their attention by having sat on a chair near to them both, remained silent and steady until Gulliver spoke once again.

'Ashanti Akintola?'

'Yes. That is me.'

Although she had not spoken much, it was already noticeable that there was a significant resemblance between the anonymous caller and the elegant woman now sat before them. The official language of Nigeria being English, it was no surprise that her spoken idiom was excellent; but her recognisable Ajebotan accent was unmistakable.

An educated woman, Ashanti Akintola chose her words carefully and spoke at a pace that commanded respect. She was a good-looking woman, large and strong, big eyes, beautiful dark features. She was, according to their notes, fifty, but she could have easily passed for a much younger woman. She was tall too. Catherine had already decided that her feet were at least a size nine: her painted nails the colour of a passion fruit shell.

It was a total surprise to them to learn that she had spent the last ten years of her time in Nigeria, and on her own, living with family in Abuja, the capital.

'Like most in Nigeria, extended families are the backbone of our social system. I couldn't have managed without them. I attended Ladoke Technical University for two years and completed a mortuary science degree before finding work in the capital.

My father died last year – times have been hard for my mother since. I returned to be with her. *Massey and Sons*, my last employers, have a temporary vacancy for me, this coming March: maternity cover. I will be able to support my mother then.'

'So Mr Lexton is not their father?'

Ashanti Akintola looked both shocked before she seemed amused. Even Catherine was surprised by Gulliver's question.

'Trinity and Cala? No. No children. They are my sister's. I wanted children.'

There was a pregnant pause before she spoke again – more composed now, angry maybe – aggrieved for sure – she leaned forward like a tree bearing fruit.

'I have not seen Neil since the morning of the day when he and I were to move permanently to Nigeria. I embarked on the plane, alone. I neither heard nor saw him after. We could have never had children – he had had a vasectomy many years earlier. I didn't want children then.'

It was obvious now Akintola held some deep resentment towards her previous lover. All the while, she held the gaze of both officers; when she spoke of her past lover, she vented an admirable level of controlled bitterness.

'How long were you together beforehand?'

'Almost two years. I had worked many years at *Massey and Sons Funeral Directors*. I was a full-time embalmer. They taught me the trade – I liked it there – joined them in my twenties. After my first University degree. I had spoken to Neil many times over the years – before our - our relationship. He was one of two gravediggers Massey liked to use. Always reliable. How is it you feel I am able to help you? Have you heard from Neil?'

'We recently received an anonymous phone call. I have a recording with me, if you'd like to listen to it. It is the voice of a woman that we need to trace – the accent is not too dissimilar to your own.'

There was a pause. A long pause. Gulliver was about to open a black backpack he was shouldering when Ashanti began to speak.

'It is I who made that call. Before my father died last year; he visited me in Abuja. He wanted me to come home. I was so happy. You see - when my father learned about my relationship with Neil, he was disgusted. Neil is a married man – and almost his own age. He forgave me. Eventually. But I never saw him again, after he boarded the plane. He had cancer. He did not tell me. He died before I sold what little I had; he died before I returned back to England. He told nobody. Not even my mother.'

'We are sorry to hear that Miss Akintola. Would you mind explaining the reasons for the call you made? You understand the claims made, are both unusual and alarming?'

'I decided a long time ago that if I visited England, I would tell of the things Neil had told me in confidence. I did not want them on my conscience. I suppose too, I wanted him to know I was here, in England. I am still angry.

I gave everything up to be with him. Missed out on many years with my family. Missed out on being a mother. Wasted time. And money. He had the money for our fresh start – half of it was mine. He kept it and sent me on my way. One way ticket. I had nothing when I arrived in Nigeria. I had to labour and study for many years before I worked as an embalmer again. I thought I'd never return home.'

'We have been unable to trace Mr Lexton. It appears, so far, that no-one has seen him since he left for Africa. We were certain he was with you. We were hoping you could point us in the right direction.'

For a short while Ashanti looked perplexed – baffled. If she was lying, it was a good act. Her face even seemed to show regret before she suggested in an accusatory tone that he had probably flown abroad in an altogether different direction with all of their hard-earned cash. Still, she didn't seem sure.

Baffled, the party parted in the hope the investigation could reveal more. It was a mystery to be sure. As advised, Ashanti agreed to return to the station with her family lawyer, before making a formal statement. She was adamant that there were more undiscovered bodies to be found, not just at Southport's main graveyard but at several similar locations about the town.

28

MRS LEXTON AND Mrs Tanner are both in the front lounge discussing Mr Lexton, when they hear their singular front gate swing quickly open. For a few moments they play musical statues – freeze frame – hadn't seen the detectives coming. The box seat below the window is only four feet ahead of them – ahead of the front window; for a moment they both look to the base of it, as if pleading Mr Lexton to stay silent.

Mrs Tanner zealously motions for Mrs Lexton to step back quietly; she does so with her right hand – the gesture plays out in slow motion – it is not too dissimilar from one that communicates to a driver who is reversing and parking into a difficult space. It is in the shadows that they must disappear.

Both sisters are now at the back of the room. Mrs Tanner is deep in thought: it is fortunately a grey and miserable day outside - she suspects the detectives will stick their noses where they are not wanted, up close against the bay window, and hopefully see nothing. The fading white net curtains that have never twitched, should do their job. Mrs Lexton concentrates on them – they have always reminded her of her wedding veil: hers too had a small floral pattern. She didn't have a white veil. Nor a white wedding dress. *I, Joan Bond, take thee, Neil Lexton, to be my wedded husband, to have and to hold, from this day forward, for better, for worse, for richer, for poorer, in sickness and in health, to love and to cherish, till death do us part, according to God's holy ordinance.*

Knocking. More knocking. Mrs Tanner is worried. Poor Mrs Lexton looks like she is about to cry. Her eyes are fixated on the window box – her ears on the door. Her right hand grips her wedding finger. They're coming for her. For a moment she visualises her husband's rotten corpse, his knuckles rapping against the wooden frame: she studied *The Tell-Tale Heart* at school. They're coming for her.

Knocking. More knocking. Their knocking has a determined sound about it. But Mrs Tanner remains stoic: they cannot get in without a warrant. It feels like they'll get in, but they won't. Mrs Tanner holds her sister's right hand and squeezes it gently. There are tears running down her wrinkled face. Her slight green eyes fixated on the window. Her entire small frame shaking like a bird's breast.

Mrs Tanner whispers into her sister's ear that the detectives will eventually grow tired and leave soon. *They have no idea if we are in or out.* They could easily be out: they used to trundle to the shops almost every day. They could be anywhere. They could even be fast

SISTERS

asleep – they do both own ear plugs: they both snore very loudly.

The back door. As usual the back door is open. If one moves along the outer side of the house, via the tunnel, to the back - goes for the gate – tries to look over, they'll see the back door is open. If they call out, and neither of them answer, then, it could be argued that, out of concern for their well-being of course, they would need to enter the premises in order to check on them – they are after all almost seventy.

Moments later, the voices of the two figures appear to crawl steadily away; they are shifting towards the back of the house. Mrs Tanner quickly signals to Mrs Lexton not to move – a right finger to her lips. She then swings swiftly out of the lounge door and disappears. In the kitchen now, Mrs Tanner seizes the key with her right hand whilst quietly pushing the door closed with her left palm. Locks the door quick as a wink. It's a quiet flick to the right. She'd like to bolt the door but that will just have to do. Too much noise. The lights are thankfully off. She listens.

Voices. Quiet – lingering silence. Voices. A muffled conversation. *Jesus fucking Christ!* Either one of them or both is climbing the gate – it's at least eight foot – that won't stop them. It's one of them. The man is over. His voice is closest. Mrs Tanner backs away from the kitchen and steps into the hallway. Her eyes on the door. The lock is undone at the top. The lock is undone at the bottom. Both bolts to the left. Noise of metal clanging and wood groaning. The gate lock flicks upwardly before it is open. Drawn back. Voices. Mrs Tanner checks the window with her eyes before she heads back to the front lounge, pulling the kitchen door closed behind her. Her sister. She must check on her sister.

Like trapped animals they look nervously about in their front lounge. Should they head upstairs. Should they stay put. The back door is shaken. Even Mrs Tanner feels sick now. The smell in the room isn't helping. If they get in, Mr Lexton will give them away.

More knocking. Mrs Tanner looks at Mrs Lexton – she looks like she has been crying again. Mrs Lexton has been picking at a scab that was an invisible irritation at the top of her thumb for a week now. It is bleeding again but she is yet to notice. Mrs Tanner smiles and holds her sister's hand in hers. *Come what may, it will all be okay.* She whispers that.

Last night, when they were talking before bed, Mrs Tanner convinced her sister that if push came to shove, she'd take the blame. They'd prepared their story. There was no point both of them going away. And Mrs Lexton had done her stint at Greaves Hospital. No salutary benefits. Burned to the ground. Ashes to ashes, dust to dust. Mrs Tanner doesn't have that many years ahead of her anyway, she said. Her sister cried. Last night, like when they were both children, they fell asleep in the same bed – the one from Cider Drive – the one they slept in together as small girls. Before their parents died. Before they married a useless cunt and then a selfish bastard. Before the beating and the cheating, and the crying and the lying. Before they took an iron and a hammer into their hands and put an end to it all. And now they're both threatening to give them away.

Eventually, after they have peered through almost every window and gap – and probably taken a good look in their garden – shed locked - and knocked on every possible door and window once again, the frustrated detectives head off, only to make enquiries with some of their neighbours. Mrs Lexton looks at Mrs Tanner and breathes a sigh of relief.

'I TOLD YOU THEY COULDN'T GET IN MRS LEXTON.'

'I CAN'T STAY IN COOKED UP IN THIS HOUSE ANY LONGER MRS TANNER! IT'S BEEN DAYS SINCE WE LAST WENT OUT.'

'TWO DAYS MRS LEXTON. TWO DAYS. MIND, WE NEED TO BE SEEN. IF NO-ONE SEES US – IF ANYONE SHOWS ANY CONCERN – NOW THAT THEY'VE BEEN TALKING TO THE NEIGHBOURS – GOD KNOWS WHAT THEY'VE BEEN ASKING – THE'Y HAVE THE EXCUSE NEEDED TO CHECK-UP ON US!'

'THEY'LL KNOCK THE FRONT DOOR DOWN MRS TANNER!'

'NO-ONE'S GOING TO KNOCK THE FRONT DOOR DOWN MRS LEXTON!'

'AS SOON AS THEY'RE GONE, WE'LL CALL IN ON A COUPLE OF NEIGHBOURS. WE NEED TO THINK OF A REASON MRS LEXTON!'

'WE'RE RUNNING OUT OF GIN MRS TANNER!'

'AND TOBACCO MRS LEXTON!'

'AND MILK MRS TANNER!'

'THAT'S IT MRS LEXTON! I'LL CALL ON MR AND MRS STONE TO BORROW SOME MILK – TELL THEM WE'VE HAD A SICKNESS BUG – TELL THEM WE'VE RAN OUT. WOULD HE MIND LENDING US A PINT?'

'I FANCY A NICE CUP OF TEA NOW MRS TANNER!'

'YOU CAN CALL ON *THE CURSED HOUSE* AND TELL THEM WE'VE GOT NO WATER – ASK THEM IF THEIR WATER SUPPLY IS OK.'

'SHALL I GO NOW MRS TANNER?'

'IF WE GIVE IT A COUPLE OF HOURS, GIVE THE NEIGHBOURS TIME TO TALK, THEY'RE BOUND TO ASK OR TELL US SOMETHING – HOPEFULLY THEY'LL LET US IN ON THE QUESTIONS THE DETECTIVES WERE ASKING TOO!'

Mrs Lexton nods. For a short while their nerves have the better of them. They cautiously head out from the kitchen, into the hallway and to the front lounge. The two detectives are speaking to Mr Evans. Pipes held between their teeth, they peer at a safe distance, smoking, watching in unison; the detectives come and go as they work their way around the close.

Only three neighbours appear to be in. They were inside, at the Rimmers' for approximately ten minutes. Only a couple of minutes at *the cursed house*. They spent the longest, from the little they could see, at the Stones'. Mr Stone walked them to the gate and shook hands with them both before re-entering his home. Yes, they were with him the longest. Mrs Tanner will make sure she calls in on him later - after Mrs Lexton feels better.

An hour or so later, the detectives can be seen walking away towards the mouth of the cul-de-sac. Mrs Tanner heads upstairs quickly to see if she can locate their car. It is unmarked, navy. Mrs Tanner shouts down to Mrs Lexton who is now sitting on the window box contemplating.

'MRS LEXTON. THEY'RE IN THE CAR NOW. THEY'LL SOON BE DRIVING AWAY!'

Moments later, the unmarked vehicle snakes its way back to where it came from – left again, away from Crossens village, probably right, along Preston Road, probably towards the coastal road – probably on their way to the station. Probably.

But Mrs Tanner is unaware of what Mrs Lexton is doing downstairs. In the front lounge. If her husband was alive and kicking, he'd probably say she has lost the plot: he used to like using that phrase a lot. When all she'd done was lose a baby. Mrs Tanner is still thinking on her feet when she suddenly hears the crunching of wood below. Downstairs.

Mrs Lexton has pulled away the purple window seat cushion, that matches the curtains before throwing it behind her. Even in death, the useless cunt is determined to ruin her - there is no peace to be had with him still there – threatening to bring them down – exact his revenge. His carcass needs burning – whatever there is left of him. And as she hammers at the wood with her thin fists, but with so much force, the rotten planks, mouldy on the inside from the damp that has risen out of the front garden, give way and collapse. The smell is indescribable.

In the sick and chilling darkness, Mr Lexton awaits.

29

A MONOTONOUS AND dreich coastline, grey after grey, one bleak shot taken after another, eyes blink, light rain carried by an energetic wind, more usual in April, appears never-ending. It is just the sort of weather the English should have grown accustomed to by now. But never have. Just the sort of weather Catherine intensely dislikes. Its beyond her why people walk in such weather conditions – but they do.

'I'm counting on the BBC getting their weather forecast right this weekend. Cold but dry. Looks bloody miserable out there!'

'Let's park across from the cul-de-sac. We'll wait a while – hopefully one of them – or both of them will leave the house to go to the shops at some point. Are you sure you heard the back door being locked?'

'I did. Positive. Let's wait and see if any of the neighbours have any joy! They might open the door to one of them, if they think we've gone. Mr Stone said he'd keep calling until he got a response – that the sisters usually switch on the lights about four, just as it's going dark.'

'We'll see. He's got our number. We can't see the front door from here but we will be able to tell if a neighbour is awhile before returning. If we're lucky, we might catch them with the door wide open. Fingers crossed they don't slam it closed, when they see us.'

'I wonder what they're hiding?'

Almost two hours had passed before Catherine Shakespeare called it a day. Gulliver was pleased. He wanted to call Olivia – a burning desire to hear her voice growing. In the last twenty minutes, Catherine had spoken about her relationship with Hermione Folkard. They'd been working together on an unusual case, only next door.

'I still can't believe it. Can't seem to get through the day without thinking about it. Not what happened – just her – she was my boss before she was my friend – never judged – intuitive, had a sixth sense about most things. I always wanted to be like her. I learned so much from her. I could do with her right now – no offence.'

For a slight moment Catherine looked embarrassed – she'd probably said too much. She didn't know Gulliver from Adam. Who was he anyway? Yes, they'd bonded a little after he'd unexpectedly slumped backwards. But he was a stranger. In many ways, a total stranger. He pretty much kept himself to himself; although to be fair, he'd made a bigger effort than she had. In just a couple of days, their families would meet. As they should – Hermione would have said. Catherine felt guilty. Yet, instinctively, dare she say it, there was something distant about Gulliver, something she couldn't put her finger on – his mind at times, very much elsewhere. What was that?

'Looking forward to Sunday. Wendy has been on the phone to Carys a few times – she's been making homemade sausage rolls all weekend. Got some back at the office – we haven't even eaten yet! Let's go back and sample them. Mr Stone will call us if he sees or hears anything. Sounds like he needs something to do whilst his wife is away with her mother. I met him a couple of years ago. Most definitely reliable. He is someone, I'm sure won't let us down.'

***

'It's me. Sorry I couldn't call any sooner.'

For a moment silence. The excitement he felt was like a sickness that came and went in waves. Did she still feel as strongly? Would there come a point, before they met, when she would cancel – the fear of him hurting her again taking over. Could he trust himself to stay in control this time?

He'd managed so far to firefight the guilty thoughts and questions, with what was to come. What was to come? He'd played it and replayed it – slowed it down more times than he could count. Had happily fallen uncomfortably asleep night after night, Carys thankfully exhausted from all the party's preparations. She'd been too busy to notice, he hoped.

He wanted to save himself. Had Carys needed him, he couldn't have refused – more guilt would have followed. The thought of sleeping separately with two women sickened him. There was nothing lucky about that. And the children. He glanced at himself in the rear view mirror. There was something almost rebarbative about him – something he didn't recognise – something more than lust – he was being greedy – wanted it all – wanted his cake and wanted to eat it come what may.

'I'm not sleeping too good.'

Her soft voice ran through his veins like a drug. He wanted her there and then. Was she about to cancel?

'I'm not sleeping too good either. Keep thinking about you. Keep thinking about tomorrow. I can't stay late.'

He was about to explain but couldn't find the words. He felt dirty – could he mention his children to her? Manon's party? He couldn't mix the two – not even in conversation – it needed to stay separate.

'I check in at two.'

'I won't keep you waiting. Text me your room number as soon as you have it.'

For a moment he hesitated. He was being presumptuous. Maybe they should take a walk along the grounds first – should he offer to take her out for a late lunch?

'I'll be waiting. In my room. I'll be waiting for you.'

And he pictured her then and there in black lace. She stood before the double bed. Her chest bulging. Her mouth parted slightly – her legs too. Her arms by her side. Teasing him. She wouldn't come to him. He'd go to her.

***

Carys' car wasn't on the drive when he arrived home. He still hadn't fully decided what to say to her. In the ten minutes it took for her to return home, he still remained undecided. Manon and Brody spilled through the front door following after Carys; in turn she headed directly upstairs. He emerged from the back kitchen to discover that Manon was furious: she'd been set homework for the weekend. Brody needed the toilet. And within seconds, they had dispersed three separate ways – all of them shouting for different reasons.

'I'm going out with Joanna tomorrow night for a couple of drinks. I'll only be a couple of hours. What time will you be back from work?'

'What time are you going out? We're working overtime whilst on this case.'

'I need to leave by eight. Won't be late – the party won't organise itself!'

'I'll be back for eight.'

No matter. He didn't need an excuse then: he just needed to be back for eight. He stood feeling a little relieved; despite everything, he hated lying. The least said, the better. He'd learned that at work. Criminals talking themselves into jail. No comment. He unintentionally caught himself in the hall mirror on the way upstairs – he needed a haircut – and a shave.

'DAD! DAD!'

Brody's trouser zip was stuck.

'DAD! DAD!'

He looked away from the mirror disappointed. He'd let himself go since their move from Conwy. He'd recently noticed his inability to move his wedding ring in circular movements; something he was always able to do with the same hand – thumb and smallest finger - now failing to twirl without the assistance of his right hand. It was a habit like any other – he'd always done it without thinking in the past – it annoyed Carys, for some reason.

His father used to do it too. Exactly the same way. Thumb and smallest finger twirling the thin yellow band. Used to mostly do it whilst watching television. His parents had married as teenagers. He'd always suspected the wedding had been rushed. Gulliver smiled as Brody was released from his zip – a kiss to his forehead. Brody's face red. But then unexpectedly, an uncomfortable childhood memory presented itself – possibly a time when he was too young to understand. He thought about it before he chose to dismiss it. He could only remember that his mother had cried. Something or nothing. Still, he wasn't sure.

30

HAD MR LEXTON remained buried, as he was meant to in the first place - had he remained tightly bound by the taut tape, in the dark tarpaulin sheet as intended, then an intact corpse of his former person would have presented itself following Mrs Lexton's determined efforts to rid herself once and for all of her useless cunt of a husband.

Before them now is a gaping hole. Pieces of broken pine-wood planks surround Mrs Lexton; in her right hand she is holding a long splinter-like-knife. She is on her knees rocking slightly back and forth. In the darkness, amongst the dank smell, is a folded human shape – the remains of someone they both knew and disliked. The remains of someone much smaller than they had remembered.

Mrs Tanner is lost for words. In the past, they had often talked about moving the body at some point – but her sister's unpredictable actions have, of course, made matters worse. Now is not the right time for moving a body. Looking at her now, Mrs Lexton looks exhausted, angry even. The smell soon persuades them both to move back, onto the sofa.

The darkness surrounding his corpse seems to dissipate as their eyes adjust – the curled body as it was, ten years ago, folded to fit, in the gaping hole. To the right and further back, tucked behind Mr Lexton, is the iron; it still looks like it is in good working order – not too rusted – the coil and plug in sight. Then the hammer – now the iron. Bin day is days away. You couldn't make it up if you tried.

Finally taking charge, Mrs Tanner takes Mrs Lexton to the kitchen for a much needed cup of tea – with plenty of gin. She has locked the front lounge and replaced the key above the frame. For a moment she almost loses her balance standing on the old chair. The house is colder than usual. Like her frail sister, she is exhausted.

Mrs Tanner will have to put off visiting Mr and Mrs Stone – they are likely to detain her for longer than she can endure. Maybe later, it is already getting dark, she will pop over the road and visit the Evans'. Borrow some milk. In the morning she will make sure she calls on the Stone's.

An hour has passed and both sisters are sitting quietly. Mrs Tanner is hatching a plan. Maybe Mrs Lexton should go to bed; it is obvious from her face that it has all become too much. Her hands are shaking. Her scab at the top of her thumb is bleeding again – scarified and infected now. But Mrs Lexton won't be redirected anywhere.

'USELESS CUNT HAS TO GO MRS TANNER!'

Mr Lexton's corpse, obvious from the weight, has been slow to decompose. There is a slushing sound coming from the inside of the plastic as they begin to move him – they both hope it is only water. The plastic has come undone by his feet. They avoid looking at what seems to be a mixture of rotten flesh on bone.

Eventually, his body is settled at the back of the room, behind the sofa. For a moment, the two women gasp for breath. Mrs Tanner leaves the room only to re-enter with a bin bag and a tea-towel. She picks out the iron whilst holding the tea-towel in her hand, then expertly places them both in the garden refuse sack.

'I'LL STICK IT IN THE SHED NOW – UNTIL BIN DAY MAYBE.'

'I THINK THE CLOCK'S STOPPED WORKING. IT SAYS IT'S ELEVEN MINUTES PAST TEN MRS TANNER!'

'MRS LEXTON – IT STOPPED WORKING YEARS AGO. DON'T YOU REMEMBER?'

Mrs Tanner's soft voice is appreciated by her younger sister; she has a headache – nauseous. She looks to the silver clock before she thinks that she can remember something important. Aware now that her hand is bleeding, she leaves the room for a plaster. Mrs Tanner closes the door before leaving. On the way back from the shed, she must remember to pick up the thick bleach from underneath the kitchen sink.

'BACK IN A JIFFY MRS LEXTON.'

Once in the shed, and for a lengthy moment, Mrs Tanner stares at the space between the two nails where the old hammer once hung. It was a great hammer – weighty - good for pounding and extracting nails – and other things. It was their father's. Mrs Tanner was sorry to see it go. It has recently been replaced with another. To Mrs Tanner, one hammer looks much like another; she sometimes says this about babies, but she doesn't mean it. But the handle on this lighter version is considerably thinner.

At the hardware store, Mrs Tanner was offered *a ladies hammer*. At first she balked at such a thing. The store manager seemed unsurprised. Then having held each alternative tool in turn, really so that she could dismiss such a feeble and useless version of the original, she decided upon the less weightier hammer after all – its structure, size and shape rather pleasing. It could still be as effective – deliver a good blow. In fact, the alternative now suddenly seemed cumbersome and outdated. Pleasantly surprised, Mrs Tanner paid for the item and left.

Looking around, there are more places than she at first thought of, to hide the bag, hopefully for only a few days. After moving several boxes, Mrs Tanner decides upon burying it underneath a box of potatoes, kept for planting outdoors in the spring. Only a couple of weeks ago they had been kept under her bed wrapped in newspaper. Now they were regularly heating the house, the potatoes had to be moved before they break from dormancy and begin to sprout. Their mother grew many varieties of vegetables. There is nothing as good as picking your own vegetables out from the earth, cooking and consuming them within the hour from when they were born – raised from the soil, washed and boiled – salted and buttered.

Twenty of so many minutes have passed. Time for something to eat. They need to get their thinking caps on. Mrs Tanner retrieves the hammer. She intends to at least pull the seat apart tonight – burn all she can and address the rot. In the garden now, she looks at the back of their house, cosily nested between the house on the left, belonging to the newly married couple, who argue less and less since they were enrolled on the infertility programme with their doctor, and the house on the right. Mr and Mrs Eccleston are both as deaf as dodos; they both wear hearing aids that doesn't seem to help either of them that much. Both sisters fell out with Mr Eccleston years ago after he grabbed Mrs Lexton from behind in the front garden.

The dark is on its way. With exception of the geese, who noisily dart across the sky above her, all is quiet. The chill in the air is uncanny. It seems impossible to not accept this as an omen.

31

BETWEEN 1986 AND 2007, Mr Lexton had worked as a private gravedigger for Merseyside council. If Miss Akintola was right, and there were more bodies buried in different graveyards, they would need more than just manpower. The media would soon pick up on the story and like ripples in a pond, they would spread far and wide.

The exhumation of a body was never a pretty sight. Although generally rare, the psychological trauma for any family meant that courts were very unlikely to allow any deceased body to be unearthed willy-nilly unless there was evidence to support Miss Akintola's claim. The expense would be immense, and any disinterment could take a very long time to arrange. How on earth were they to persuade families to allow a loved one's exhumation just on the chance that another body had been sneaked in the night previous?

Since Superintendent Reid had retired, budget cuts had resulted in an area commander taking over – Superintendent Gary Griffin's monthly on-the-spot visit was imminent. He'd known both Hermione Folkard, and her husband, Walter. It was obvious from his comments about filling big shoes that he felt the team was yet not up to his expected standard. It was hard to meet such high expectations – so many changes. Administrative tasks and e-mails swamped them daily – too many forms – not enough hours in the day – no pay rise – cut backs.

There were three main cemeteries and over thirty-three churches, all with their own graveyards. Since at least twelve had closed in the last twenty years, record-keeping would not show exactly who had worked on what job. Detective Sergeant Cunliffe and McKenna had a mammoth job ahead of them.

'I'll put together a list of graves that Mr Lexton had signed off on. Then a list that he could have been working on, considering there were only four of them working in Southport at the time. If it helps, it does seem to me that Mr Lexton worked mostly on digging plots south of the town.'

'Thank you Charlotte. That's a start – some good news at least. Luke, can you assist Charlotte? If at all possible, I need this list before Monday's interview. Superintendent Griffin will have to be informed at some point, especially if we are to expand the investigation. Who knows, Lesley Litt may not have been telling the truth when he claimed he had no recollection of his father or Mr Lexton doing anything improper. We will re-interview him after Miss Akintola makes her statement.'

Catherine was home for the weekend – family leave booked until her return Monday. Gulliver was about to leave when Detective Constable Stanfield mouthed Mr Stone's name. Gulliver paused before he signalled for him to take a message.

'Ring me if important, otherwise, I'll speak to him on Monday Omar, thanks! Need to leave – its 12.30 already!'

***

Olivia: 'Checked in early. In the bath. Waiting.'

Gulliver: 'On my way. An hour tops. Room number?'

Olivia: '12'

Gulliver: 'Same room. Same place.'

Olivia: 'The door is unlocked. Waiting.'

Gulliver's mouth had gone dry. For a moment he stood still – dazed even. No-one had noticed. He headed outdoors avoiding polite conversation. Outside now, he drew a deep breath. It was a dry afternoon – bright but bitter all the same. He didn't take the time to fasten his jacket. He needed to get going. Olivia decisively on his mind.

Once in the car, and for a moment only, he couldn't think of his way there – he visualised the route then pressed the ignition. Should be no traffic. He knew better than to use the *Sat Nav*. He had hoped to call home; he checked himself in the mirror – he was already perspiring. Home would have to wait.

Earlier that morning he'd taken longer than usual in the shower. He hadn't noticed Carys enter; he was embarrassed. He first spotted her on the toilet. She got up before washing her hands – she didn't even speak to him – yawned a fair bit though. Maybe she had spoken to him – although he was sure she hadn't. She hadn't stopped for the last two weeks. Seemed daft going out the night before Manon's party. What time would she be home?

He did unintentionally notice she had painted her nails. It wasn't quite red, an orange red, pretty. She had short nails, but all the same, the colour suited her skin – he'd noticed when her left hand pulled the door closed behind her.

***

Gulliver's stomach rumbled – if he was hungry, he didn't know it. Unlike the last time they met, he instinctively knew there would be no walk amid the grounds – or even a late lunch – no polite conversation. He checked the time on the dashboard. He'd arrive about two. He'd leave as late as he could. He'd leave when she was done.

There was no point listening to music: it was distracting him. Gulliver turned the radio down, then off. Neither was there any point either managing or marginalising guilty feelings now – he'd longed for this for months – Olivia too it seemed. He hoped to find her as she'd promised. *I'll be waiting. In my underwear. I'll be waiting for you.*

And he pictured her then and there, again, in black lace. It was important that he could see more flesh. She waited for him at the foot of the double bed. Her chest swelling. Her mouth parted slightly – her legs too. Her arms at either side. She was teasing him. She wouldn't come to him. He'd have to go to her. And she wouldn't move. He knew her well enough to know she'd hold back – she'd watch his every move – never losing control.

He'd lost all sense of time last time. He did things he'd never dreamed of before. He'd owned her in every way because she made him.

No was a word she tended not to listen to.

32

IT IS DARK now. Quiet too. Peaceful even. Looking up at the vast sky is what both Mrs Tanner and Mrs Lexton loved to do as young girls with their father. It is so easy to be that little girl again here, outdoors. Everything in the universe seems to be as it was back then – up there, little appears to change, despite the passing years.

Mrs Tanner sighs before she wipes her hands clean on her red pinafore – the hammer tucked under her left armpit. The cold air smacks her fresh cheeks – a lonely star that she has located quickly, is in fact an aeroplane in the distance – but there are so many other stars to admire. Some no longer exist. Staring into the past. A snapshot light years away. The souls of the departed long gone – some say.

The back door is now closed – the cold air shut out; she is about to head for the kitchen sink, to retrieve the thick bleach, when she thinks she hears a familiar voice. She retraces her steps before she dismisses a worrying thought. For a moment she thinks of sitting down: she can neither fathom what is happening nor come up with a solution to their problem.

A familiar voice. An unmistakable voice – confident, and energetic. Mrs Tanner puts the hammer down quickly and heads for the lounge before she quickly returns to retrieve it. In all honesty, she cannot think straight – what on earth was Mrs Lexton thinking about, when she allowed him into their home – into their front lounge of all places?

Mr Stone and Mrs Lexton stand facing the vacant and damaged window seat. They look like Ben and Gus in *The Dumb Waiter*. When Mrs Tanner reaches the doorway, the hammer behind her back, Mrs Lexton is making polite conversation. And of course, Mr Stone, is enthralled by the mystery of the ghastly smell. Mrs Tanner is either the audience looking in or a visitor imposing.

'AND HOW MANY MORE DAYS UNTIL MRS STONE RETURNS FROM VISITING HER MOTHER MRS TANNER?'

'TOO MANY MRS LEXTON – TOO MANY – ALMOST ANOTHER WEEK!'

Mrs Tanner still cannot understand how on earth Mr Stone has ended up in their front lounge. Obvious from his demeanour, he has not seen what lies at the back of the room. What was her sister thinking? Tense now, her grip tightens about the neck of her trendy hammer.

Without drawing any further attention, Mrs Tanner urgently decides she needs to get Mr Stone out. What on earth was her sister doing allowing him to enter the house in the first place? Did she invite him in?

'A dead rat did you say Mrs Lexton? What a stink! I'll make some enquiries if you like, as to how you can rid yourself of that smell!'

'THANK YOU MR STONE – THAT IS VERY KIND OF YOU! OH HOW GLAD I AM THAT YOU CALLED IN ON US TONIGHT!'

Mr Stone returns her half-smile. For a moment, he seems to be staring at her mouth. Unbeknown to Mrs Lexton, she has some greenery between her two front teeth. Mr Stone decides to not mention this to Mrs Lexton. Mrs Stone is always complaining about her teeth – last year she had to have two wisdom teeth removed.

Mrs Tanner makes a mental note of the smell – yes, it does not seem as offensive since the box has been laid bare. Determined to get Mr Stone out, she points to the window pane – but Mr Stone is now looking to the back of the room. She is about to ask him to look at the wall from the outside of the house – she is even moving out of the room and raising her voice, when he begins talking again.

'I also said to Mrs Lexton, Mrs Tanner, that I have a number for a damp-course specialist. He did a fine job on the back of our house only last year. Injected stuff into our walls – all clear now. Its living so close to the sea – and the marshes. Too much damp. I say, I haven't seen wallpaper like this in a long time!'

'DO YOU LIKE THE WILLOW PATTERN? MY SISTER CHOSE IT – I HATE IT MYSELF!'

'There was a time when this wallpaper was the trendiest to have – covered many blemishes – a multitude of sins!'

'MRS STONE IS AWAY VISITING HER MOTHER MRS TANNER! HE CALLED TO LET US KNOW OF THE DETECTIVES' VISIT WHEN HE REMARKED ON THE GOD-DAMN AWFUL SMELL COMING FROM THE INSIDE OF OUR HOUSE!'

'Yes, I'm afraid I pretty much invited myself in – offered immediately on the spot to help out. Looks like you're getting on top of the problem though?'

Mrs Tanner's incredulous face is a picture – she cannot believe how composed her sister seems. Of course, she is drunk. Mrs Tanner is now glaring at Mrs Lexton; she is now comfortably seated in an armchair looking at the gaping hole. In the meantime, Mr Stone has taken a closer step towards the back of the room.

'CAN I SHOW YOU FROM THE OUTSIDE MR STONE? I THINK I HAVE DETECTED WHERE THE PROBLEM FIRST BEGAN!'

But Mr Stone's eyes are fixed now on something of interest. For a moment he adjusts his spectacles – his right hand checks his white beard. Even from the side, it is easy to tell that he has a puzzled look on his face.

'MR STONE! CAN I SHOW YOU FROM THE OUTSIDE MR STONE?

'Yes, of course Mrs Tanner.'

Silence. Mr Stone has not moved. In contrast, Mrs Lexton is still staring at the gaping hole. Mr Stone has now turned around; he too is staring at the gaping hole. The room's silence is discomforting. Mr Stone looks at his naked wrist before he stares at the silver clock on the mantelpiece – the time stopped at eleven minutes past ten. More silence. No tic or toc from the clock. Only the intake of their breath.

It is obvious now, from the look on his face and calculated steps towards Mrs Tanner, that he wishes to leave the room and head outdoors. How much he has seen, Mrs Tanner cannot be sure. He has seen enough. She is sure of that. She is sure he has put two and two together. His face is red. He is not smiling. He is holding himself very still. Mr Stone looks at Mrs Lexton for a moment and says nothing. Steps away. Looks outdoors again. He has now noticed Mrs Tanner has one hand behind her back.

'I'll take a look at that wall now Mrs Tanner. If that's okay Mrs Lexton? It's chilly outdoors. Best look before it rains. We're forecasted rain tonight. I'll head home and fetch my torch.'

Small conversation. Mrs Lexton sits back in her chair and yawns loudly. And just for a split moment, a fragment in time, Mr Stone looks to Mrs Lexton, a look of passing horror flashes. Is this really happening?

Quickly, Mrs Tanner has already made the significant decision as to which end of the hammer she is about to use. Only a few minutes earlier, she moved her right hand down the handle until she reached the lower half; she gripped it before she gently swung it against her own back so as to feel the impact. In the end, she decided that the blunt end of the hammer might stun Mr Stone enough for her to have time to hit him again. She was sure the one blow would not suffice. And when she does – as Mr Stone gestures towards Mrs Lexton, Mrs Tanner delivers her best blow to the side of his head, hitting him just above his left ear.

Mr Stone is neither a tall nor small man. He is still standing. He is still looking at Mrs Lexton. There is no blood. In response, the sound of the blow is disappointing, mismatched with the effort behind it. Mrs Tanner swings it the second time. The noise satisfies her for all the wrong reasons. It was not an option the first time – he might have seen her coming at him – she could have even missed. Then where would they be?

When Mr Stone landed almost across Mrs Lexton's lap, before her arms rejected him and he both rolled and slumped over onto the carpeted floor, at her feet, Mrs Lexton did not move. Instead, Mrs Lexton lifted her booted feet out of the way, an unexpected response considering how inebriated she is. Mrs Lexton looks incredulously at what her sister had done. Mrs Tanner shakes her head before she wipes her hammer on her red pinafore.

'WAS THERE ANY NEED MRS TANNER? POOR MR STONE. WHAT'S MRS STONE GOING TO SAY WHEN SHE GETS BACK?'

Mrs Tanner has no time for this. What else was she to do? She quickly leans over Mr Stone to check for a pulse – below his ear, bloodied now. The seeping red liquid trickles along his neck into a shape that resembles the map of Italy. No pulse. His wrist. His hands are clammy despite the cold room. She is sure he is dead. It is when she looks to her sister and demands she be quiet, when Mr Stone lets out a sound that alerts them to the fact that he is very much alive.

Mr Stone is no threat to them at all. But neither of them know this. They are not defending themselves or righting a wrong. This is kindly Mr Stone, who lives with his wife and his cat – the neighbour everyone can count on for something or another.

Quite suddenly, Mr Stone's right hand reaches out towards nothing. He cannot see, but neither of the sisters know this. Mrs Lexton screams – it is a horror movie; she stamps on his head several times before her sister tells her to shut up. Half-gently, half-rough, she guides Mrs Lexton out of the room, removing her boots for her. She tells her to go upstairs and wait for her. Her sister is crying. She does so as quietly as she can.

Mrs Tanner waits at the bottom of the stairs until she hears her sister flop onto her bed. She returns to the front-lounge where Mr Stone lies very still; he is still breathing. The hammer is still in her right hand. She closes the door behind her.

33

CARYS SLAMMED THE door behind her when Gulliver finally arrived home. He'd wasted his time checking himself constantly for any signs of unfaithful behaviour. He'd even showered before he left. Although he did not do so alone.

He watched Carys drive away before he took a deep breath – he hadn't planned on being late but he had grown careless the last twenty minutes before he'd left Olivia untidily behind - her lithe figure no longer restless.

For a moment he pondered on Carys – his last observation. She did not kiss him on the way out – her bright lipstick accentuating her lips. He tried to recall what she was wearing, why he was not sure. He was so busy in the moment – of course, he couldn't, she had already put her coat on. He'd watched her walk a little along the path before she clambered into her car. He should have offered to drive her – drive her where? Where was she going? Out with friends she'd said, he thought.

He had noticed she was wearing heels – black office heels – the ones no-one ever wears. High stilettoes. Her short coat had revealed thin legs and tight calves. A snapshot of his wife from behind. She looked great. She'd smelt great too. He'd noticed that briefly. Something familiar. Intense rather than fragrant. He then thought of Olivia. She'd been wearing penitential colours as he entered the bedroom.

Manon was still awake whilst Brody was sound asleep - his thumb loosely hooked onto his top lip like a fish. Small transparent nails like pearls. Gulliver turned his side light on. He'd managed to reach the toilet the last two evenings. The hall landing carpet needed replacing. If you knew where to stand, despite all the scrubbing, the smell was rank. A kiss to the top of his wide forehead followed, after he briefly moved aside a mass of rusty hair with his right hand. In no time at all, it sprung back into place. His hair needed cutting. Preferably before the party.

From the landing Gulliver could see several discarded outfits that had been flung onto their bed. Carys had made some effort. Where was she going? He was about to enter their bedroom when he heard Manon call.

'I'm still awake daddy.'

Gulliver smiled before he whispered back. 'You need your sleep for the big day tomorrow young lady. Double figures! Ten!'

'Mum said I had to go to bed early. A whole half-hour early!'

'You'll want to look your best then?'

'I'm so excited daddy! I cannot sleep daddy!'

'It's going to be a great party Manon. Close your eyes. You need your rest. Close your eyes princess.'

'I love you daddy.'

'I love you too princess.'

The BUZZ of a text interrupted the calm that had replaced boredom and restlessness. Gulliver stood half-resentful, half-curious. He knew instinctively it would be from Olivia.

'Close your eyes princess.'

***

It was early autumn when Gulliver first met Carys. October. In a primary school with a daft name. At the Harvest Festival. It was the Lawn something – like tennis maybe. Yes. No. The High Lawn Primary School. That was it. He'd almost forgotten. Was it okay to forget small details?

Carys was almost twenty-five; he'd be thirty then. Her not long a teacher. Him a copper in attendance – green but cocky despite his age. Ambitious. Sure of himself – like many of the lads then. Not many where he lived had settled down yet. Lived at home with their parents, for as long as they could. He lived with his mother and father too. You went from living with your parents to living with a wife – and kiddies followed. He wasn't ready for any of that. He wasn't even going to think about it. He was seeing Bronwen then. She was the local barmaid. He'd only known her five minutes.

He'd been standing not too far from the school stage, safeguarding the local MP – he couldn't remember his name. He thanked the crowd, the staff, everyone for raising money for the homeless community. He sounded nervous. He remembers thinking that. He unveiled a mural after delivering a poignant panegyric – an elaborate tribute in memory of the school's previous headteacher who had since passed away. He didn't hear much. He didn't care about people back then like he did now.

Carys wasn't too far from where he was standing. He'd first noticed her eyes – well, maybe he'd noticed her figure – but then he'd definitely noticed her eyes. He'd seen many blue eyes before of course. Maybe it was the combination of her chocolate hair and pale skin that accentuated her large eyes – blue, but bright, if that's possible. When she smiled politely his way, her eyes smiled too. She hadn't noticed him at that point. She didn't until he made sure she had. He might have been green but he was keen, never shy – he didn't lack confidence. Was she even his type?

Her eyes were a sapphire blue – not Atlantic, not that deep; they were paler, clearer. She'd worn a blue sweater that clung – it showed off her eyes. And everything else, but not in an obvious way. He could see her in that sweater now. He'd always see her like that. She rarely painted her nails then. He couldn't think of when he'd seen her in high heels, although he'd known her to wear them – for work. She looked great that day. She was wearing jeans, and trainers maybe. Her hair was down. She'd never let her hair pass the bottom of her shoulders. He'd always liked the way it fell from both sides across her face, just a little – and the way she tucked it back behind her ears.

Maybe that was it. Even now, for leisure, it was jeans, flat brown boots or her yellow wellingtons. Had he ever seen her wear black stilettoes before? He was sure he must have. She'd painted her nails in the past. She'd more often thought of painting her hand nails than done it. She always painted her toe nails – left them wearing the same colour until she couldn't put it off any longer.

What colour were her toes? He thought purple – but he didn't know. He was sure she wouldn't wear a different colour to her hands now. Her hand nails were orange or red. She'd always worn lip colour for work. Her underwear always matched. He'd always liked that about her.

The thought that he suddenly seemed to know so little about his wife's present wardrobe momentarily amused him. A mirror being held up for him, A bizarre awakening to the fact that he'd quite happily taken his eyes off the ball. Somehow she was different but of course, she was not. A ridiculous thought crossed his mind. Seed planted. A ridiculous thought ignited by guilt or suspicion? Of course it had to be guilt.

34

FROST LIES LIKE a thin cellular blanket across the historic village of Crossens. At one end, the coastal road end, the tide is far out; its wild terrain, one declivity chasing after another, is divided by remote marshland and threadbare boardwalks. At the other, is a picturesque village that dates back to the Domesday Book: Churchtown. Pretty thatched-roof cottages align the oldest of roads – a panoramic black and white conservation area surrounded by walks, pubs and parks.

It is early in the morning. A veiled sun peeks between several houses whilst most inhabitants still lie asleep. A lone dog-walker pauses resentfully by a wall – the steam from the pup's urine trailing along the pavement. Soon after, an unpopulated bus passes through the village on its way to town. At this time of the day, few alarm clocks disturb sound sleep. At this time of the day, the temperature is lower than a morgue chamber.

Mr Stone is dead – stone cold dead. Almost twenty-four hours have passed since Mrs Tanner put him out of his misery. Quietened, he now lies at the back of the front room lounge with Mr Lexton for company. Mrs Tanner had to move him on her own, in case anyone looked through the window. She'd exhausted herself moving him in the early hours, well dragging his upper half, before dragging his lower half after him. She was so tired, she left him, and the mess she'd made. She needed some sleep. She set her alarm for five. It was past 5.30 in the morning before she rose – the onerous task ahead of her looming like a giant boulder.

For a woman in her late sixties, Mrs Tanner is incredibly strong. She has been trying to scrub the blood from the carpet, for almost an hour when Mrs Lexton can be heard making her way down the stairs.

'CUP OF TEA ANYONE?'

Mrs Tanner shakes her head before she rises to join her sister at the bottom of the stairs.

'GRAND MRS LEXTON. JUST GRAND. NO GIN MIND – NEED TO KEEP MY WITS ABOUT ME TODAY.'

'AND WHY'S THAT MRS TANNER?'

Mrs Tanner looks incredulously at her sister. In the meantime, she had better lock the front room and pocket the key. Mrs Tanner shakes her head from side to side. Her sister is already reaching into the cupboard under the sink for the gin.

'IT WAS NICE OF MR STONE TO CALL IN ON US LIKE THAT LAST NIGHT WASN'T IT? HOW LONG DID HE SAY MRS STONE WAS AT HER MOTHER'S?'

'I THINK ANOTHER WEEK MRS LEXTON. ANOTHER WEEK I HOPE.'

Mrs Tanner begins to make them both some breakfast; she is not quite sure why but last night she did not make either of them something to eat. Come to think of it, they only ate a cheese sandwich earlier on in the day – with pickle – like when they were at school, cheese and pickle sandwiches – they would have gone nicely with a bowl of steaming tomato soup to dip them in.

'FANCY SOME SCRAMBLED EGGS MRS TANNER THIS MORNING? I'LL DO US A COUPLE OF RASHERS TOO AND A FRESH POT OF TEA!'

'LOVELY MRS TANNER! JUST LOVELY! WHAT TIME DID YOU SAY WE WERE GOING TO VISIT MUM AND DAD TODAY?'

'SORRY MRS LEXTON – WHAT DID YOU SAY?'

'MUM AND DAD! WHAT TIME ARE WE GOING AROUND TODAY?'

'CIDER DRIVE YOU MEAN?'

'WHERE ELSE MRS TANNER? THEY'LL BE EXPECTING US!'

'AND WHY'S THAT MRS LEXTON? IT'S SLIPPED MY MIND, WHY'S THAT?'

'BILLY'S BIRTHDAY PARTY MRS TANNER! OH, DO KEEP UP!'

Silence. Mrs Lexton is scratching an invisible spot on her left hand – it is already red, just above her thumb, red like a birth mark. Mrs Tanner is looking at her sister scratching her thumb before she approaches her and takes each of her hands in her own.

'NOW MRS LEXTON.'

But Mrs Tanner cannot find the words to say to her sister – it would be like stealing sweets from a child. She bends down and looks into her sister's eyes. She looks so tired, and haggard. Her eyes look smaller too – tiny dark pins – so many lines about her eyes.

Mrs Tanner holds her sister's hands a while longer before she pulls her forward and embraces her. When she stands, she places a kiss on her sister's forehead. For a moment or two their hands shake. It is very cold in the kitchen. Mrs Tanner puts the kettle on and fetches the gin.

Breakfast over, Mrs Tanner looks inside their empty fridge for a small while. What is she to do? Like a baby, Mrs Lexton sleeps in her chair. The look of contentment on her face is welcomed. She has been through so much, all of her life. One sorry bombshell after another. At least the useless cunt got what was coming to him in the end. Mrs Tanner wakes her sister to assist her up to bed. If she makes a start on cleaning the walls, she is unlikely to hear if her sister slumps from her chair. She is clearly in shock and needs her rest.

There is never any rest for the wicked. She'll have to clean the mess up on her own. It is a mystery to her how she will dispose of two bodies now. She has thought of going on the run, with her sister. The idea is ridiculous. They have some savings, yes. But sooner or later, they would be found. And her sister cannot be counted upon. To be honest, she is not sure at all how they will cope. No, they are better off where they are. At home. Sooner or later the detectives will come. And take them away. Come what may.

By twelve, Mrs Tanner has had enough. Her freezing cold hands are sore and raw from all the scrubbing and the bleach. For a moment she thinks about letting go, the need to sob growing like a tidal wave inside. Rising now, she leaves everything behind before heading to the kitchen to put the kettle on. She'll make her sister a nice cup of tea and suggest they go for a walk to the shops. Tonight she will heat some nice soup and add lots of vegetables; she'll add a couple of potatoes too.

Upon entering her bedroom, Mrs Tanner sees that Mrs Lexton has kicked off the covers. The red bow to her pinafore looks neat. From the look of the only hand on show, it is as cold as hers. Mrs Tanner covers pulls the fleece blanket over her sister's back before tucking it under her chin. Her chin is warm like a child's neck.

There is a white light that enters the bedroom from the first window on the right; it lands squarely at the foot of their three-quarter-bed. Only limp shadows from two spider plants intersect. Outdoors the mist grows; it mantles and cloaks what it can – unaffected, the tallest of trees in the neighbourhood look on. Mrs Tanner cannot see her sister's face – she has her back to her.

It is very difficult letting go of someone you've loved so deeply all of your life. Their mother urinated the sofa, before she died too. It does not matter. It could not be helped. Sitting on the edge of the bed, Mrs Tanner begins to sob. She hasn't cried like this since she killed her husband, and then, beforehand, since she lost each child. When their mother died, before their father, she sobbed then too. They both did. For years.

Mrs Tanner climbs onto the bed, she lies close to her sister, holding one of her hands. Rubs noses. Like they did as girls. Babs and Jo. Girls with hopes and dreams. Girls who played at being nurses who were going to marry doctors. Girls who'd have babies. Hearts filled with love.

After crying for the very last time, Mrs Tanner falls into a deep sleep. There is nothing else to do now but rest.

Knocking. More knocking. Mrs Tanner awakes with a start; she takes a deep breath and heads downstairs. It is a relief to not have to clear anything up. Not anymore. Key in her pocket, she unlocks the front door.

35

CATHERINE WOKE MUCH earlier than usual. Since being a child, she'd never slept well on Sundays. She'd gone from dreading the return back to school in her teens to dreading the return back to work as an adult – still behaving like a child in her forties. But it wasn't work that had disturbed her sleep. Nor the relentless wind that had swooned like an ice-skater swapping direction – Axle – Lutz – one chaotic blast after another, the window closest to her side of the bed hit repeatedly by gale-force winds.

It was Wendy that first alerted her to Carys' indiscretion – if that was what it was. Wendy had asked her to fetch Zita's mobile from her car only to follow her outdoors herself. She knew from her face that something was wrong.

'Are you sure it was not unintentional? He could have done it by accident!'

'It wasn't just the way he brushed his hand against hers; for the tiniest moment, he tipped his curled fingers inside her own. I know he did. It was – it was intrusive – and – and it was the fact she didn't react in the least. Like she knew who it was – she didn't flinch an inch. It was no accident. There was something tense about it all. It was very foolish of him!

Wendy just wasn't the gossiping kind. And she was rarely wrong about such matters. The party had now been and gone. Catherine and Wendy were amongst the first to leave. Zita's dark and unruly long hair was in desperate need of a wash – she had a lock stuck to her muggy forehead, Her tiger face had almost disappeared. The castle was awash with the smell of perspiring children – the time had now come for them to cry in turn. Most parents were either arguing or negotiating with their offspring: *No. It's school tomorrow – five more minutes!*

Despite everything, and having gone to some effort to entertain their visitors, Carys and Gulliver appeared pretty settled; neither had ever lived beyond the Welsh border. Both already settled in their neighbourhood, and at work, they had made a new life for themselves and seemed apparently content.

Gulliver had not stopped all day; he had been preoccupied with either seeing to the BBQ, putting logs on the fire or fetching drinks for guests. In return, Carys had taken a well-earned break by taking the back seat in the proceedings – relaxing after all the preparation. She was the perfect hostess. She looked fabulous in her blue silk dress, although to Catherine, her heels seemed unnecessarily high for the occasion.

The dry weather had helped, and for the time of year, it was not too cold. To Catherine, there were many unfamiliar faces; Wendy knew most of them though. Other than family, most of the adult guests were either parents from their children's year or family visiting from Wales. Younger siblings had attended too; one in particular played nicely alongside young Brody most of the afternoon, even though his nose was constantly running. The bouncy castle in the garden was a God-send: it entertained them right up to the time when parents had concluded that it was late enough and time to go.

Children that had earlier appeared in frocks with matching tights, headbands and painted faces left sweaty, their smeared faces and bare legs resisting the calls to quit the day, head home for a bath, prepare for school and the following day.

Most parents had drank their lot in wine and beer; conversation had been polite, even pretentious for the first hour or so, then, as they eased into more comfortable seating, about the open-plan sitting room and yellow lounge, as they ate more freely and laughed a little louder over the music Gulliver had chosen, they soon forgot to overcheck their brood – the need to prove their overqualified parental status gone.

To some parents, the interruption by crying was now resented – now was not the time for such trivialities. How differently they had all seemed when they had arrived earlier. Now their conversations mingled and steadily flowed. There were few disagreements of any sort. Tired overworked parents and grandparents united. Most had even adopted a similar response to any complaint or interruption from an aggrieved child. Their initial differences melted and the crowd morphed into the tail end of a pleasant dream. What did the phrase *Run along and play nicely* really mean?

Then she saw it for herself. Had Wendy not alerted her, she would have missed it. She'd intentionally watched Carys and Gulliver's behaviour for most of the afternoon. Zita was having the time of her life; it was great having so much fun – not a care in the world. What a pity Harry had not been able to make it. For too long he had rendered himself obscure – a master at obfuscating when asked for his plans. Survival masked as avoidance.

Zita had disappeared once more into the garden, after handing over her sparkly shoes and dirty tights. Wendy had called after her; she'd leaned forward to call her back before she ended up following her too. Zita lunged onto the first ballooned step belonging to the orange castle head first.

Manon had been waiting for her. They firmly held hands as Manon helped Zita back to their chosen corner – the one by the windowless space that had invited them both to climb and ride, one leg at either side. How they laughed. The other children looked on enviously. There wasn't any room for anyone else – besides, as Manon had shouted, it was her party. Their faces disappeared looking in the opposite direction, intruders all around, before they reappeared. Wendy was smiling despite Zita's ungraceful behaviour: she adored her. They both did.

Catherine had deliberately not asked Wendy whom the person was that had made physical contact with Carys. Sadly, the thrill of working it out for herself had entertained her more than making mundane conversation with bystanders who had taken it upon themselves to begin most conversations by confessing their part in a minor crime. Topping the lot was movie piracy, streaming being the least of her concerns: Wendy herself had either downloaded or acquired a fine collection of movies over the past few years.

A parent who had arrived late had been her first suspect. He wore a fine indigo blue jacket with jeans – his crisp white shirt had been unbuttoned twice. He seemed the type. She was being judgemental. He fancied himself; he'd sat for a while amongst a group of women before walking over to Carys. What he had said, to make her laugh unnecessarily loud, she was not sure. Then Catherine realised, Carys' laugh had been too indiscreet.

Yes, she knew this game. Carys had laughed for the benefit of another, someone within earshot. Someone unfamiliar to them all, it appeared. The man in the indigo suit was not interested after all; he had at least checked his watch on two occasions.

Armed with BBQ utensils, Gulliver had then joined Wendy at the kitchen sink; they laughed merrily themselves, satisfied by their children's talent, dominating the windowless frame, in cahoots together. Manon and Zita were *the kings of the castle* and everyone else were *the dirty rascals.*

Then the parent with the indigo-blue jacket stood up to welcome his partner; his excuses for having arrived an entire hour later than expected immediately forgiven by the small crowd that now succumbed to their infectious banter – exchanged glances signalled to the apprehensive that all was now forgiven. Catherine laughed to herself, her gaydar was seriously off.

Carys' actual love interest, if that was what it was, had been dismissed early on. He'd sat firmly by his wife for most of the afternoon. She'd firstly dismissed him on the basis of their matching wedding rings – their impressive golden width noticeable to all. To Catherine, they had appeared the most committed of all the couples. His pale pink shirt complimented her own blouse; but at different intervals she exchanged glances like a frightened rabbit – her left hand to her stomach – an obvious pregnancy being the second reason she had dismissed him in the first place.

Gulliver had been standing by Wendy's side when Catherine saw him leave his wife's. It was Carys' face that almost immediately gave him away. For a split moment in time, she looked resentfully his way as he moved in her direction – he was about to tentatively pass her, when she suddenly got up and walked away. In response, he halted momentarily and looked after her before heading to the downstairs toilet. He did not ask anyone for its whereabouts. Had he been there before? Surely not.

When his wife got up to head outdoors, Catherine followed. She could rely on Wendy to keep an eye on matters indoors. She'd check on Zita and remind her they'd be leaving soon. His wife couldn't have been more than a few months pregnant. Not much younger than Carys herself, she seemed so much slighter in many ways, frail even. She smiled back when Catherine approached her.

'And another one on the way? When's your due date?'

'May. End of May.'

'Congratulations. Is this your second?'

'A complete surprise! Our first, new to all this! None of these are mine. Needed the fresh air – still get nauseous from time to time.'

'Yes. It can take you by surprise, children. I'm Catherine. I work with Gulliver, Carys' husband.'

'Fleur. I'm Lewis' other half. I'm afraid I don't really know anyone here. Lewis works with Carys at St Patrick's. Guess I've got all this to come now. Goodness. Sorry. I'm really not feeling much better. Would you mind fetching me a glass of water?'

A minute or so later she had returned with the glass in hand. She thought of fetching Fleur's husband, an opportunity to meet but then she thought better of it. If Fleur collapsed, she'd be to blame. She was about to ask a passing grandparent to find Lewis when he appeared before them.

'There you are! Are you ok? Feeling any better?'

'Oh Lewis. This is Lewis. I'm afraid I'm not feeling any better. I'm sorry: I think we'd better head off home.'

Not long after the two said their goodbyes, Fleur had headed to the car whilst Lewis made his apologies at the door. There was something yuppified about them. Different. Strangely it seemed to unify them. Carys had noticed too. Her composed smile lacked grace although she looked radiant herself in comparison to Fleur, not a hair out of place, her pale blue dress accentuating her eyes – her face poised yet unfalteringly tense.

Gulliver's firm handshake and earnest smile assured Catherine that he knew nothing about something. Lewis smiled uneasily at him before he excused himself and quickly followed his wife; he apologised again to Carys, who in response thanked him in a clinical fashion for dropping by.

'They seem a nice couple. How do we know them?'

'Lewis is the deputy head at St Patrick's – fairly new, like me. Only started this last September.'

'New job. New baby. Their lives ahead of them. Before they know it, they'll be knee-deep in nappies and bottle-feeds. Don't envy them one bit. Glad our two are that bit older – don't fancy going through all that again.'

Catherine joined Carys at the front door after Gulliver had quickly shifted in the direction of the hallway, She admired her near-to-perfect nails that matched her painted smile. Gulliver excused himself: Brody had wet himself waiting for the toilet.

In unison, Lewis and Fleur half-waved before disappearing into a silver car. He looked much older than his partner; his greying features suited him – there was something quite composed and handsome about his whole demeanour. He had blue eyes, like Carys, like Gulliver. The front door closed firmly behind – the light fading as evening advanced.

'They seem nice. It's been a lovely party. I know Zita has had a wonderful time. Must get her home and bathed before bed - she'll sleep well tonight after all that exercise.'

'Thank you Catherine. I'm sorry: I meant to spend more time with you both tonight. Wendy's been cracking – a great help – and thank you for Manon's bicycle helmet.'

For a moment, Carys seemed to re-examine the closed door, the empty darkening street behind her. Her laughter had left her now; she looked empty, tired even. She kicked off her high shoes before she suddenly excused herself. Her eyes searched Catherine's for a moment. Did she want to ask her something?

'I'd better check on Brody and change these shoes. My feet are killing me! I'll be back down in a minute.'

***

It was almost lunchtime when Catherine and Gulliver headed out towards Crossens; come what may, they were determined to see the two sisters that day - a voluntary interview back at the station was preferable. For mid-January, the unusual warm climate had been welcomed in the hope that an early spring would follow.

Gulliver seemed pre-occupied; he hadn't said much since his arrival to the office that morning. Unintentionally, he had fallen asleep downstairs that evening after tidying up. Carys had done more than her fair share – by the time he was finished, it was almost midnight.

He'd both texted and rang Olivia, twice. She had not replied back. He had not heard from her since Saturday night. Saturday night. After his return home he'd slept soundly. Heavily. Despite this, he'd still woken up when Carys arrived – she'd been drinking. He couldn't recall how he knew but he was sure of it.

He was too tired to ask about her car. She'd returned in a taxi, he'd heard her say so, or had he? He glanced at the clock before he fell asleep again – almost 3 am. He thought he'd heard her giggle – a bright mobile light had bothered him before he fell into a deep slumber. It couldn't have been his – his lay face down in the bedside drawer. He later thought Olivia had texted back. But his mobile was on silent. *Cracking. Night night,* he heard Carys say.

'What's it like in Wales? Well the part you came from Gulliver? At this time of the year?'

'Much the same – although many say February is far worse than January. It's the mountains. Most land is over 150 metres. Maritime climate. Mostly cloud, wind and rain. You get used to it. You don't have any choice but to get used to it!'

'Zita and Manon got on like a house on fire didn't they?'

For a moment they both sat in silence before Gulliver nodded. Even he pondered on her unfortunate choice of words. They both laughed uneasily.

'You seem more quiet than usual. I imagine you're tired. Come September, when Zita turns eleven, we'll be sure to hold her party on a Saturday. Bet you're both exhausted?'

For a moment Gulliver paused before speaking. Had either Catherine or Wendy overheard him on his mobile? He'd left the house on a couple of occasions to ring Olivia – one of the messages had been quite lengthy – he'd told her he loved her. Why did he do that? Had he frightened her off?

'I'm sorry. I'm tired – we both were. We'd been out Saturday as well – Carys met with a work colleague and I with an old friend. You're right too. Sunday's a killer - with work and school the next day. Manon was

insistent on having her party on her actual birthday –
and we thought, being a Sunday, that guests were less
likely to overstay their welcome – well, leave late. That
sounds awful, but last year, Brody's fifth birthday, we
had children screaming until almost midnight whilst
the parents were having a whale of a time! It was a
good party though. Most of us ended up in the bouncy
castle – even my mum and dad!'

Catherine smiled. She had told herself that it was
none of her business. Still, she was curious as to which
work colleague Carys had met up with. Working in a
job like theirs, it was easy to miss the most obvious
signs, even when it was happening under your nose.

'Not far now. Let's approach the road from the
Preston Road end. We'll park by the factory and walk
up – approach the house from behind – we might be
able to look into their garden – see if their back door is
open beforehand.'

When Mrs Tanner opens the door, after only
knocking a couple of times, both Catherine and Gulliver
pause before re-presenting their badges. It was
obvious from her face that she has been crying. Where
was her sister, Mrs Lexton?

'Mrs Tanner, is that right? May we come in?'

36

THE TEMPERATURE IN the custody suit at Southport's station warmed and soothed Mrs Tanner's ageing body to no end. She was aching all over – all her muscles overstretched. She ached like she'd ran a full marathon. Or had participated in some unanticipated eccentric exercise. In particular, her right shoulder blade bothered her the most – understandable, she'd hammered poor, innocent Mr Stone to death.

Then, she'd scrubbed the bloody carpet before she scrubbed the flaming walls with the weeping bloody willows – a fine mess she made of that - before she scrubbed the bloody carpet again and the wooden flaming door. She scrubbed the broken window seat, as best she could. And the white window ledge. The neighbours seemed to be watching. And the dirty skirting boards. She removed the corduroy covers from the purple settee. The nightmare just getting worse. The silver clock ticking louder than usual. Time's up. Time's up.

A sharp pain bothered her just below her neck too. Muscle strain probably. Possibly nerve damage. How extraordinary it was to feel so very comforted by a little heat. Her head ached. Her chest ached. Her heart ached. Consoling, the heat - if that was the right word - to know her frail sister had passed away, so peacefully, in her sleep. To know her suffering was over. Would have celebrated her sixty-eighth birthday on the seventh of March. In turn, she herself would turn seventy this October. She could now face what was ahead of her. Despite being totally on her own, for the first time in her life.

Mrs Tanner left a right mess behind for them to clear up. She could have saved herself all that scrubbing, Had she known. In the end, opening the front door was the answer to all of her prayers and problems. A breath of fresh air. Come in. A welcomed relief. Take a look. Help yourself. I'm done. I'm exhausted. The look on the officers' faces. Mrs Tanner felt sorry for them. Everything looks so different when you see someone else's reaction. The red-head, Sergeant Pope, had taken the key from her as she pulled it out from her red pinafore pocket. She handed it to him.

'THEY'RE IN THERE.'

The other, the Inspector, something Shakespeare, took turns between staring after Pope and the two bodies, now laying neatly side by side. She now wished she'd washed Mr Stone's face – his white hair and beard thick with dark red blood and bits. It wasn't right that she hadn't cleaned him up. She was about to open the back door, when she heard detective Pope call after her. Mrs Tanner took the Inspector's arm half-way.

Although her eyes were hard, they didn't lack compassion – she could see that.

'MY SISTER'S UPSTAIRS. DEAD. SHE PASSED AWAY LATE MORNING. IN HER SLEEP. SHE MUST BE BURIED WITH OUR PARENTS. I'VE SAID MY GOODBYES. SHE PLAYED NO PART IN ALL OF THIS.'

There is a clock on the wall in the custody suite. The time is twenty-one minutes past three. The walls are blue – the type of blue that some might associate with peace and calm. Mrs Tanner feels calm. Even though she's had two cups of tea without any gin – just sugar. It's not until now she realises how much the gin helped. She wants to sleep. She feels very tired now. Her neck is bothering more than her shoulder.

Earlier, a different officer took her details and wrote them down. It was explained that a forensic officer was on his way – they would have to retain all of her clothes. Even her underwear. She felt embarrassed then. She wasn't sure when she'd washed last. Hours had merged into days, over the last few weeks – she knew she had but wasn't sure when.

She thought then about her underwear. Cringed at the thought. Her mother was right – important to always wear clean. Her personal items would be kept in a safe place. Returned to her at the appropriate time. Mrs Tanner hasn't any personal items on her: she left her pipe at home. She's never had a mobile. She's never wanted one. *They're complicated, heavy and make too much noise.* She does have a number of overused tissues in her pocket though. *That's all.* They're welcome to them.

There's some equipment on the table that she leans on from time to time. Especially when her neck hurts. She lowers her head. The officer watching her asks if she's okay. She means well. Earlier, the detectives, Inspector Shakespeare and Sergeant Pope, pressed a button on the fancy equipment – a gadget like a bigger mobile phone, but on its side. They elucidated to the fact that she was allowed a solicitor. *No thank you.*

It was odd – she'd hardly touched it. Not a sound. Just a tiny red light. Technology these days. Not a big tape that has a button that you press down on and it makes a clunking sound - obvious when something is being recorded. Like in the movies. Or TV. In the seventies, she loved the detective series *Quincy*. Fancied him a bit too. Even though he was old. And a bit round. Her sister Jo was into *Charlie's Angels*. Jo was Sabrina Duncan. Boring but clever. She was Jill Munroe. Clever and sexy.

Poor Mr Stone. For a moment Mrs Tanner wonders if the *Southport Visitor* will post pictures of her sister and herself on the front page. She hopes not, but deep down she knows they will. She's glad their parents aren't around to see what's become of them both. Sisters who became sisters who became abused wives, and motherless women, who then became killers. If that's what they've become.

Although not Jo. They needn't pin a thing on her. It was all *her* own doing. Which explains her sister's reaction the first time the detectives came to the house. She had no idea Mr Tanner had been killed. Her sister Jo thought he'd died of a heart attack. So she never knew anything. She'd lied to her own sister. See. Until recently, of course. The shock. She died in the end of a heart-attack, in her sleep. You have to kill three times to become a serial killer.

So far, she's confessed to killing both Mr Tanner, Mr Lexton and Mr Stone. But she's not really a serial killer. Well, she sort of is, but she's not.

No-one will remember her for being a nurse, or a sister, or a daughter; she'll be known for being the serial killer who lived next door to a father who murdered his own daughter, Mara, who was fifteen and had tried to kill herself. Left to die in the bird-shed. She's glad her sister died today. When she did.

She took her sister on a day out many moons ago. They took the train to Bingley in North Yorkshire. It was 1978. They never forgot that. She was thirty at the time. Jo needed a day out – as did she. Jo was on sick leave. It was not long after Christmas. The useless cunt was seeing someone. Her bastard husband had drank too much in the New Year. One bash follows another. What a nightmare that was for both of them. Getting through Christmas. The season of goodwill. Everyone else with a smile on their face whilst she was nursing a black eye and her sister struggling with depression again. They went out for the day, last day in January.

At the time they didn't know of course, what had happened - that day – not that far away, in Huddersfield. They'd even joked about it on the train. What a miserable life they'd had. All they needed, heading into Yorkshire, was to come across the Ripper. That'd be their luck. And they'd laughed. With depression and a black eye. They didn't hate their husbands then. They didn't love them either.

Helen Rytka. A girl. An eighteen year old prostitute and a twin. Didn't matter she was a prostitute. Her age helped. The media saw her as a girl. Her life ahead of her. They said prostitute – the papers – but the world saw her for what she was. His eighth victim. Somebody's daughter. Rita Rytka's twin. Hammered in a wood yard. Her life ahead of her. Hammered by an animal. Not by someone who'd snapped after thirty-nine years of domestic abuse.

Now *he* really was a serial killer. She forgets his name. He was *The Yorkshire Killer*. Not as glamorous as *Jack the Ripper*. And on that day, when they went to Bingley, in Yorkshire, he'd killed a young woman, a bit of a girl, a sister out working with her twin, trying to get by, whilst they strode along cheering themselves up, thinking the world had been placed heavily and unfairly on their small shoulders. Shit parents.

Jo said days later she felt guilty that they'd been having such a good time whilst the poor girl was hammered and then knifed to death. Jo cried. She always thought of others. Saw the good in everyone – even in the useless cunt of her husband.

Their parents once took them to Bingley market as teenagers. Neither could remember much about that day – except that it was a great day - sunny. They'd eaten cakes. No scones. Maybe lunch too, but they'd had scones in a black and white cottage-like house. A tea room. And they'd walked, afterwards. For ages. It had been a fine warm day. They hadn't enjoyed the long walk, even though it was by a canal. All they could see was more canal and more walking. They didn't understand then - that every step taken, every golden moment together, was precious. And temporary.

But they'd loved the market. Dad had bought sweets for them. Mum bought lots of stuff too – she couldn't remember what. But she remembers her mother smiling like the war was over – and their father kissing her – on the mouth – and how they didn't like that – and tried to stop them – and how they'd all laughed.

That afternoon, before she died, Jo had asked if she remembered Bingley. *With mum and dad. And the tea rooms. And the market. And the walk by the river. How we screamed and jumped up and down when dad kissed mum. It was a canal. Oh. It was boring. It was. Mum and dad held hands. They did. We held hands too. We did. I love you Babs. I love you Jo.*

They'd walked past mums holding their children's hands. Jo didn't say it. *Billy would have been ten this summer.* They were sisters when others were mums.

Mrs Tanner had taken her sister's hand and looped it into her own. *There, there, there. Do you remember how you dropped your ice-cream when we came with mum and dad? You licked it and off it went. What is it with you, always letting the ball of the ice-cream roll off your cone? Or dropping your popcorn in the cinema? You're always the one to drop your popcorn on the floor. And it's always almost full!*

And they laughed then. They walked laughing, looped, arm in arm heading towards a tea shop that looked like the one their parents took them to once upon a fabulous time. They couldn't say for sure - and Bingley's not a big place. There's lots of tea-shops, and on the same street. But the one on the corner, thatched it was, black and white, with the big front window and the structure to the side, yes, it looked like the one. And when they entered, they smiled. It was. They *saw* mum and dad sitting there. Kissing again. *Was it there? It was.*

They caught him in 1981. Three years later. *The Yorkshire Ripper.* A monster with no face. A cold-blooded murderer. It was appalling. It was exciting. Then they said he was called Peter Sutcliffe. He had family. Brothers and sisters. And a mother and father like them. And a wife. A bloody wife. What's that all about?

Thirteen victims they said, or more. Off to Broadmoor. For the mentally insane. He'd hammered her, then knifed her, gone home and put the hammer back with the others and the knife back in the drawer. Sunday dinner didn't bear thinking about.

He had the voice of God in his head – God had sent him to rid the world of prostitutes. Even though he was a regular user himself, of prostitutes. Of sex workers. Even though he had a wife. And was a father.

Huddersfield is five miles from Bingley. Not all of the women were prostitutes. It said it in the papers months later, And he was born in Bingley. Of all the towns in Yorkshire.

No tourist sign says so, of course. Had they even passed any of his relatives in the street on that day he played away? It didn't bear thinking about.

37

GULLIVER HELD THE door open without looking behind. A newly-qualified officer hoping to impress him had passed and thanked him; he neither noticed nor acknowledged him. He ran his left hand through his coarse rusty hair; he still hadn't heard from Olivia. And Carys had refused to talk to him that morning.

She'd been quiet since she'd awoken. He only asked after her. The look she gave him seemed to suggest something else, something deeper, a revelation of pain or frustration – something unexpected. Did she know? For a while he looked after her, the children waving enthusiastically from the back seat of their car. On their way to school. Was she onto him?

Of course, he was also concerned with the transformation that had taken place before his eyes. He'd lost sight of it all – had no idea when it began. Had she lost weight to impress someone or was she working too hard, even ill? Sadly, there was a case for all arguments. What was he doing? It was his own fear taking hold – guilt – paranoia. Carys was probably angry over something trivial, spilt milk. They'd talk tonight. They were both overtired from the previous night – and the night before that. He never did find out where Carys had been. He hadn't asked afterwards about her evening. He'd neglected her. His mind elsewhere. Guilt. Olivia. Why hadn't she replied?

When he arrived at the custody suite, the one holding Mrs Tanner, he noticed Sergeant Ludwig at his desk looking though Mrs Tanners arrest file, an empty *MR ROBOT* mug in his left hand. Did that mean something?

'Well, she neither wants legal advice nor anyone contacting. From what it says here, she has no living relatives.'

'She won't make bail. Seems harmless enough. Compliant. Probably relieved to get it all off her chest. But she's strong. Hammered an innocent man to death less than twenty-four hours ago. She's strong for a woman of her age. '

'Seventy October. Did Sergeant Cunliffe manage to get hold of the victim's wife?'

'Not yet. Mrs Stone is apparently staying with her mother – none of the neighbours can tell us where. Charlotte and Luke are at their house now looking for an address. Three deaths in a row now on North Road alone.'

'Unlucky cul-de-sac I say.'

'She's admitted to killing all three of them then?'

'All three. A victim of domestic violence – years of it. She hammered her husband to death. Battered her brother-in-law to a pulp with an iron because he was leaving and cheating on her sister – bad temper – but I just don't know. And Mr Stone, our very own marplot, and just because he spotted Mr Lexton at the back of the room. She only regretted killing Mr Stone – *he'd been the best of neighbours*.'

'So the sisters weren't in it together then?'

'Who knows? There's no evidence to show otherwise. Mrs Lexton most definitely reacted as though she had no idea about Mr Tanner's death – like her sister had hidden it from her. But I do wonder. About Mr Lexton.'

'I heard one of their husbands had been buried in their window box for years!'

'Ten years Floki. Ten years. Apparently they got the idea from a play they'd read. A play lent to them by Mr Stone of all people.'

'I've heard it all now Sergeant.'

'*Arsenic and Old Lace*. That's the one. Catherine Shakespeare knew all about it. The sisters in that story eventually moved the body to the cellar! And before you ask – there's no cellar at their house!'

Sergeant Floki Ludwig seemed pensive. He'd been a long-standing officer with Merseyside Police since he'd joined almost forty years ago; he had a jocular personality – had rarely been seen looking so unhappy. From the look on his leonine face, it appeared he felt sorry for his latest detainee.

He tutted. He'd searched for some understanding of the whole situation. Found little. Some extenuating circumstances maybe – his father had given his mother and him a dog's life. Nursing his beard single-handedly for hours since her arrest hadn't offered him any of the answers. It wouldn't be long until she would appear in a magistrate's court and spend the rest of her life in prison.

'She's been photographed, fingerprinted and processed; we've taken a sample of her DNA too – over to you Detective Pope. Inspector Shakespeare about?'

'On her way. She's picking up the initial post-mortem report from Mansell. Toxicology report should follow soon after. How long did they say for the DNA match?'

'Possibly later today. The duty solicitor is on her way. She's a candidate for New Hall Women's Prison don't you think?'

For a moment Gulliver rattled his brain. Unfamiliar with most English prisons, he could not call to mind this one. In Wales you were either sent to Usk, Cardiff, Parc or Berwyn. Scotland had its own women's prison, he knew that, England had at least ten but in Wales there were none. They were kept in units or held within men's prisons – suited most families, although there'd been investigations in the last few years over the handling of gender specific issues. Staffing shortage hadn't helped.

'Sorry. You're probably not familiar. It's in West Yorkshire - for the older kind. Nice one if you can call it that. One of the better prisons in Yorkshire.'

Gulliver's mobile rang then. For a moment he stared at the screen, then swiped right. He nodded in Floki's direction before heading off. Moving in the opposite direction. He chose an empty custody suite before speaking. It had been almost forty-eight hours since he'd last heard from Olivia.

'Hi. I've been trying to reach you. Are you ok?'

'I am. I'm sorry. Had a lot on my plate. I'm sorry Gulliver.'

For a moment Gulliver's mood dipped. Her voice had a tone to it that immediately concerned him. Impending doom. It was probably for the best, but he still didn't want their relationship to end. He'd been preparing for the worst all day Sunday. He'd kept busy fortunately. With the party. Overthinking. Carys had even picked up on it. He hoped.

'Gulliver, are you there?'

'Yes. I am.'

'I love you Gulliver. I've thought of nothing else since Saturday – since you said you loved me.'

Gulliver felt immediately uncomfortable. There was a long uneasy pause. He could hear her intake of breath – laborious at times – like she was searching for something invisible. Why did he say he loved her? He wasn't entirely sure that he did.

'I have asked for a separation - from Claude. I needed the time to think – make sure I was doing the right thing. Acting in my best interest. I didn't want to do it, tell you, and put you under any pressure – I had to decide on my own. Be sure this was what I wanted.'

There was no two ways about it. Gulliver suddenly realised what her last words had imparted. And although a part of him did not jolt like a horse, he felt more than just a pang of fear – even panic. He was lost for words. He wasn't entirely sure he was understanding her.

'Olivia. What do you mean?'

'I've asked Claude for a separation. We are still working out the logistics. Sounds strange, hearing it said out loud. In time, a divorce. Gulliver, I no longer love him. I don't think I ever did. I love you.

Since the summer – and your move to England, I haven't been able to – get over losing you – I thought I would in time. Move on. But I couldn't. I feel – altered – changed. Everything's changed – and so quickly.'

And for some strange reason, her final words, they made him immediately think of Carys. And the children. Manon and Brody. And for some strange reason his parents.

Fear and panic intermingled with dread returned – stronger than ever. He had been compliant in all of it, yet here he was, about to lose all control. And for what? He was not sure. What did she want from him? Was Olivia indirectly asking him to leave Carys. What did *he* want? Whom did he love? He loved them both. Didn't he? He couldn't explain, not even to himself -the unforeseen and sudden emotional reversal punching him in the ribs. Panic. He loved Carys. Of course. He couldn't leave the children. Could he? He wouldn't.

He pictured Brody then – he still wasn't toilet trained. He pictured Manon – blowing her ten candles out on her cake. Her face. Carys. She was smiling. He pictured Carys. He'd break her heart. He'd break all their hearts.

'Gulliver – we should talk – meet up. I know you haven't asked for this. It's my choice. I have been with Claude for many years. He knows me well; he has known there was something wrong since summer. Has asked me about it. I haven't told you this: I didn't want to frighten you away. And we'd gone our separate ways. But I'm not the sort of person who is comfortable with lying, cheating – I've never been unfaithful in my life!'

And then Gulliver knew what she was about to say. She had of course confirmed her husband's suspicions that there was someone else. Had she told him his first name? His occupation? Would he come looking for him? Probably not. Maybe. Would he turn up to the station? He didn't feel he loved her then. Did he love her? He wasn't sure he cared – or that he wanted to talk to her any longer. How strange? How odd that feelings resembling both love and hate can so quickly interchange like two sides of the same coin.

And he saw the children again, this time in the family portrait that had presented them as a unit to the world – a portrait that stood framed on a side table in their bright and sunny lemon lounge – a room they had decorated together, all four of them. He'd complained to Carys at the time, because of the cost. He hadn't picked up that portrait in ages. Maybe not even before they had moved. Since they had lived in Wales, before Olivia came along.

He'd forgotten its significance - laid it mentally aside. And he knew he was blaming Olivia, somehow, more than himself perhaps, when in fact, he was very much to blame. She was a fantasy, a desire, he thought, unsure of himself. Yet, he couldn't deny it, he'd played the lead in this relationship. The drama his end was about to begin. The metaphor of *shit hitting the fan* came suddenly to mind.

He thought of Carys. He used to see her, back in Wales, proudly dusting their family portrait from time to time. A wide smile on her face. A moment captured for the world to see. This is my family. I love this family. This is us. United. In love.

Had she stopped looking at it? Had she lost interest in him too? Fallen out of love? Her stilettoes. Her nail varnish and lip colour. Her aloofness. His fear and guilt. Was he losing her? Did she know of his affair? Would he abandon her? Was she simply adapting to change and a new set of friends? Who were her friends? Suddenly he knew, when he got a chance, he'd check her mobile phone. He knew he would.

'Say something Gulliver. Can you find time to meet up? Later or tomorrow? It's important. I have something else to tell you.'

'Detective Inspector Pope?'

Behind him at the door of the empty custody suite, Sergeant Ludwig held an invisible mobile in his hand.

'A call for you. I have your wife on the line.'

38

ON SATURDAY THE third of June, Mary Elisabeth Rimmer wore, to her parent's horror and to her groom's delight, a bright red pair of Mary-Jane shoes. It was her wedding day. Her mother had begged her over and over again not to do so – her reputation – the shame. Had the vicar spotted them on her feet, he would have most definitely forbidden the ceremony. Fortunately, her virgin-white silk dress covered her small feet for most of the day – it was an entirely different matter later that evening.

Two years earlier, September 1948, William Bond, or as he was affectionally known to his mother, Billy Bond, then aged twenty-six, courted Miss Rimmer, aged twenty, for the very first time. They'd first met on Southport's busiest of roads: Lord Street. Not too far from where the Winter Gardens showcased Southport's very own Opera House.

Almost half a century later it would become the Mecca Bingo Hall – inconceivable at the time – preposterous to consider – yet it still went ahead, change as reliable as death itself. It is only when one looks beyond and above the garish and offensive multicoloured blue sign that the remnants of the divine edifice reappear. With the three windows to the centre, and what a shape they were, elongated like candles, it is only then that the observer can be reminded of the past and all that was truly golden in the 50s.

And nearby, not too far from where they would meet for the first time, by the nostalgic and robust lantern-slide-boulevard, in its Parisian fashion, stood a lean paper boy in a thick brown jacket and cap selling the *Southport Visitor,* the Town Hall behind him. Soon after, when the rain fell more heavily, he crossed the road, narrowly avoiding an expanding thick puddle, in order to shelter below the glass terraces of *The Scarisbrick Hotel* – built on the site of the former Scarisbrick Arms. Above the double entrance doors its inscription still physically evident: 1881 – one of the few untouched landmarks from way, way back then.

There had been a great deal of flooding that summer; elegant cars waded their heaving curves slowly through the water – the rain relentless. A newish matt-black MG four-door saloon refused to budge from where it was parked, the driver visibly exasperated, whilst a Morris eight series, of a similar shade, fortuitously manoeuvred its way past – the sole female passenger showing profound relief at their departure from the whole desperate situation.

To everyone, it seemed as though the torrent would never end. Rainwear House, of all the bespoke shops on Lord Street, had failed to expel the rainwater that had flooded the bottom floor! Gasps of horror and sympathetic expressions of regret invaded the bitter air that now raided the stores along the busy Boulevard.

For some, a difficult decision needed to be made – ladies rubbed their gloved hands together and fixed their hats in place. Should they risk the downpour and the bitter cold or remain indoors? Should they leap out of the frying pan and into the fire? Their husbands looked on helpless – they shrugged their shoulders in unison whilst their wives frowned angrily at them.

The ongoing London Olympic Games, or as it was then known, *The Austerity Games,* had a pronounced influence on women at the time. Cinema icons like Elizabeth Taylor, Lauren Bacall and Marilyn Monroe, were mostly responsible for the sudden interest in the latest Parisian fashion. The recent war over, unsatisfied independent womenfolk parted with their hard-earned cash, procuring outfits with full skirts mid-calf lengths, fitted jackets with nipped-in waists and bold shoulders.

Neat hats resembled the Hattie-Carnegie on the front cover of *Vogue*. This appeased their collective regret at not having indulged in an off-the-shoulder dress first modelled at London's *Dorchester Hotel* earlier on in the year. The shopfronts on Lord Street had all this and more on offer for the new season. The new season's collection should have sold out, had it not been for the weather.

Billy Bond had come to Mary Rimmer's rescue. Like a knight in shining armour, he was suddenly there; he literally scooped her up and carried her across the road. Right time. Right place. Right face. Picked her up in his arms, like some scene from a black and white movie. It was raining - but she'd been rescued by a fine-looking chap in a matching tweed cap and jacket. And a lovely face it was.

He had marvellous blue eyes too. Pale blue. And large hands. She could tell by the span of them on her back. The way he held her confused her. Strong too. She knew he wasn't going to drop her. He was gallant. He was too forward. For a long while, after their initial meeting, she was disturbed by thoughts that revisited her nightly and aroused and awoke her impulses as was yet to be explored beyond her limited imagination.

She'd been trying to cross the road for almost ten minutes. He'd been watching her. Said later that it was her light blonde hair that caught his attention. Her hat had shielded her face at first. It suddenly seemed important to see her face. A conclusion of many sorts. No rhyme or reason. Just an irresistible urge. An itch to scratch possibly.

And although the sky was grey, a scathing light fell upon the back of it, in a peculiar manner – possibly a waterfall of some sort; he was not entirely sure what it was that caught his eye. He continued to observe her at a distance. Became amused by her efforts to cross. She was right-handed; he knew that. Her leg and hand had

SISTERS

come forward whilst her body resisted the impulse to jump forward told him so. Go for it.

Her thick navy-blue coat, wrapped about her tightly resisted any further energetic outbursts - her movement restricted. Her hands gloved. He wanted to catch sight of her hands. Was she married? He hoped not. He thought he'd follow her first, to see if she would be met by anyone. He knew it then and there; he needed to find an opportunity to talk to her. For a moment, he questioned his own sensibility.

In total, he'd watched her for fifteen or so minutes. As each minute passed, he learned or noticed something different about her. How dainty she was from where he stood, not twenty or so metres away. He liked her ensemble, not too glamorous but elegant. His mother would like her. He liked her facial expressions. He was amused by them. Frustration once turned to laughter. In her laughter he saw something he wanted to engage with. She was both charming and amusing.

Surrounding her, were many others alike in their distress – all along Lord Street, men, women and couples struggling with their indecision to cross, like runners bolting ahead of gunfire, back and forth like waves. There were those crossing regardless of the consequences – many of these had children. Those who began to cross but then turned back. Those who did nothing but seal themselves with anxiety. Very few waited patiently. And it was now raining more than ever. And there Billy Bond stood. Motionless.

Inspecting her from afar, under a shoe shop's veranda. The commotion surrounding him like a comical farce.

He'd asked her to the cinema that very afternoon. Introduced himself. She'd refused of course. She hadn't wanted to. She was still blushing from his confident grip. His careful hands. He'd somehow awoken something in her, possibly an unknown desire caged within. Then he apologised. He saw she was offended – embarrassed. She apologised. How childish of her to expose herself – such a lack of discipline and control. She then laughed. He did so himself. She could neither control the urge to run away or overstay. She was still blushing when he apologised again. *What for?* She heard herself say.

On their first date they went to Southport's *Picture Drome* on Lord Street, opposite end and opposite side of the road. There were thirteen cinemas at the time to choose from – even one in Ainsdale called *The Plaza*. Had they known that they lived fairly close by to one another, they could have visited *The Savoy* in Churchtown.

He didn't live too far from where she did. She'd passed his house on Cider Drive many times. Had never laid eyes on him though. Set unusually far back from the unobtrusive street, the elongated front lawn was at least one-hundred feet – a path to its left running alongside the next-door neighbour's fence. The front door was a sage green then, like the side gate that led to the allotments in the back. Lived with his parents – an only child.

She'd stopped and admired their busy garden on occasion; there was an impressive patch of asparagus to the middle of it. Everyone knew the house with the asparagus plot – had she paid more attention, she might have met him sooner. She might have had him for longer too. Their two girls, Babs and Jo, eventually missing out on them both.

The asparagus patch was smaller then. Only three mouths to feed. His parents ate so very little. They were kind to her, like Billy, kinder than her own parents had been. Billy's father used to say that growing asparagus was a labour of love.

When Billy Bond turned up on her doorstep, to pick her up, he did not expect her to be literally wearing a pair of bright red shoes for their first date. He thought he loved her already for it, although he thought he might feel a tad embarrassed to be seen with her. Neither of her parents came to the front door. It was a relief in more ways than one. He'd guessed from the little she had said that she was younger than him – how much younger, he did not wish to enquire.

Her father resisted the temptation to rise, sat in his armchair smoking his pipe, unengaged physically, mentally taking it all in. Mary's twin, Margaret, had already been taken from them, not long after birth. He'd prepared himself for what was to come. When he learned that the young man lived nearby, he felt some relief. What he was relieved about, he could not be sure. Maybe it was because he'd know where to find him, her mother had said.

What's his job?

Don't know – I didn't think to ask. He dresses well. Lives on Cider Road – the house with the asparagus to the front.

Oh. I like asparagus.

The cinema was packed. There wasn't an empty seat around. It was wise of Billy to buy the tickets ahead. At first they both looked about before they spotted their allocated seating. *Excuse me. Excuse me. Excuse me.* They sat somewhere in the middle. It was a relief to them both not to be sitting towards the back.

Mary Rimmer had wrapped up warm. Worn the full-skirted and belted pea-green dress that she had purchased on the day she had been rescued by Billy Bond. She was still cold in the cinema, yet she undid her coat enough to let him see. Her curled hair looked magnificent, showcased in such a fashion; it fell beautifully onto either side of her newly-acquired dress. He smiled approvingly, although he made very little conversation. This did not matter to her: she wasn't one for conversation either. She learned though that he worked for a large bank. Had a clerk's post at Martins main branch on Lord Street – on the counter. He'd been with them since he had left school. Mary Rimmer smiled. Her father and mother would be pleased.

On the bus, on the way to the cinema, she had crossed her ankles several times. She was regretting having worn such ridiculous footwear for the sake of frivolity, wistfulness and adventure. Yet, when she arrived, she spotted another girl wearing a similar pair to hers. They knowingly admired one another. A relief of some sort. They raised their noses in triumph.

An older usher showing them through the first set of doors complimented her footwear whilst another opposite clearly thought them to be vulgar. His face said so. For a moment, she almost linked Billy's arm.

But Billy Bond was proud. Nothing about Mary Rimmer was vulgar or eccentric - she was kind, gentle and spirited. This he knew then. She was full of life and traditional ambition.

In later life, he soon learned that she was also hard-working and very organised. Yet he noticed at times a frailty he could not comment on, not even to himself. A slither of nervousness that was only exposed in her laughter. A nervousness that she was able to control for most of their lives together – at least whilst he was physically there to protect and support her. Something that he recognised in their youngest child.

This was unfortunately a nervousness that up-reared like septicaemia after he died – her mind rather than her blood corrupted by negativity and grief. They had teenage daughters then, Babs and Jo, eighteen months apart. He had bowel cancer, and would not survive beyond a couple of months. The grim reaper took him sooner. Sooner than they had expected. Sooner than the doctors had promised. There weren't any final goodbyes.

Mary Rimmer knew before they were even to be married, that she would execute the curse that so many before her had chanted both insincerely, although with affection, that she could not live without her husband by her side. Although she tried. For the girls. She tried. They forgave her because they truly loved her. Their father would have wanted them to. And so they did. And they lived on. As best they could.

The Red Shoes was the top-selling film in 1948. The movie poster itself had raised a few eyebrows, both by the men and womenfolk. In it, the elongated image of an attractive dancer in a black leotard, bare legs and long-flowing blonde hair, looked innocently sideways whilst the print to her right informed interested audiences that *Dance she did and dance she must – between her two loves.*

If one considered the female form, about two-thirds of her figure belonged to the bottom half below her waist. Desirable yet naïve. She was, of course, wearing red ballet shoes – her entire body weight supported on the tips of fully extended feet *en pointe.*

Being innocent of the film's purpose and plot, Mary Rimmer had been waiting for an opportunity to see the film, ever since she had seen the poster. Hans Christian Andersen's childhood tale of the same name, had since her youth fascinated her, that and the story of *The*

Little Matchgirl. Billy Bond found, not long after the film had begun, that the story was not to his taste, but that did not matter: he was delighted to please his shy admirer, happy to be her escort for the evening. Stupidly happy to be her escort ever after.

The lead character, a dancer by the name of Vicky, inevitably and predictably fell in love with her fetching co-dancer Julian; of course, the musical director Lermontov was also in love with her. Infatuated. Unable to control his jealousy, he fired Julian, and in turn Vicky abandoned the theatre and her love for dance and the ballet.

Already Mary Rimmer was feeling uneasy, the unexpected rising tension in the plot confusing her expectations. She herself knew not of a character by that name. What sort of name was that for a ballet dancer?

She knew of Karen, the spoiled girl who had complained to her good mother, who had adopted her by all accounts after she was orphaned, of her rough red shoes, insisting she should be bought a new, more expensive pair – a pair fit for a princess. One day, Karen disobeyed her mother by wearing her red shoes for church. It was then that a soldier with a red beard placed a magic spell on them, by touching each one in turn.

On the occasion when Karen left her mother ill at home, in favour for dancing in her red shoes at a grand ball, her shoes took control, rejecting her pleas for her to stop dancing. Desperate, Karen requests an axed executioner to chop off her feet: even after they have been amputated, they continue to dance! The executioner provides her with wooden feet and crutches; she returns to her church changed and repentant. Eventually, when she dies, her soul goes to Heaven.

Mary Rimmer's mother read the story to her from a book she herself had as a child. In those days, it was quite common to find such gruesome stories; the penurious *Little Matchgirl* living in fear of returning home to her mother, having sold no matches. In the end she died. Frozen to death. Why were women and girls so very often presented in such a miserable light?

Yet despite the common nature of stories at the time, Mary Rimmer, who blenched for years when her mother reread the tale over and over again at her request never really understood her fascination with such stories. As a mother, much later in life, she altered certain details in the story. Her girls clung to one another spellbound, whilst their father warmly looked on. Every shadow at night was a villain. Or an evil step-mother.

Still, the character of Vicky, in the movie version, seemed to be far more gracious. Well, that was until she was torn between the desire to dance and the love for her husband, Julian. *Really?* Mary Rimmer felt a tad embarrassed. How childish she had been to expect anything other from a film such as this? She sensed her date was not enjoying the film. She could see him from the side, despite appearing to look right ahead at the screen. Then she glanced momentarily; she sensed he had seen her. He smiled at her as she turned back.

In truth, she doubted there and then that anything would ever come between her growing affection for Billy Bond and anything else in life. It would be three weeks from their first date until he would pluck up the courage to hold her hand. This time, they watched a movie of his choice: *Red River* starring John Wayne. And so their love of Western films began.

To Mary Rimmer's satisfaction the plot took an unexpected turn. Vicky chose to dance at the ballet, choosing to reject both her husband and Julian. In the belief that he had lost her for good, Julian headed for the train station. Suddenly, at the ballet, the red shoes took hold of Vicky and led her, against her will, out of the theatre and towards the train station. The horror-struck audience looked upon the final scene from the theatre stalls, aghast. The end seemed inconceivable yet predictable. Cinema onlookers prepared for the worst; the music suggested it – *Swan Lake* playing its final overture. In it Odette had been resigned to death following Siegfried's betrayal.

About to embark the train, Julian becomes aware of his wife, then dancing above the platform on a bridge. Alas, she gracefully leaps from above, onto the path of an oncoming train. Her death is prolonged – the music enthralling – then Julian removes her red ballet shoes and she dies.

To her mother's relief, and on her wedding day, there was no soldier waiting for her with a red beard at the church. Instead, Billy Bond patiently awaited her arrival, by the altar, proud as Punch, his eyes fixed upon the woman he loved and was forever to remain by his side. *Till death do us part.*

39

THE TRILL OF the office phone had irritated Sergeant Ludwig on the spot. He'd almost completed his crossword. It sounded like a hysterical bird. He took a deep breath before he prudently took the receiver and answered it.

Gulliver had been standing in the empty custody on his mobile when the Sergeant interrupted him. He couldn't think straight. He couldn't think at all.

'I'll have to call you back Olivia.'

He didn't wait for a reply. He should have. He should have apologised. He should have said more – maybe added a more concrete indicator as to when he would call her back. Added that he would meet her, of course he would. He hadn't meant to be rude; he simply wasn't prepared to commit himself to anything when he couldn't think straight – certainly not there and then. For God's sake, he had Carys on the other line.

He wished Carys had called his mobile. On top of everything else, he had no alternative as to where he could have a conversation, having to stay put by the custody desk, within Ludwig's earshot. Afraid that the tone of his voice would betray him, Gulliver opted to say very little, instead adopting the appropriate tone expected from a husband who is dedicated to his wife and family. A responsible adult – not an adulterer.

'Carys? Is everything okay?'

'Sorry. I tried your mobile. It was engaged. I don't have long: it's my lunch break.'

For a moment he thought he should explain himself but then Floki would know he had lied. He nodded several times. He didn't mean anything by it. Just that he was the sort of husband who listened. There was nothing to be alarmed about. He avoided her question. He knew that she was in a hurry. He then laughed, smiled. At nothing. How ugly he'd become. A two-headed serpent.

His father once told him a mythological story about such a serpent; he loved that story. The two heads were constantly clashing with one another. In the end, the serpent brought about its own self-destruction – both heads continuously at odds. One head, he couldn't quite remember how, ate the other. Problem solved.

'What time will you be home tonight? I wanted to apologise – about this morning. I can't explain on the phone Gull. You're right, of course. We should talk.'

'Of course. I'll be home about tea-time.'

He wanted to say more. He really did. Ludwig smiled as he handed him the receiver. He should have said something else, but chose not to. If his words hadn't given something away, his face must have, for Gulliver Pope looked like a man who had the weight of the world on both his shoulders. He had no choice but to meet both Olivia and Carys. He would hopefully escape early, after Ashanti Akintola's interview. He'd leave to meet Olivia. Nowhere near where she lived. He didn't want her husband to see them together. Think they were serious about each other.

How stupid he had been. How selfish and crude it all seemed to him now. Why did she move the goal post and confess their relationship? It certainly had never crossed *his* mind?

***

They had both met at a café that had recently converted part of its coffee grinding room into a seating area. The aroma, as he entered, from the largest of roasters within view, comforted him. How different he felt now, searching amongst the seated customers for Olivia. No longing. Just anxiety. And doubt. And regret.

Olivia smiled from where she sat in a corner, at the window. He resented her. Why? He had been a willing participant all along. In return he waved – raised a smile: she looked worried. He felt stupid doing so. Waving. Smiling. Instinctively, he looked about – was there anyone about he recognised?

'Hi Olivia. Thank you for meeting me here: I know it's out of your way. But I have to get home early.'

He was going to say more. He didn't want to. He didn't have to explain himself. Not to Olivia. He couldn't explain why he felt to angry. Guarded. He was angry at himself. Angry with Olivia. Olivia sensed it; he saw it in her face. She looked down at her hands; her smile disappeared. He hadn't meant to offend her. Again.

'Iron Men.'

'Sorry?'

'The Coffee I'm drinking. It's lovely. That's the owner. Jack. He started out in his mother's kitchen, just around the corner - 2014 – look at him now.'

Gulliver was grateful for the small talk. He requested the same coffee before apologising for his behaviour.

'I'm sorry. I don't know why I'm stuck for words. Only a few days ago everything seemed so different. I feel like in a small space of time, everything has altered. Like a console game. Another level.'

Olivia's warm smile matched her relaxed gaze. She looked well – radiant. In harmony despite the difficulties she had endured the last couple of days. He was glad to see her like this. In control. Deep down he thought he knew where the conversation was going; he needed to steer it in the right direction – before it was too late. Before everything that was dear fell apart. He hesitated before taking her hand in his. He wasn't sure of what he was about to say. But he hesitated. So Olivia spoke first.

'I'm pregnant.'

***

When Gulliver arrived home, he could hear the children playing outdoors. Of course. The inflatable castle was still with them – would be with them until Tuesday – a two day hire. He'd always wanted more children. Never like this though. He resented *it* already.

He'd called Catherine on the way home. Asked if they could meet for a drink later. After Carys. He thought she might have put him off; it surprised him that she accepted, although she did pause and seemed to sigh before speaking. Maybe she hadn't. Maybe he imagined it. Gulliver felt exhausted. Isolated. Was it fair to share his dirty secrets with Catherine? Whom else though did he have to turn to?

'I'll be down in a minute! Watch the children Gull – I'm going to take a quick shower. Why don't you make us a coffee?'

It seemed early in the day for Carys to take a shower. He was doing it again. Guilt. Paranoia. He was diverting the real blame onto someone else. Deflecting.

Screams of laughter. He approached the kitchen window. He waved but they did not see. How well Manon and Brody played together. Something smelled good. Homemade soup. Carys could make soup from any bone left over from a roast. She'd save the stock, and left over vegetables. And chick peas – or rice. She'd always add a piece of belly pork – to fatten the soup up. He could smell lamb though. He lifted the lid whilst glancing episodically at the children. Snapshots. A series of snapshots. The soup busting with vegetables – butternut squash, potatoes, cabbage. And still the children leapt about like spring lambs – not a care in the world. No sign of Carys' mobile.

Who were Carys' friends now? He looked about the kitchen. He'd never leave his mobile lying around – he'd keep it close by. And Carys was in the shower; he doubted she'd taken it in the shower with her. Now that would arouse suspicion. To think of it, her mobile was always around. One of his sole jobs was to ring her mobile – help her find it. When was the last time she'd asked him to ring it?

For a moment he felt ashamed. Was he thinking like a husband, a cheat or a detective? Maybe all three. He moved upstairs casually, half convincing himself that he was going to change – his eyes as sharp as pins. He should have made them coffee. Had the excuse of being upstairs, bringing it up to her. But time was of the essence. He thought.

For a moment he stared at her mobile before he picked it up. The sound of the shower helped. It was ideal. The movement of the water within the cubicle informed him more or less of what she was doing. He only had a few minutes. Of course, his fingerprint wouldn't work. He dearly hoped she had not changed the passcode. Their wedding day date. Why would she? She had.

Gulliver sat perplexed on their bed. She was still showering. He felt sick. A nebulous plan with an unintended outcome. Confused. A hypocrite. He'd changed his passcode. For a short while he observed her in the shower cubicle. He thought long and hard. Nothing. No concrete evidence. Just a hunch.

***

Catherine was already there when Gulliver arrived; he spotted her car not too far from the entrance to the local pub. It was a relief to see so many unoccupied spaces, would be no good if it was too noisy inside – could be difficult, awkward even, if it was too silent.

It was always easier to spot Catherine's car in any parking lot – it was often the dirtiest. He'd overheard, in some past conversation at work, her defend her deliberate avoidance of any interaction with both its interior and exterior - now a corporate joke. *It's a car. It's a means of getting from A to B*. It was clear from her short responses that she preferred her car very much that way. *They're not human! They're just a car!*

Catherine had never been either graceful or elegant; like she'd said to him only last week, there was nothing sparkly about her. He'd surprisingly learned, over a short period of time, that there was also nothing superficial either. She was raw, thoughtful and honest – and understandably private. She'd grown on him despite her initial cold demeanour and if truth be known, him on her.

'Griffin dropped by after you left.'

Gulliver was quietly thankful: he wasn't in the right frame of mind to talk yet. He needed a drink. He wasn't sure where to start. He wasn't even sure whether he should: the ugly truth of it all choking him. Catherine noticed that a puzzled frown formed across his forehead before she saved him from asking.

'The Superintendent. Gary Griffin? He said he might drop in last time I spoke to him. Remember? After we'd interviewed Miss Akintola. More concerned with fire-fighting than solving the mystery.'

'Understandable though, isn't it? Mind, if there's nothing concrete? Mrs Tanner has no knowledge of what her brother-in-law was up to. If her sister knew anything, that has since died with her. DNA's inconclusive. Could cost a small fortune to exhume all the graves he'd ever worked on. Media would have a field day!'

'I know. Hearsay he said, before he left. Lesley Litt still claims he knew zilch. There's only her word. What Mr Lexton related to her, could have been invented or even exaggerated, and to be fair, she has no idea of the extent of burials.

Personally, I think we are sitting on a ticking bomb. But Griffin thinks otherwise. He's choosing to chalk it up for now as nonsense. A lover showing off, trying to impress his latest mistress. Not sure I agree, although it does relieve us from further investigation. Case closed. Killer processed and on her way to prison for life.'

'Maybe we'd better prepare a statement ahead of it all.'

'It's done. Griffin wants me to do it.'

'No disrespect, but wouldn't it be better coming from him?'

'That's the point. If someone high-ranking publicly speaks, the media will dig even deeper. They'll know there's more to it. Best coming from us. It could, although I doubt it very much, die a death in time. Strangely though, many things in life do. Today's news, tomorrow's fish and chip paper. Depends if there's bigger news on the day. Might be a blessing in disguise.'

'I've been having an affair.'

It was obvious from Catherine's face she had been expecting him to say something much different. For a long moment she said nothing. A weighty silence. She neither looked disappointed nor upset. Just shocked. It was strange how stunned she seemed; what had she expected him to say?

'Wow. Sorry. How long?'

'On and off, since summer. Since before Carys and I even moved to England.'

Gulliver looked into his pint of bitter. He didn't need to confess, that wasn't why he'd asked her to meet him. Catherine's opinion of him did not matter. Or maybe it did? He needed someone to talk to, someone whom he respected; who might be able to help – although the entire situation was in truth, beyond help. He did hope though, Catherine wouldn't mind it being her – whom he'd chosen to talk to. He wasn't entirely sure why he felt sure he could talk to her: aside from work, they had never been close.

'So, I thought I loved her. Maybe I still do. I'm not sure. Actually, I was sure I loved her. And then suddenly, I wasn't sure. I'm not making sense. So much has happened in the last forty-eight hours. As ridiculous as it sounds, I'm really not sure where to begin.'

'Well, take your time. We can talk for as long as you need to. I'm not sure how I can help, but I'll try. If you want that.'

'Catherine. I've been so stupid.'

'Haven't we all!'

'She's pregnant.'

For a moment, Catherine's stunned look of surprise returned; she sat rigid in her seat, the news taking everything to another level. She thought of Hermione – her shrewdness: she would have touched her arm at this point or something – reached out to her – known what to do. She wished she was there sat beside her. She wanted to help but wasn't sure how. Even Wendy would have done better. And Carys. She too was having an affair. Obviously, it seemed, he had no idea.

'Gulliver. I'm sorry. How – I mean, not how but – Jesus! Does Carys know?'

'No. I've just left Carys. To meet up with you. I think, no - I'm sure. I'm sure she's seeing someone herself. I've been so wrapped up in myself – in Olivia – I hadn't noticed. I have no real evidence? But I'm almost sure she is. And what's worse – when she told me we needed to talk – I thought the worse. I thought she was going to confess. Possibly leave me. But she said nothing of it. And I can't put my finger on it – yet – but something isn't right.'

'What do you mean?'

And then Gulliver communicated through many broken sentences – leaving Catherine in no doubt that his suspicions where for good reason – that his choices seemed doomed whatever happened next. His life has become entangled like frogspawn trapped in a dark pond of impermeable slime. He wiped his nose and eyes. In truth, he looked frightened.

'Then Carys sat me down, after she'd showered, and told me she was pregnant too. Incredible is not the right word.'

For a moment Catherine stared open-mouthed. She felt stupid beyond belief. She instinctively inched closer towards him before taking his right arm.

'And I am left wondering if the child she carries is mine. And if it's not, and Olivia chooses to not carry on with the pregnancy, what right have I to question her? I couldn't, you see. It's my fault either way. Before Christmas, I could be a father – twice over.'

Songs of Innocence

Nurses Song

When the voices of children are heard on the green,
And laughing is heard on the hill,
My heart is at rest within my breast,
And everything else is still.

'Then come home, my children, the sun is come down,
And the dews of night arise;
Come, come, leave off play, and let us away
Till the morning appears in the skies.'

'No, no, let us play, for it is yet day,
And we cannot go to sleep;
Besides, in the sky, the little birds fly,
And the hills are all cover'd with sheep.'

'Well, well, go and play till the light fades away,
And then go home to bed.'
The little ones leaped and shouted and laugh'd
And all the hills echoed.

William Blake, 1789

Songs of Experience

Nurses Song

When the voices of children are heard on the green
And the whisp'rings are in the dale,
The days of my youth rise fresh in my mind,
My face turns green and pale.

'Then come home, my children, the sun is come down,
And the dews of night arise;
Your spring and your day are wasted in play,
And your winter and night in disguise.'

William Blake, 1794

ABOUT THE AUTHOR

Sally-Anne Tapia-Bowes graduated from Hope and Liverpool University with a B.A. in English Literature and Contemporary Art followed by a P.G.C.E. in English and Drama. She has been a full-time English teacher for as long as she can remember.

HIS MOTHER was her debut novel, with sequels HER FATHER and SISTERS, released in 2017 and 2019.

Sally-Anne's first children's story-book *The Star that Lost Its Sparkle!* was published Christmas 2015. She has since gone on to write several other children's stories. She is a proud member of the SFS – *Society for Storytelling* and *Patron for Reading* at a local primary school.

Sally-Anne lives in Hightown, England, with her husband, children and two cats.

Official website: www.purplepenguinpublishing.com

Praise for Sally-Anne Tapia-Bowes

★ ★ ★ ★ ★

'Yet another brilliant psychological thriller by
Sally-Anne Tapia-Bowes. Her novels get better and better!

A page-turner until the very last word. Once again,
I couldn't put it down. Read it through in one day. Forgot to eat,
I was so carried away with the twists and turns.

The breathless pace which is created, in part by staccato
sentences and punctuation, all added to the heightened sense of
anticipation – only to find another surprising turn of events!

Brenda Giblin

Chairperson of Hightown Community Library

★ ★ ★ ★ ★

'A taut and tense psychological thriller – yet another
accomplished and emotional read. Sally-Anne has
developed a real niche, packs quite a punch. Superbly
crafted and lyrical, she paints imagery and feeling with
words. Her observations of life are delightful.

To write such a well-paced and clever plot with twists
and nuances of emotional turmoil with a feeling of
claustrophobia is rare .

Sally-Anne is a star in the ascendant.'

Tony Higginson: Beyond Books Media

20724828R00192

Printed in Great Britain
by Amazon